TRUTH IN MAGIC

IN MAGIC SERIES
BOOK TWO

KJ WARAWA

MYSTIC
CITY
PRESS

Twenty-Two Years Ago—Simon, Age Twelve

Simon Hughes hugged his foster mother tightly, knowing he'd never see her again.

After a moment, his foster mother pulled back and cupped Simon's cheeks. "We're going to miss you, Simon. I know we said we talked about you joining our family—" Pulling away from him, she took a tissue from her pocket and wiped her eyes. "You know we would keep you if we could."

Simon nodded and swallowed against the lump in his throat that threatened to strangle him. He waved his hand in front of his eyes to look like he was sweeping the bangs off his face, a move he'd mastered two years ago after his parents died. His non-magic foster mother would never know he was magically drying the tears that threatened to spill over. He wouldn't cry because it never helped. His tears just made people feel guilty. They didn't change anything. He swallowed again and pushed his shoulders back.

"I know." He told her what she wanted to hear, but it was

a lie. He had no problem lying when it made someone else feel better.

"Simon, please wait in the car while I speak with Mrs. Nelson." The social worker's voice was soft, the corners of her lips barely curving up in a sad attempt at a smile. "I'll only be a few minutes."

His foster mother pulled him in for one last hug, then Simon picked up his backpack loaded down with his comic books and walked out the door. He got into the backseat of the social worker's car and watched the two non-magic women as they stood on the front porch and talked about him. Pulling in energy from around him, he sent some power to his hearing to temporarily enhance it with magic, so he could listen in.

"We are so sorry to lose Simon." His foster mother paused and used the crumpled tissue in her hand to wipe her eyes, already red and puffy from days of crying. "He has become a real part of our family, like he's one of our own." She paused, dabbing at her eyes before continuing. "I know this sounds strange, but I think he even looks like he could be our biological child. Sorry, I'm babbling. It's been a tough time."

"I understand," the social worker said in an empathetic voice that was almost like a purr.

"He just seems so much like my husband, reading the same types of books, liking the same sports, and even learning about my husband's hobby in antiquities."

The social worker nodded as if she could fully comprehend what the other woman was saying. But she couldn't, no one could.

"I'm new to Simon's case, but everything I've read in his file shows he truly did become a part of your family. I know it's going to be a huge loss to your family to move him, and for him too, but you need to concentrate on your own family now. I understand that getting your husband the care he needs to beat this horrible disease should be your top priority."

Simon turned his head, looking out the window at the kids playing down the street. He stopped listening. He had tried so hard to be what they wanted so he could fit in. He'd magically darkened his hair, a little bit at a time over the months so it would look more like his foster father's. Every night for months, he'd spent hours in the back yard practicing his golf swing so he could keep up with his foster father. Simon swallowed again, and rubbed his chest as the feelings of loneliness overwhelmed him. Learning new hobbies and how to cook, being polite, never complaining— none of it had been enough.

Being a part of the family and helping his foster father get well was something he yearned for, and he didn't understand why he couldn't stay. He'd be one more person to help and he wouldn't get in the way. He wanted to belong.

He'd been in several foster homes over the past two years, but this one felt different. He'd felt a connection to these people, and they'd even shared inside jokes. Like *ask the kid on the bike*. One day his foster dad got lost and a little kid on a bicycle had to give him directions. After that, when someone didn't know something, a family member would yell out "Ask the kid on the bike!" It wouldn't make sense to anyone outside the family, but he understood.

They had trusted him to do what he said he was going to do, and they did the same, like he was a true part of the family. It didn't matter that they were non-magic people; he'd felt like he belonged. Why hadn't that been enough?

When his parents had died, he was tossed into the state's foster system among non-magic people and he'd lost all connections to others like him. There was no one to teach him about his magic. He had been completely alone. Then he had joined the Nelson family and he didn't think he'd ever be alone again.

His parents had told him all about magic people—or magics—and that they were born with their magic essence inside of them. They'd explained that like all magics, his powers would continue to grow, and when he hit puberty, he'd come into his full power. Then he'd have to learn how to master using it.

His parents had also told him that some magics had special gifts, just like some people were talented at playing sports or music. Knowing all this didn't help because now that his abilities were growing there was no one to teach him. He'd have to figure it all out on his own.

His dad told him that specialties were passed down like other types of genetics. Just like families with mostly brunettes could have a blond or red-headed child, magic families could have a child with a specialty not seen in generations or even no specialties at all.

Thinking of his parents and wishing they were there, not just to help him but so he'd still have a place he belonged, he closed his eyes and pictured them in his mind. It'd been two years since the accident that took their lives. The pain was still a constant, living presence in his soul. Some days he looked down at his chest and expected to see scars, big and ugly, marring his body. The ache was a continual reminder of what he'd lost.

When he used his special power, he could pretend he was someone else and sometimes even go a day or two without thinking of them. Just like belonging to a new family might ease some of the ache. It was enough to keep him going. He never wanted to forget his parents, but he'd do anything to lessen the pain.

He expected he'd hit puberty any day now and come into

his full magic. But until then he practiced with what magic he did have every chance he got, and it was paying off. He could now do things he couldn't do even a month before. Somehow, he knew these new skills were the key to his future because he would be able to pretend he wasn't the lonely boy that no one wanted.

With his next family, he would use his powers more and try even harder to fit in, to make himself into a boy that they wouldn't want to throw away.

Twenty-One Years Ago—Jo, Age Six

"Jo, sweetheart, you need to listen to me." Jo's mother crouched to her eye level. "I've already told you that Daddy and Dylan are dead. They died in the fire and no matter how much you want them to, they are not coming back." Her mother's voice cracked as she said the final words and she briefly closed her eyes before looking back at Jo.

Jo, dry-eyed, patted her mother's cheek like she'd seen her mother do to her and wiped away her tears. Everyone had been sad and crying for days. Half the family was gone, dead in a fire. At six, Jo understood fire. Had stood with her mom, aunts, brother, and cousins and watched the huge cabin burn with some of her family trapped inside. But her family were magic people, and her father was extra special. "Mommy, you don't have to be sad. Daddy will come back when he's ready, and he'll bring everyone else back too. He promised."

"No, Jo, he's not coming back. No one is coming back. They're all…" Her mother didn't finish the sentence as she let out a sob, but Jo knew what she wanted to say. Dead. Her dad, her brother, her two uncles, and her three cousins were all dead. But they couldn't be.

After getting into a car accident on the way to the family's cabin, she was afraid her father was hurt because he'd said he bumped his head. He had picked her up and looked her straight in the eye and told her he was okay. He promised he'd live a long life and watch her grow up and get married and have her own children. Her dad never lied to her.

She knew the cabin had gone up in flames. She'd stood beside her mother and her brother, Reece, her aunts and cousins while everyone watched in horror as the flames engulfed the huge structure. The heat was so intense it forced them back, closer to the lake. They watched as the smoke grew thicker, like a cloud fallen to the ground, choking out the sun. The roar of the fire was deafening as the crackle and popping of the flames consumed the log cabin in minutes. She saw the fire, but her dad never broke a promise. He'd come back.

At the funeral, three large coffins and four smaller ones were buried in the ground. Reece stood on one side of her with his arm wrapped around her, snugging her into his side, her protector. Her two remaining cousins, Meredith and Rowena, stood on her other side, their faces awash with tears. Everyone cried except Jo. Her mother and aunts huddled together, and the minister's words echoed throughout the grounds, drowning out the three women's sobs.

After that, life went on. She started first grade and found a new best friend, Jessica, and Jo continued to wait. Days turned into weeks and every morning she wondered if it would be the day her father came back.

Three months and six days later it was Jo's birthday and she stopped waiting.

"What's wrong, Jo?" Jessica asked, blue icing smeared around her mouth.

Jo hadn't touched her birthday cake. "My dad has never missed my birthday. He's not coming back." Her father had lied to her.

Eighteen Years Ago—Simon, Age Sixteen

SIMON HAD MOVED SO many times, he had a routine—efficient and always the same. He put his stuff away in his latest bedroom's age-worn dresser. Besides his prized comic books, there were only a few pictures and some clothes, so it didn't take long.

He would share the room in the group home for the next two years, until he aged out of the system. If they let him stay that long...

He put everything away neatly, folded in a drawer or hung up in the small closet. Afterward, he sat on the bed and looked down at his hands as if they would have the answers for where he had gone wrong. Four foster homes in six years and they all said he was part of the family. That he belonged. Until he didn't.

He'd made subtle changes to fit into each of the families, but it was never enough. Not even after he had come into his full magic. He knew from his father that his magic would continue to mature as he did, but so far nothing was ever enough.

Glancing around the room, his eyes focused on the cheap, plastic picture frame he'd placed on the nightstand by the bed. Holding out his hand, he used his magic to float the frame over to him, landing it softly on his open palm.

Everyone in the photo was laughing and leaning over to one side. Simon smiled as he remembered his dad setting up the camera and tripod, then flashing into the picture before the timer went off. His dad had flashed too close to his mom, shoving her to the right, and they'd all started to topple over like dominoes. They'd taken it a few months before his parents died. He ran his finger over the glass, tracing the shapes of first his mother and then his father. A yearning welled up and threatened to consume him from the inside out. He took a deep breath and swallowed. He often wondered what they'd think of him if they could see him now.

Would they think he hadn't tried hard enough to fit in? Or maybe too hard? Would they think the families hadn't been polite or kind enough and that's why they didn't want him? His parents had always said how important manners were, and they had been the nicest people he knew. Maybe he wasn't nice enough or he'd focused on changing the wrong parts of himself.

His parents had been only children. They'd had a huge circle of magic friends. His dad had even been a member of the magic council, but at home, it had just been the three of them. They'd spent every free moment together. He had been so loved he couldn't have imagined how it could have all changed in an instant. After their deaths, he lost all touch with magics when he was swallowed up into the social system.

His parents always told him to be true to himself. Be the best he could be. And he had tried. He tried in each foster home, but it was never enough.

But, for the first time in his life, he began to think his parents had been wrong. Maybe even the best Simon wasn't enough. No matter how good he tried to be, no one loved him enough to keep him. He was lacking something and didn't know what it was. Being the best Simon was never going to be enough. So maybe he shouldn't be the best Simon he could be. Maybe he should be the best someone else.

He cocked his head to the side and listened, making sure no one was around, before he put the picture frame back in the drawer. Magics were forbidden from telling non-magics about their power, and he never wanted to get caught doing something he shouldn't. It was even physically difficult to mention it around non-magics. Probably another design by Mother Nature.

Since Simon had never been in a foster home with another magic kid, he only practiced his magic when alone, like now. He held his hand out in front of him, palm down, and pulled his magic from within. Using the energy in the room, he focused it onto his hand and he stared at a poster on the wall above the twin bed opposite his.

Ever since he'd figured out he could magically change his hair color, he knew changing his appearance was going to be his magic specialty. He'd been honing it since he'd come into his full power.

He listened for movement in the hall again, and when he heard nothing, he decided it was time to see what he could really do.

The musician in the photo had a tattoo of an electric guitar covering the top of his hand from his knuckles, up past his wrist. Simon focused all his attention on the image, guiding his power.

He first fixated on the bridge and saddles of the guitar, the dark shadows covering the man's knuckles where the tattoo gradually faded out. Then the pickups and strings. No detail was too small for Simon as he continued to draw in energy and use it to work his magic. His eyes never wavered from the poster as he concentrated on each section of the photo before moving his focus onto the next.

As his focus on the details intensified, he continued to guide the energy and magic into his hand.

Then it happened.

A strange sensation raced through him, like a caffeine buzz, but not a normal one. An all-encompassing buzz that he felt throughout his entire body. One like he'd been mainlining caffeine right into his veins.

As the sensation continued, his hand transformed into the guitarist's hand and the tattoo appeared.

He giggled like a small child and sat up straighter, glancing around the room again to make sure he was still alone. Then he let loose and laughed like he hadn't since his parents had been alive.

He stood and paced the small room, walking back and forth between the two twin beds. A rush of adrenaline coursed through him as he stared down at his hand.

Transformation. His specialty was transformation. Years earlier, at his first foster home, he'd had his first hint that was his specialty when he'd been able to change his eye color and lighten his hair to match his foster father's, but now he knew for sure.

He sat back down on the bed and concentrated on the poster again, but this time he intensified his gaze to take in the entire man, not just his hand. Simon pulled in more energy and focused his magic throughout his entire body. He would become the best someone else—someone who would finally belong.

Nine Years Ago—Jo, Age Seventeen

Jo STARED at her best friend, Jessica. They sat together at a picnic table on the school's lawn, facing the street. "Really?"

"Uh, yeah, I told you I was going to the library last night."

"Alone?"

"Yeah." Jessica twisted a strand of her long blond hair around her finger.

Jo had been friends with Jessica since first grade and she knew her tells. Right now, Jessica was lying.

"I went by the library last night. I thought I'd study with you."

Jessica's eyes widened. "I must have missed you."

"I was there from five until it closed at nine thirty."

Jessica stood. "Okay, so I wasn't there. What do you want to know, Jo?"

"I want to know if you were with Travis last night."

"Travis?"

"Yes, Travis, my boyfriend." Jessica was lying and now Jo wanted her to confirm it.

"No, I went home after the library."

"Really, Jess?"

"Yes, I went home and was by myself all night. What's with all the questions, Jo?"

Jessica had lied to her and betrayed her. No matter how you looked at it, lying was wrong—it hurt people. And now she knew it could also ruin friendships. It hurt even more when the lie came from someone you trusted. Maybe if Jessica understood how much the lie had hurt, they could salvage their friendship. "After I left the library, I stopped by Travis's house and you were on the front porch with him."

"Well, I got bored at home and decided to stop by Travis's. He was helping me study."

The more Jessica talked, the more she lied, but Jo couldn't let it drop. "Anatomy?"

"Huh?"

"Jess, I saw you! You were sucking face with Travis on his porch!"

Jessica dropped all pretense of innocence. She placed her hands on her hips and thrust out her ample chest. "Well, he likes me better than you. He was only waiting until you gave it up to him, and now he's mine, like he always should have been." She stormed off like a woman scorned instead of the one doing the deed.

Jo sat at the picnic table, dry-eyed, and wondered where she'd gone wrong. They were best friends—they'd even bonded over their grief. Jessica had lost her own dad to a heart attack. Now in their senior year, they had already applied to the same colleges like they'd planned. Had their friendship all been a lie?

"Jo, come on." Jo looked up to see Meredith and Rowena in their car at the curb. Jo had forgotten her cousins were picking her up after school today.

Once Jo was in the back seat, Meredith turned around, not taking the car out of park. "What happened?"

"What do you mean?"

Rowena turned to face her as well, and Jo knew Meredith wouldn't drive until she'd gotten the truth out of her. The truth was supposed to set you free. Yet Jess's truth felt like it had ripped a hole in Jo. "Travis and I broke up."

"Oh, sweetie, I'm sorry. Are you okay?" Rowena asked.

"Yeah. Travis and Jess are a thing now."

"Travis and Jess!" Meredith's voice came out as a screech, and Jo winced.

"Yeah, they lied to me."

Rowena and Meredith glanced at each other. They both knew how much Jo hated lies.

Jo's eyes tingled with the threat of tears, but she didn't cry or show how she was feeling on the outside. Inside, she seethed with anger at the betrayal and the damage lies continued to bring to her life. They also took away those closest to her. Lies had no place in the world and Jo wouldn't tolerate anyone who told them. There had to be someone out there, besides her family, who wouldn't lie and cause her more pain.

2

Nine Years Ago—Simon, Age Twenty-Five

Simon nodded a thanks to the agent who showed him to the office and stood waiting for permission to enter.

Ben Davis, head of a special FBI task force, hadn't mentioned what the task force covered when he'd introduced himself a few minutes ago. The soundproof room he'd led them to gave Simon an idea though.

After graduating from Quantico, Simon was assigned to the Blue Mountain, Colorado, division, and it was working out okay, but he wanted more. He had a driving force inside him to be indispensable and in turn that would make him part of a team and give him a place where he belonged once and for all.

He'd made a few friends, and his supervisor seemed pleased with his work, but this meeting came out of the blue. Yesterday, his boss told him he had a meeting at zero nine hundred this morning to meet with Deputy Assistant Special

Agent in Charge Ben Davis, or DSAC Davis as he was referred to.

Excitement hummed through Simon. This could be what he was waiting for—a place to belong in the organization.

"Thanks for coming, Simon. Please sit down. I've just got to finish up this report."

Ben gestured for Simon to take a seat and turned back to his computer. He'd heard Ben's name bantered around, but that's all he knew about him. Discovering he was a magic person had been a surprise.

The older man was probably in his mid-fifties and looked like a friendly professor. The serious but kind type, non-threatening and approachable. Someone who could blend into a crowd.

He could blend in too, but for a completely different reason.

Ben turned away from his computer and focused his gaze back on Simon while he took a sip from his coffee. Simon fisted his hands on his knees and forced himself not to fidget or move his gaze away from Ben's.

He wasn't easily intimidated, but the silence was becoming awkward.

Simon's patience wouldn't be considered extraordinary, but he had persistence, and the FBI had honed that skill over the past year.

As the silence drew on, he expected it was some kind of a test, but of what he had no clue. He stayed silent and studied the other man. Ben's eyes were hazel in color, and as the clock ticked on, the effort to resist seeing if he could match Ben's eye color became harder.

Another minute went by and Ben glanced at the computer. With the older man looking away, Simon took the momentary reprieve from the silent staring and pushed magic to his eyes to change their color. Without a mirror, he couldn't tell if the match was exact, but it felt right.

"I knew it." Ben whipped back to Simon and a smile curved his lips.

Shit. He turned his eyes back to green but feared it was too late. He'd always been so careful to hide his skill, but his magic had spurred him on this time. Like its essence wanted to preen like a peacock and let Ben know what it could do.

"Simon, do you know why I called this meeting?"

"No, sir."

"The task force I'm in charge of is called missing persons, but it's a cover. It's made up of magic agents like yourself and we investigate cases involving magics."

Ben paused. Was he waiting for a response?

Simon nodded, not sure what to say. Perhaps Ben hadn't seen him change his eye color and his earlier comment was in response to something on the computer.

"We are looking for magic agents with different specialties and powerful bloodlines. I believe you have a gift that we can use."

"What is that?" *Shit.* He'd never revealed his unique specialty to anyone and didn't know how Ben had even suspected. Had he given himself away before? Had someone seen him use his gift?

Ben's expression was serious but not unkind when he answered. "We've met before, you know. I used to be friends with your father when he was a council member, and I knew your mother."

Simon schooled his features to avoid showing his shock.

"After your parents died, I thought you'd gone to live with relatives. You were already in college by the time I discovered you had gone into the foster care system."

"That was several years ago."

"Yes, and when you graduated college, an FBI recruiter came to see you."

"And I told her I wasn't interested."

"I know, she told me. I sent two more recruiters before you finally said yes."

Simon wasn't sure what to think of Ben's involvement in his life without him knowing. "Why didn't you approach me yourself?"

"I almost did at one point, but you seemed like you were doing alright and I didn't know if you'd remember me."

"No disrespect, sir, but that's a cop-out."

Ben chuckled. "I suppose it is. I also felt guilty when I found out you hadn't been taken in by relatives. I should have checked in on you after your parents died. I was close with your parents and their deaths hit me hard. I couldn't wrap my head around their accident, but again, that's no excuse."

Simon had felt so alone for years and would have given anything for someone like Ben to have found him. But wishing wouldn't change the past and Simon had been through too much to feel the need to assuage Ben's guilt. "It's done."

"Yes, it is, and it's not why I brought you here. I believe you can change your appearance to match that of someone else. Am I right?"

"Yes, sir." His neck heated and his back became sticky with sweat, but he didn't hesitate to answer. Ben could be what Simon was looking for, giving him a place to use his specialty and fit in.

Ben smiled. "Can you change into anyone?"

"No, sir. Only men and there are limits." He had come this far and since Ben clearly knew about him, there was no point in hiding it. If Ben was going to reveal his secret, it wouldn't matter if Simon transformed or not so he may as well show him. He stood in front of the desk and reached out his hand to touch Ben's. "May I?"

Ben nodded and watched him intently.

Since that day in his bedroom at sixteen, Simon had been honing his skill. He laid his hand on top of Ben's and closed his eyes, gathering in energy and pushing his magic throughout his body while absorbing all the details that made up Ben's appearance.

The first time Simon had completely transformed into someone else, it took several minutes, but over time it became easier and easier, and he no longer had to touch the person or look at a picture, but it was faster if he did.

He kept his eyes closed but heard Ben sharply inhale as he imagined Ben feeling like he was looking in a mirror.

"Remarkable," Ben said with awe in his voice.

Simon could feel the successful transformation and opened his eyes to look into ones that he knew were now identical to his.

Ben stood and walked around the desk to stand in front of Simon, looking him up and down.

"I can only transform my body within reason. The most I'm able to change my mass is about three inches in either direction. I can make myself narrower in build, but I can't hold it for more than a couple of hours at a time."

"Wonderful," Ben said as he walked around Simon, taking him in.

"Simon, I have a special place for you in my task force," Ben said, and held out his hand to shake one that looked just like his own. "Welcome aboard."

Things were finally falling into place. Simon would finally be the best someone else he could be.

Nine Months Ago—Jo, Age Twenty-Six

"You lied. You all lied!" Jo threw out the accusation from the doorway. "How could you do that? For twenty years you lied. You hid everything from us." Her voice rose with each subsequent accusation, but she was too upset to care.

Her aunt stayed where she was at her desk, looking Jo straight in the eyes. Sadness and grief overwhelmed the older woman's expression, but Jo wasn't backing down. Nothing could excuse the lies she had been told for most of her life.

Elise put down what she'd been working on and took a long, slow breath before fully facing her niece. "We lost our husbands and our children. What else would you have had us do? Wait for our surviving children to be harmed or possibly killed?"

A part of her wished she could take comfort from the words, knowing that her mom and aunts had been protecting them, but her anger burned too deep. She wasn't ready to let it go. It was like a festering scab eating at the best parts of her, leaving only ugly and infectious remnants.

She had lost her mother less than two months ago and just yesterday Jo learned she had been lied to for twenty years. A lie that had caused her mother's death. It seemed so unreal to think she wasn't just a normal human. That there was something special about her. The news hadn't fully registered yet.

Giving her head an internal shake, Jo concentrated on the present. "We're magic, and you actually thought it was okay to keep it from us all this time? You thought it was okay to take away what is innate to us?" Her words were quieter this time, but she couldn't hold back the anger. She was losing control over herself, the anger taking over, and her need to inflict the pain she felt onto someone else was a driving force within her.

Her aunt's eyes were shrouded in grief and rimmed with tears, but her shoulders were rigid with steely determination. "Don't you dare judge me, Josephine! You have no idea what we were going through!"

Aunt Elise's voice was harsh, but Jo didn't flinch. She refused to give in, clinging to her anger at the lies. Deep down she could only imagine the sorrow her mother and aunts had felt. They had each lost their husband and at least one child.

But that didn't make lying to their surviving children right. They had spellbound them, denying them the truth of what they were. Wouldn't life have been easier if she'd known about her magic? At least she would have been saved from all the hurt caused by those lies.

If no one had ever lied she wouldn't have had to endure the teenage heartbreak inflicted by Jessica and Travis. Without lies, her ability to trust others wouldn't have been destroyed. Nor would her ability to have strong relationships been affected. And because of her mother's lies, she was now even questioning her own memories.

"No, I don't know. I can only imagine, but you didn't give us that chance. And even worse, your lies killed Aunt Lillian and my mom! Lies hide the truth and hurt the people you're closest to!" She felt a rawness inside from her grief and anger, but she wouldn't let it go.

Aunt Elise got up from the chair and came to stand in front of Jo. Her eyes burned with fire as she tilted Jo's chin up with her fingers. It was a move Aunt Elise had done since Jo was a little girl when she wanted to make sure Jo was listening. "You think we wanted to bind you? Take away your magic and lie to our children? We had just buried our husbands and some of our children and feared for your lives. It was the only way we knew of to keep you safe."

Jo whipped her face out of her aunt's grasp and straightened her shoulders as her aunt continued. Aunt Elise lowered her voice, like a hissed whisper, an edge to it that Jo hadn't heard before. "Don't you question what we did; you don't know what it was like. We had no choice but to keep you safe. If getting rid of all traces of your magic and ensuring no one hurt you to get to it kept you safe, then we were willing to do it.

"Jo, I know how you feel about lying, but sometimes there are no other options. Life isn't a black-and-white, always-tell-the-truth type of place like you want it to be." Aunt Elise's voice was back to her usual calm, with no censure in her words.

Elise grasped Jo's hand and pulled her over to the small loveseat in the office. Jo sat stiffly and looked down at their joined hands and the truth of the moment hit her like a truck hitting a brick wall at a hundred miles an hour. She would never again have a conversation like this with her mother.

The full force of the realization enflamed Jo's anger, creating a seething resentment for the times she'd lost and would never get back. For the lies she'd been forced to believe.

She had twenty years of lies to look back on and would never be able to question her mother again. She'd never be able to talk to her mom about magic and have her explain why they did what they did. Never have her mom's guidance to help her adapt to her new reality.

Her aunt turned toward her, their knees bumping, and their hands still clasped. "I've had to live with this lie for twenty years and not only was the guilt heavier than I thought I could bear at times, it killed my two sisters."

Bringing one hand up, Elise waved it softly in front of herself and her tears disappeared. Like magic.

It pulled at Jo's heart, the anger bubbling up even more from knowing that the magic her aunt just performed without thought was one more thing Jo's mom would never be able to teach her. Twenty years of opportunity gone. Her mother could have taught her how to do it and so much more, but instead their time together had been bathed in lies that ended up taking her mother from her years before her time. Her mom had lied every time she'd used her magic and hid it from her children. Every time she could have made Jo and Reece's lives easier with magic, she had denied them that. Were they the only lies they had been told or had there been more?

"Jo, hopefully you will never know what it is like to watch a spouse or your children die. Spell binding you lessened some of the pain you and your cousins felt from losing your siblings and fathers because it got rid of so many of the memories you had with them. It allowed us all to keep you safe so we could move on with our lives. If I had to do it again, I would, and I know your mother and your aunt Lillian would too. We always did whatever we could to keep you all safe."

"I love you, Aunt Elise, but I don't know if I can ever forgive you, my mom, and Aunt Lillian for denying us our magic and hiding the truth for so long."

"You may think that now, Jo, but one day you'll realize there is a place for lies. Sometimes we have to lie to protect those we love, and it's always worth it." Aunt Elise's voice trailed off and she gave Jo's fingers a final reassuring squeeze before dropping her hand. "It was worth it to keep you all safe and for that I have no regrets."

"I did it because I love you and Reece more than anything else in the entire world," Jo said softly.

"Did what?" Aunt Elise's eyes narrowed.

Jo's eyes were dry, but she squeezed them tight for a moment, willing the familiar tingling sensation away. "Those were the last words Mom ever said to me. I didn't understand what she meant and thought maybe it was the pain speaking." Jo stopped and took in a deep breath. "She didn't regret the spell binding, even when she was dying because of it." Jo squeezed her eyes shut again and then looked at her aunt.

Tears fell freely down Aunt Elise's cheeks. Her aunt seldom cried. "No, your mom had no regrets. Neither did Lillian, not even during her final days. We made a pact twenty years ago that we would protect all of you, no matter what it cost us. Now, were there times over those years when we questioned whether we had done the right thing? Yes, absolutely, but then we would see how carefree you were all able to live, not worrying that someone would try to harm you because you came from a powerful bloodline and you had magic they could take. We always came back to the conclusion that we made the right decision."

Jo stood and turned, looking down at her aunt as she shook her head. "Aunt Elise, you lied and took decisions away from us that were rightfully ours to make and I'm having a hard time forgiving that right now."

Aunt Elise stood as well but walked by Jo and returned to her desk. She sat down and turned her chair so she could look at her niece. "What more do you want me to say? That I regret what I did? That your mother regretted it? Well, we didn't and you're not a child anymore, so you just have to accept that we lied because we loved you."

Jo left the room, her heart heavy. Once more a lie had changed her entire life.

Nine Months Ago—Simon, Age Thirty-Three

"It's go time," Ben said without preamble when he flashed into the office where Simon was studying some video footage. "Lucas Jenkins is dead."

Ben took the seat across from Simon and opened his laptop. The office was pretty sparse, a rent-by-the-month place in a large building complex. They brought their laptops with them, never leaving behind any identifying information when they left.

Simon had been to the FBI offices in the last ten years, but not often. When he wasn't working on a case, he'd come to this rented office. Ben kept him informed of everything that was happening with regard to the other agents and magic business in general, but Simon didn't have anything to do with them. Even though they may know his name, no one had ever met Simon, not even Jack.

When Simon first started working for Ben, he'd explained it was for Simon's protection more than anyone else's. If it got out what Simon could do, he would be a hunted man and it could blow his cover. Even worse, if every magic person knew that someone could take on another's form, trust would be lost between magics.

Ben looked at something on his computer before glancing back at Simon. "A unit was following Lucas's car when it hydroplaned in a storm and went off the road. Our agents were able to keep his body alive and mask the incident from non-magics. He's in the local hospital with magic ER staff protecting him from view. You'll go in as planned, copy his appearance, and it will look like Lucas was able to walk away from the incident unharmed. After that, our people will deal with his body."

Ben continued to go over a few details that Simon already knew by heart. There was no need for him to respond as he started to mentally prepare himself to become Lucas. This was what he lived for, what he knew best. He would become someone else for as long as needed.

The task force had continued to grow in the years since Ben had recruited Simon, but some things hadn't changed. There was still no North American council after it had fallen apart not long after his parents died. No council meant Ben and his brother Frank had to make decisions without guidance and hope they wouldn't come back and bite them in the ass. Simon had heard rumors that it wouldn't be long before a new council was started. He'd believe it when he saw it.

The task force had identified Lucas a couple of months ago and had been watching him. They knew he was spoiled and selfish, from a wealthy family, and had a penchant for power. He'd worked his way into an organization Ben and Frank believed was responsible for the deaths of many council members and their families years ago. The task force hoped Lucas would be the key to identifying the organization's leaders.

Simon had worked with Ben for months to come up with a plan. When the time was right, they'd offer Lucas immunity for his crimes in exchange for what he knew and put him in protection, allowing Simon to take his place. They hadn't expected Lucas to die, but there was a contingency plan in place if he did.

Simon had been studying Lucas for several months, learning his habits, his mannerisms, and as much as he could about his past. He'd studied everything the FBI could find on the man, including video footage, in the hopes Simon could easily pass himself off as Lucas when the opportunity arose.

Just over a month ago, Simon went to Lucas's gym to bump into him. Literally bump into him, allowing skin-to-skin contact. With that brief contact, Simon was able to perfect his transformation into Lucas in seconds, instead of minutes.

To test his transformation, Simon did a trial run by meeting up with Lucas's college friends for a drink. It went off without a hitch. The only person still an unknown was Lucas's mother, Catherine.

"I assume you've got his ID, wallet, and personal items to give me, but what about his car?" Simon asked.

Ben passed over the items in a clear plastic bag. "You can claim the car was written off and that you were damn lucky to walk away from the accident. You'll call for your family's driver to pick you up from the hospital."

He knew everything there was to know about Lucas Jenkins, and now he would assume his identity. Everything from his home, his over-privileged life, to his friends and mother would be his. Simon Hughes would cease to exist for now. This was everything Simon had worked for.

Two Months Ago—Jo, Age Twenty-Seven

"You don't have to stay, you know," Reece said as he settled himself onto the other end of the couch. "I'm just going to read for awhile and then go to bed."

"I know. It's just comfy here on the couch and I'm not ready to go up to my apartment yet."

Reece let out a huff. "Pinky, I'm okay."

"You just seem like you've changed. I worry about you, Reece's Pieces." Jo grinned, knowing how Reece felt about the nickname she and her cousins had come up with years ago. She didn't need to mention how weak he'd gotten or how he seemed quieter ever since a spell had been cast on him at the ceremony to remove the spell cast on them by their mother and aunts. Life could be ironic.

Reece chuckled. "Oh, I see, I use your nickname and you have to dredge up that horrible name. Beware, Pinky Pie." Reece wiggled his eyebrows at her and relief flooded through her. Her brother was still somewhere inside this new, somber guy he'd morphed into since the unbinding spell.

He'd started calling her Pinky right before her high school graduation when she'd cut her hair into a short pixie cut and dyed it purple. Reece didn't care that the My Little Pony character was really pink, hence the name Pinky Pie, and not purple. He'd said it worked and it stuck.

Reece sobered, his expression becoming serious again. "Look, Jo, I know you're worried. I am too. But there's nothing we can do about it. It is what it is."

Reece shook his head and Jo's heart broke at the look of defeat on her brother's face. "We'll find a way."

"I know you want to believe that, but the Emissary and the other council leaders have already tried."

Jo wouldn't accept defeat. There'd already been too much loss and suffering in their lives. They'd lost their mother in the last year and losing Aunt Elise recently had been the latest blow. Jo was determined their aunt would be the last person they lost to spells and people using magic for evil. She would find a way to save her brother.

"Jo?"

"Hmm?"

"You seem lost in thought. What are you up to?"

"Jack asked me to do something."

Reece reached forward and took her small hand in his far

larger one. She squeezed his hand and forced herself not to comment on the loss of strength in her brother's grip.

"Jo, tell me."

"Jack asked me to look for an ancient book that he believes is hidden in the downtown library. He says they need it for the new council."

"Jack and Meredith don't even have the new council set up yet. What is this book supposed to do and why do they need it now?"

Jo shrugged. "I think it's supposed to help them find the magic box that Copeland was looking for before Jack killed him. They need to find it before his people do…"

"You hesitated. There's more, isn't there, Pinky?"

"The book is hidden, because duh, magic." She winked at Reece and he chuckled. The sound helped to heal the cracks in her heart just a tiny bit.

"Being a historian, no one will think anything of me researching in a large library, so I'll be able to look for the book without it looking suspicious. Like I said, Jack needs it for the council, but there's something else in the book…" Jo took a deep breath and looked her brother in the eyes. "The Emissary and other council leaders believe that the book contains a spell that will heal you."

"No!" Reece dropped Jo's hands and sat back. "That's the real reason you're looking for it, isn't it? And you said others are looking for it too? What if you get in their way? It's bad enough you could be putting yourself in danger to help the council, not that I like it. But I know you—you'll take bigger risks because you think it will help me. You can't put yourself in danger because of me."

"Reece, it's not just you. Before Copeland died, he said he wasn't alone and that there are more people looking for that magic box. If it's opened, it could release all kinds of bad shit."

"First, it's never been proven the magic box is even real. It could be just a myth. And secondly, there are lots of other people who could look for the book." Reece leaned forward again and put his hand on Jo's leg. "Pinky, what happens if you end up in the same boat as me? What if the magic book has a spell on it and you get hurt too? I couldn't stand for anything to happen to you."

"That's just it. Don't you get it? I feel the same way. You're already hurt and if there's anything I can do to heal you, I will."

"Come here." Reece pulled Jo into a hug. It felt like it'd been eons since she'd felt his brotherly embrace. She got up on her knees and scootched forward, sinking into his arms. "You're determined to do this, aren't you?" he asked softly.

Jo looked at her brother, his face leaner than it had been just a few months ago. He'd always seemed bigger than life and since he loved to weight lift, he'd been big too. Now his shoulders didn't seem as broad, and his face looked gaunt. Even his biceps and thighs didn't have the muscular girth she was used to seeing on him.

She'd do anything to fix that. "I don't know if Jack asked anyone else, but it makes sense for me to look for the book. Besides, I'll just be in a library and nothing will happen there."

Reece started to speak and Jo held up her hand. "Please, let me finish. I'll be careful, I promise. Plus, there's an elder magic person who will help me—Viktor Szabo. He's a legend at the university. Although I've never met him and didn't know he was a magic person." She snorted. "Hell, that would have been funny if I had, considering five months ago I didn't even know magics existed."

Reece grasped Jo's arms and looked her in the eyes. "I need you to promise me that if you ever think you're in danger, or something doesn't seem right, you'll stop. Let Jack and the FBI take over. It's what Jack does."

"I promise I'll do my best."

"Pinky." Reece enunciated each syllable in her nickname. "That's not what I meant."

"Reece, I won't lie to you and say I'll stop looking for the book when I don't know if I can. But I promise I'll be careful." She was just going to be in a library, what could possibly happen?

3

Present Day

*J*o breathed in the delicious smell of fresh bread. She should add the smell of fresh-baked bread to her mental list of things a woman needed, a list she'd decided upon in college. Coffee, chocolate, wine, a good book, an occasional good fuck, and now fresh-baked bread. There wasn't much more a woman could want. Okay, some really great shoes would be nice, and maybe more than just an occasional good fuck, but that was pretty much it. And her family healthy and happy.

Maybe a woman needed more than she'd thought. Well, she'd concentrate on the smell of the bread for now.

The early morning sky was still dark and the bakery hadn't opened for the day. Normally, it was far too early for her to even have her eyes open, but she loved the quiet time with her brother and she popped in a couple times a week. Something deep within her was telling her to spend more time with Reece, even if it was just spent stirring stuff and making small talk.

He was still strong enough to work and she took that as a good sign. "Hey, Reece, where are you?"

A sound like a groan came from the kitchen and before she realized what she was doing, she flashed to the back. A second later, her feet landed on the stark white linoleum floor by the large stainless-steel worktable. The place seemed empty. "Reece?" Another groan came from near the freezer. Jo rounded the table and dropped to her knees with a gasp.

Reece was on his hands and knees by the freezer. "Reece, talk to me." She surprised herself with how calm she sounded when she would swear her throat had just landed in her stomach. Kneeling in front of her brother, she laid one hand on his shoulder.

"I'm… I'm fine." He shrugged Jo off and struggled to his feet, using the counter for support. "Just got a bit dizzy."

"Let me help you." She put out her hand, but Reece ignored it. The snub hurt, but she didn't let it show.

"Jo, I'm fine."

"You don't look fine. You were on the floor, for shit's sake."

Reece straightened and turned to the table, bracing himself with his hands, his head bent forward. She tried to catch his gaze, but he wouldn't look at her.

She rounded the table and faced him. Being eight inches shorter than her brother, she didn't have to bend down to meet his eyes. "What happened, Reece?"

He looked up and Jo held back a gasp. Reece's cheeks were hollower than they had been even two days ago. His broad shoulders now looked narrower and his skin looked sickly pale. He was getting worse by the day. "Reece? You going to answer me?"

"I did. I got dizzy. What else do you want me to say?"

"I want you to tell me what's wrong and when you're getting worse. I'm worried about you." Once more she managed to keep her voice calm when she wanted to shout to the world, *not again!*

Reece dropped his head as if all the fight had gone out of him before he looked up at Jo again. "There's nothing anyone can do to fix this. It's been nine months since the unbinding spell. Ha," Reece said on a huff. "That's so fucking ironic. With everything that's happened, I never really thought about it that way before."

"What do you mean?"

"In the ceremony to unbind us and save Aunt Elise, someone binds me again, but this time it's killing me. And Aunt Elise is fucking dead anyway. If no one has solved the problem in nine months, likely no one will."

Jo's throat tightened at the mention of their mom and Aunt Elise, but she couldn't bring herself to say anything. The wounds were still too fresh. Plus, she wanted to concentrate on her brother and she wouldn't be able to if she got pulled down again in grief. "I'm going to find the book and it will have a spell to break the binding."

"How long have you been looking already? Two months? It's a waste of time."

"No, don't say that!"

"And what if you can't find it?"

"Don't say that!" Jo moved closer and wrapped her arms around his waist and didn't comment on the muscle mass he'd lost.

Until the spell was cast on him, Reece had been the outgoing, friendly jokester who wasn't afraid of anything. Ever since they were little kids, she could go to him when she was down and he'd wrap his big strong arms around her and she'd feel safe, like nothing could touch them. Now, those same arms felt thin and weak, likely unable to protect even himself.

He was only two years older than her twenty-seven, but

he'd always been her hero, especially after they lost their older brother Dylan when they were kids. And that tightened her resolve to help him no matter what. "I'm going to find the book, and it will work," she said while snuggled to his chest.

Reece wrapped his hands around her upper arms and pushed her back, looking down into her eyes. "No, Jo, you need to worry about yourself. Get back to your career. Maybe date someone. We have to accept life the way it is now."

"I can't lose you too." She didn't recognize her own voice, choking on the last words. She didn't cry, and hadn't since her father had died and she'd waited for his return. But if she did, there'd be tears running down her face right now. Her throat felt constricted, and she forced a deep breath. Their family had suffered so much, including the recent losses of their mom and aunt.

Reece turned to the industrial fridge and pulled out ingredients, putting them on the table. "I've got to get back to work."

"I can help you. That's why I got up at this ungodly hour." If Reece wanted to pretend that life was fine, she could do it for a bit too. "I don't know why bakeries have to open so early. Can't people get their baked goods and coffee at a more reasonable hour? You know what I always say... nothing should open before ten a.m."

Reece chuckled. "Only you think ten is a normal starting time. Didn't you teach an eight a.m. class once?"

"Yes, and it almost killed me."

"Fine. Go wash your hands and then mix this," Reece said, gesturing to a bowl containing dry ingredients. "I've already got today's baking done, but I want to get a head start on some more prep."

Jo hurried to the sink to wash. She wasn't a good baker, but she could mix. "Have you tried using your magic yet?"

"A bit."

"And?"

"And nothing, Jo. It's the same. Jack and the other council leaders still don't know what spell is on me. Besides killing me, it's blocking my magic."

Jo concentrated on mixing the ingredients and didn't look up. She'd find the book and break the spell, but right now, she needed to enjoy this time with her brother. "Well… when you can use your magic to make some of this, you won't have to get up so early."

"Okay, Pinky Pie, if you say so."

"I say so, Reece's Pieces." She'd do anything for her brother, even if it meant working twenty-four seven. Nothing and no one would stop her from finding the book to heal Reece.

Simon conjured a soft cloth and crouched to wipe off the gravestone in front of him, spending extra time on his parents' names: Edward Hughes and Blaire Hughes.

When he finished, he disappeared the cloth and conjured a large bouquet of white daisies—his mother's favorite—and laid them in front of the gravestones.

"Hi Mom, hi Dad. The new job is going well. I've already told you about him, but I don't know if I told you that he's a couple inches shorter than me." Talking to his parents' gravestones made him feel closer to them, but he wished they could see how he was doing now.

"Anyway, I've grown him almost two inches in the nine

months I've been posing as him, so I'm not quite as stiff at the end of the day anymore."

Lucas was now almost the same height as Simon. He'd started to change Lucas's stature as soon as he adopted his persona, making him taller and broader, but it was a slow process that took months. If he grew Lucas too quickly, people would question it, especially his mother and close friends. The bulk was easier to explain, writing it off as the result of new and better workouts, but having Lucas grow in height in his thirties was harder to pass off.

Simon looked at the ground and waved his hand, using his magic to clean and dry the grass before he sat. He wrapped his arms around his bent legs, just like he had when he was younger. Social workers brought him here to see his parents in the first few years after his parents' deaths, before he'd come into his magic enough to flash to the cemetery.

He brought his hand up in front of his face and turned it over, remembering the first time he'd transformed. It had all started with the transformation of his hand.

Transitioning still brought the strange sensation like the caffeine buzz on steroids he'd felt that day long ago in his group home when he was sixteen. The day he transformed his hand into that of the badass, tattooed musician in the poster on the wall. That was the day his life changed.

He still felt the same excitement today when he used his ability, but as the years went on and he transformed into more and more people, guilt started to overtake him as he spent less and less time as himself. Would his parents understand that he couldn't be the best Simon like they had wanted? Sometimes he was only himself when he was in his bedroom alone, and even then, he wasn't sure if he knew who the real Simon was anymore. He'd been playing roles for so long that he often thought he might have morphed into a mixed-up version of all those different people.

He shoved his hand in the pocket of his suit pants and looked back at his parents' gravestones. "I've learned a lot about Lucas and I'm not making as many mistakes. I want you to be proud of me." He often wondered what his parents would think of his career and how he used his magic ability as this was his biggest assignment yet.

"I thought using my specialty to be someone else and helping the FBI catch bad guys was the right thing to do. Now, I'm not so sure.

"I mean, aside from upholding the law, I sometimes think you'd be disappointed in me." His voice hitched, and he took a deep breath. The feelings of inadequacy as he was shuffled from one foster home to the next threatened to suffocate him, even so many years later. He stared at his parents' engraved names. "I don't mean to whine. I'm grateful for what I have, I just wonder how my life would be different if you'd lived."

"They would be really proud of you."

Simon jumped up and spun toward the voice's source. He'd been so lost in his own misery he hadn't sensed anyone nearby.

"Ben, I didn't hear you." His boss stood about five feet away, his black pants, white shirt, and shiny black shoes immaculate.

"I didn't want to interrupt, but you're wrong, Simon. They would be proud of you."

"You don't know that. Parents always tell their kids to be the best they can be. You've probably said it yourself. I don't think I've done that."

"Are you sure about that?"

Simon frowned. "Of course. I pretend to be someone else every day."

"Yes, and by doing that, you're using your specialty in the best way you know how. And are you sure you're not you?

You haven't made Lucas a nicer person?"

"Making Lucas a nicer person didn't take much. He'd been quite the asshole." If only everything were as easy. "What are you doing here, Ben?"

"I was getting ready for work when I saw the date on my phone."

Simon nodded, a sudden lump in his throat prevented him from speaking.

Ben closed the distance between them and stood beside Simon, shoulder to shoulder as they looked down at his parents' grave. "Your father was an amazing man. He was the perfect blend of strong and soft," Ben said quietly. "I know calling a man soft could be considered weak, but your father wasn't. Most great leaders are strong and assertive, but it takes a special person to know when the opposite is needed and still be able to lead. I remember sitting in on a council meeting once when Daniel Knight was swinging his weight around as council leader and wanted things his way. I can't even remember what the topic was now. But your dad was able to talk Daniel down without pandering to him and eventually a compromise was reached." Ben chuckled softly. "I don't think Knight even knew what hit him."

Ben faced Simon as he continued to stare at his parents' names. "I see a lot of Edward in you, Simon. You're both strong and soft. You are being the best you, even when you take on someone else's persona. I think you bring your all to each role you play. Your parents *would* be proud of you," he said, emphasizing his point.

Simon looked at Ben and nodded, then said a silent goodbye to his parents. He turned and walked toward a large monument about thirty feet away, Ben at his side. "I don't think I'm getting anywhere on this case. I've infiltrated Lucas Jenkins's life completely, and I've met with the people Lucas was trying to ingratiate himself with, but so far, I haven't moved up the ladder."

"Patience. You will. It's only been three months since Louis Copeland was killed. He may have been the face of the group looking for the magic box, but I don't think he was the mastermind behind it. Someone else is looking for the magic box too, and I have a feeling they won't be patient much longer."

"Why do you say that?"

"Just a gut feeling. It took twenty years for everyone to come back together to look for the box, and in the last few months, there have been more magic children taken, and a few attacks. Something will happen soon, I feel it. And if they find that box, they will unleash evil on not just all magics but non-magics as well."

They reached the monument and walked to the back so they were in shadow. "I believe in you," Ben said before he flashed away.

Simon wished he had the same faith in himself that Ben had. And if he did succeed, then what? Would he forever be someone else? He shook his head and inhaled deeply through his nose. Enough melancholy for one day. He needed to get back to being Lucas.

4

"*M*orning." Jo nodded at Jack and Meredith who were sitting at their kitchen island when she walked in, making herself at home. "Didn't you make coffee? I really need some."

"Here." Jack conjured a mug of coffee and passed it to Jo.

She took a sip and closed her eyes. "Ambrosia."

Meredith chuckled. "Why didn't you conjure some yourself?"

Jo leaned her hip against the side of the kitchen island. "I can't get it right." She took another sip. "I just went to Reece's."

Meredith glanced at her phone. "He's still at home? It's past seven, I thought he would have been at the bakery for hours by now."

"Me too. But he seems to be getting weaker by the day, so I went to check on him and he was still in bed."

"I'll go see if I can give him a bit of a magic boost." Jack leaned over and gave Meredith a kiss. The kind of kiss that had Jo looking down. Then he flashed and was gone.

Jo sat on the stool Jack had vacated and sipped her coffee. "What have you got on the agenda today, Mer?"

"The normal stuff. Meeting with some contractors. We're almost finished with most of the condos and they'll be starting on the gym soon. You know, as much as I love just chatting with you, I can tell there's something else going on. Should I call Rowena to join us?" Jo didn't even get a chance to answer when Meredith closed her eyes for several seconds before looking back at Jo.

"Morning!" Rowena said when her feet touched down in the kitchen. Rowena flashed everywhere she went. She said it was the best thing about magic because it saved her a ton of time.

"Holy shit, Mer, you need to stop that." Jo stared down her cousin. It wasn't fair that Meredith could talk telepathically to someone who was on a different floor of a building when the rest of them couldn't.

Meredith just shrugged.

"Coffee, good idea," Rowena said as she conjured herself a cup and pulled up another stool. "What'd I miss?"

"I don't know, but Jo has something to discuss."

"Shit, Mer. I just came for coffee." She looked at Rowena, filling her in. "Reece is even weaker, and Jack went to check on him."

Rowena nudged Jo with her shoulder. "Sweetie, this is us. You can tell us what you're feeling… you don't have to be strong with us."

"Ro, you promised you wouldn't act like our psychologist."

"I know, and I'm not. Just talk to us."

These two women meant the world to her. The three of them were more than cousins, they were sisters of the heart. So corny and cliché, but Jo didn't have another way to describe how she felt. "I can't find the book."

"But you will," Meredith said.

"No, Mer. I've looked. In the last two months, I've looked through dozens of ancient tomes and I still haven't found a single clue. I don't know how much time Reece has. A few days ago, I found him on the floor in his bakery, and today he's not even up yet. I feel like he's fading away in front of my eyes."

Rowena came around the island and gave Jo a hug before sitting back down. "Have you talked to the Emissary about this?"

"Not me, but Jack and Mer have. Right, Mer?"

"Yes, we've mentioned it several times while Jack and I have met with the other council leaders for training. Everyone is concerned about Reece and what it would mean if the magic box were found by someone besides us. They're all looking for clues, but haven't found anything yet."

"I know finding the book to get clues to the magic box is important, but finding it for Reece is what's pushing me." Her cousins nodded and Jo felt the weight of the world settle down on her shoulders. She disappeared her coffee mug, liking the thought of it disintegrating and the energy going back into the atmosphere. If only helping Reece was that easy. "I better get going."

Meredith stood as well. "Is Morgana going with you today?"

"No, she texted to say she's got another migraine. Some days they're completely debilitating. Maybe the book will have something to help her. She said she'd try and help me tomorrow, though I'd rather she helped Reece."

Jo said her goodbyes to her cousins and flashed back to her apartment to get her bag and then flashed to a hidden alcove in the alley behind the library.

She never thought she'd see the day when she scoped out alleys. The day had come almost nine months ago when she first learned how to flash. Magics needed places to flash to where they wouldn't be seen by non-magics. Thank goodness, she'd also learned how to float fresh air around her so she wouldn't end up smelling like a dumpster.

Now, she just needed to figure out how to find clues to locate an ancient magic book to save her brother.

LUCAS JENKINS'S stride was long and confident, but not hurried. His pace quickly ate up the distance on Summer Street, one of Blue Mountain's busiest downtown roads. His dark blond hair was layered, with the top long and the front tossed to the side, the ends touching his forehead. It gave him just the right surfer-meets-high-class-businessman vibe and several days' growth of scruff added a touch of bad boy to the image. A dark charcoal gray suit ensured the perfect contrast to his golden-tanned skin and light blue eyes. He was above average in height, had a soccer player's build, and with the bespoke suit fitting his trim body to perfection, he broadcast wealth. Image was everything.

As Lucas, Simon was self-assured and had learned how to straddle the line between cocky and arrogant. That's why people loved to be around Lucas. That and his money.

Simon had learned while studying Lucas that he only loved himself. He enjoyed being amongst people because they praised him. Eliciting admiring glances from both women and men as he strode down the street, Lucas soaked them in, like rain to a water-starved, drooping flower. Every so often he threw a wink or smile to a particularly attractive young woman.

The boutique mall was a favorite place in the downtown core, lined with cafés and niche shops. He walked among the crowds, mostly made up of early morning commuters making their way to their destinations, some grabbing breakfast and hurrying on, others leisurely enjoying their first sip of caffeine before the day intruded.

Lucas slowed his stride to move around people, but more often than not, people moved out of his way as he headed toward the public restrooms in the back of the mall.

He walked to a vacant stall at the end of the row, his expression remaining the same. Outwardly he was Lucas, but inside Simon felt the usual conflicting emotions of excitement and disappointment. The feelings battled against each other as they always did just before he transformed back into himself.

Any full transformation into another person, whether it be his alter ego or changing back into his own form, brought with it the risk of discovery. There was also a mental adjustment to go through. Simon either had to assume the persona of someone else, like the arrogant and cocky devil-may-care attitude of Lucas, or come back down to earth as simple Simon.

He still longed for the day when he would be truly accepted and fit in, but he knew being Lucas wouldn't be the key to reaching that goal. The man was on a criminal path and that never ended well. There had to be someone Simon could be who would be accepted by everyone. He hadn't found that person yet—a depressing thought after ten years on the job. He shrugged off the melancholy. He'd been shrugging off those thoughts a lot lately, but he had a job to do.

He waved his hand and cast a small spell on the stall door and the gap under it to ward off any prying eyes.

The first time Simon transformed into the musician, he'd thought of Superman. Hundreds of changes later, the image of Superman always popped into his head right before he transformed. He used a bathroom stall instead of a phone booth, but it didn't matter; the change was the same.

Simon had chosen Superman as his role model years ago. After his parents died, comics became his salvation. It didn't matter where he was, his backpack full of comics had always been at his side. He would devour the images and stories, imagining what it would be like to be a superhero like Superman, to be someone everyone admired and wanted to be around.

Just like Superman, Simon's power was unique. Although there was a spell that could transform a person, it came at a great cost. Ben had once said he'd never heard of another person with an ability just like Simon's.

Pulling in energy from around him and connecting with his magic essence deep inside himself, he cleared his mind of the images of Superman and let go of his latest persona. The long, dark blond locks disappeared. In their place was a head of thick brown hair, a bit long and wavy on top with the sides closely cropped. The light blue of Lucas's eyes was replaced with Simon's green. The corner of his mouth lifted up as he felt another successful change.

The suit was gone and now he sported a black long-sleeved shirt with the sleeves pushed up that hugged his chest and upper arms, leaving his tattooed forearms exposed. He wore dark-fitted jeans, no socks, and black sneakers. He topped off the look with metal-framed mirrored sunglasses, and his five o'clock shadow was dark, like his hair.

Simon shook out his shoulders and rotated his head from side to side to loosen up some kinks. Even after growing Lucas's height over the past year, changing from Lucas back into his normal form was still like taking a deep breath for the first time all day. He could stand up straight after what felt like hours spent stooped over.

The change from Lucas to Simon took only seconds.

Simon used his magic to send Lucas's wardrobe back to his house, the same way he'd retrieved his own. It was sometimes easier and took less energy to retrieve and return the items than to conjure each piece.

Walking out of the stall to the sink to wash his hands, he blended in like everyone else. He was just another guy in jeans and a T-shirt. No one paid him any mind as he made his way through the mall and back onto the busy street. Lucas welcomed attention, but Simon liked to blend in.

He kept his pace leisurely as befitted his lax attire and casual attitude. He was a few minutes late for his meeting, but he didn't want to attract attention to himself by rushing. He'd had trouble getting away this morning and someone could have become suspicious if he'd hurried. Lucas never rushed.

He hadn't seen Ben since that day in the cemetery two weeks ago. Ben had scheduled the meeting for Simon to check in. Then he'd be right back to his arrogant blond alter ego—the cocky bastard he'd perfected over the last year. He didn't want to be Lucas forever, but when he was him, he exuded confidence. He knew what Lucas liked and how he would act. He just had to be arrogant and act like he was in command.

Simon would bet Lucas had never hidden behind comics, even as a child. He was the life of the party, the one everyone gravitated to. It didn't matter that he was an ass most of the time, because he had charm and gobs of money. His good looks probably hadn't hurt either.

Being Lucas gave Simon a security he'd never felt as himself. Lucas didn't give a fuck if people liked him or not, and never worried about what people thought. He fit in simply because of who he was. The heir to a family fortune, brought up in wealth and privilege, always knowing where he belonged.

Though, Simon loved his job and he tried to be the best someone else he could be, as soon as he shed Lucas's blond locks and light blue eyes, Simon's old insecurities from his childhood spent in the foster system simmered under the surface, attempting to rise. It wasn't intentional, it just was.

The maudlin thoughts were coming far too frequently, but he shook them off as he entered the busy coffee shop. His FBI training kicked into high gear as he scanned for threats, identifying several magics among the crowd.

Two magics and two non-magics worked as baristas behind the counter. There were also two magics at a table near the window who looked like businessmen. Their coffee cups were pushed to the side as they went over what looked like a report.

They looked up as Simon passed, giving him a nod of acknowledgment as he walked by. He returned it, tilting his chin once in their direction. They wouldn't consider him a threat as he'd perfected a casual manner and relaxed, friendly smile a long time ago. That worked for him in both his job and his personal life—average guy, nothing to see here.

He sensed another magic person in a booth at the back of the shop, among tables of non-magics. Guessing it was Ben, he made his way there, unobtrusively checking the back for exits and places he could flash from as he walked. A short hallway led to two doors for single bathrooms and an exit at the end.

"Hey, sorry I'm late," he said as he came up beside Ben at the end of the table.

"Hi." Ben stood up and reached forward, giving Simon a hug like they were father and son. It reminded Simon that his entire life was about illusion. He slid onto the bench across from Ben as his boss and mentor returned to his seat.

"No problem. I figured you might have trouble getting

away." Ben pushed a coffee across the table toward him. "Black. It was easy."

"Thanks." Simon used his magic to add some cream and took a sip. He sat back, giving the appearance of him settling in for a relaxing chat with his father.

"Just a second…" Ben said, his voice trailing off as he waved his hand. It would have looked to outsiders like he was talking with his hands or shooing away a fly. Simon knew Ben had laid a light protective barrier around them. He couldn't feel the spell, but that's what Simon would have done. It would be enough to muffle their voices. Subtle but effective as long as they were careful. A strong magic spell would be like using a large megaphone in the small coffee shop, putting all other magics there on high alert.

Ben leaned back into the bench, his coffee cup clutched lightly in his hands like he didn't have a care in the world. Even with the small barrier, his voice remained low. "How are things? It's been a couple weeks since I saw you at the cemetery, and I don't like us to be out of touch that long, especially after the problem with Copeland."

Simon was glad he hadn't been caught up in the mess with Copeland, who had been after the magic box that was believed to contain untold evil.

Mimicking Ben's body language, Simon projected a relaxed and friendly manner as he responded to Ben's question. "I had hoped to hear something by now but I can't be too pushy or act out of character or they'll know something's up. I don't think any of my actions will be enough for them to know I'm not really Lucas, but they might expect he has ulterior motives. Lucas was only starting to make contacts when he died so I've been cultivating those relationships. It's a slow process."

"I'm not pushing you. You take the time you need."

"Really? No pressure?"

Ben chuckled, keeping up the pretext that it was a friendly father and son chat. "I trust you, son."

Simon wasn't sure if the word son was an act, even though no one could hear them, or if Ben really did feel that way about him. He hoped it was the latter. He took a sip of his coffee and then let out a slow breath, controlling his frustration. He'd been in the game long enough to know how it was played. He'd figured out years ago when he could be forceful and when to back down, but he was walking a fine line here. "I know. I've been given a few tasks, but they've been pretty minor so far. Just paying my dues… that sort of thing. I'm hoping that's about to change. I think I'm about to get a real task this time."

"You have a meet-up scheduled?"

"No, but Eddie touched base yesterday just to make sure I was still around."

"You still think that's not the guy's real name?"

"I'm not sure, but it would make sense if it wasn't."

Ben nodded. "As always, keep me in the loop." He took another sip of his coffee and smiled. "Has Lucas's mother sensed anything yet?"

"Nothing concrete that I'm aware of. If she does, she hasn't mentioned it." Catherine Jenkins was in her mid-fifties and rather humble considering the wealth and privilege she'd been born into. She was kind to everyone and volunteered her time wherever she could. Lucas must have inherited more of his father's genes than his mother's, as Catherine didn't have an unkind bone in her body. Everything Simon had learned about Lucas was that he had been an arrogant ass, so that's how Simon was playing him, and it hadn't raised a single red flag with anyone that he knew of. Being around Catherine was tricky, though—she was genuinely nice, and it was too easy to respond in kind.

Ben spent the next few minutes filling Simon in on the

office caseloads. No more magic children had been taken recently, but the task force was prepared to move at a moment's notice if necessary. They just didn't know what to expect next now that Copeland was dead. It suggested that taking children could have been his idea since no others had gone missing since his death.

"Shit," Ben said and turned his back to the front of the shop.

Simon didn't look around; he knew better than to draw attention to himself. "What's wrong?"

"Someone I know just walked in. Jo Williams. She's like a niece to me and is soon to be Jack's cousin-in-law."

"Jack Knight?"

"Yup, that's the one. It would be nothing for me to run into Jo, but I don't want to have to explain your presence."

Simon narrowed his eyes when he looked at Ben, his face still partially turned toward the wall. "Why not just say I'm a friend? You've made sure Jack and I have never met. I don't see the problem." Ben had recruited Jack shortly after he'd recruited Simon, and Simon had stayed clear of Jack and the other agents. To them, he was just another name and always on assignment because Ben had kept his identity hidden.

"No, me leaving is better." Ben stood with his back to the front of the shop. "I'll go into the restroom and flash from there. Do not engage with her, Simon."

Jo looked up when Viktor called her name. She hadn't noticed him come to stand beside her.

"Did you go home last night?" he asked.

"Yes."

His raised brow made her feel like a teenager coming in late, caught with one leg over the windowsill. She shifted in her chair. "I did, I promise." He didn't have to know it was only for three hours.

Viktor leaned toward Jo and pushed her hand away from her laptop, snapping the lid shut. It made a soft thud, like a reprimand in the library's early morning hush.

"Hey! Why'd you do that?" She pushed out of her chair and with her hands on her hips, faced Viktor with her impressive height of five foot two.

"You need a break. You cannot continue to push yourself like this, *kicsim*." *My little one.*

"I need to! It's been two weeks!" she whisper-yelled, then looked around to make sure no one had heard her. "Two weeks since Reece couldn't even get out of bed. If it weren't for Jack and Meredith boosting his energy, he might be even worse! I need to find the book!"

An image of Reece sleeping on his bed popped into her head, startling her like the one of their mother on her deathbed that still hadn't faded from her mind. She wouldn't stop until she saved her brother.

"And you will. But working yourself into the ground will not help." Viktor pulled her into a hug, and she clung to him, soaking in his familiar scents of sage and cedar.

She'd been a bit leery of the older Hungarian when Jack first put her in contact with him. She'd heard of Viktor Szabo's reputation at the library years before but had never met the man. Now, after working with him for two and a half months, she'd come to care for the gruff older librarian. He was the closest thing she had to a father or grandfather. His wise insight and vast experience with all things magic had quickly won her over.

When she pulled back, he used his fingers to tip her chin up so she was looking him in the eyes. "Go, get a coffee. Everything will be here when you get back."

She knew he was right. But how long did Reece have? She would get her coffee and then she'd make sure she focused even more diligently on her task. She gave Viktor a small smile and left the library.

When she reached the street, she pulled her phone out of her pocket to text Jack and ask about Reece, then put it back. Jack or Meredith would let her know if something was wrong. Jo had never been a worrier, but in the last several months, it had become her new pastime.

She used to be more of a go-with-the-flow type of person, like her brother. Now she'd worry if someone wasn't where they said they were going to be or even if someone was more tired than usual.

The longer it took her to find clues for locating the book,

the higher her frustration cranked up. She'd been so arrogant when she'd started this task. Her first guess was that it would take two weeks tops to find the book. Now, two and a half months in, she was no further ahead.

Jo sidestepped people as she walked to the coffee shop. The warm weather had brought people out in droves. She walked around a few people chatting in the middle of the sidewalk when she reached the shop. Inside, Jo took in the smell of freshly brewed beans, one of her favorite things, as she walked to the counter.

"Morning, Jo. Usual?"

"Morning. Yes, thanks." Jo chatted with the regular baristas for a moment, and then moved to the side to wait for her coffee.

Her mind wandered back to her favorite things as she waited for her coffee. When she found the book, she'd get her brother healthy and then she'd have everything on her list. Well, it'd been a while since she'd had a good fuck. Jo considered herself a modern woman, one who went after what she wanted. She enjoyed sex, so why not seek it out? It could be a good tension reliever.

She chuckled to herself. Just the kind of stress relief she liked. But not now. She had to focus. Sex would have to go on the back burner until after the spell on Reece was broken.

Her name was called, and she grabbed her coffee. Calling out a thanks, she turned around to head toward the exit and smacked right into a hard, muscular chest.

"Sorry," said a deep voice from above her.

"Shit," she said at the same time. Pure reflex had her holding her precious coffee to the side, careful not to spill. Large hands gently gripped her upper arms and prevented her from stumbling, but it wasn't enough to stop her from face-planting into his very solid, sculpted pecs.

The scent that drifted to her temporarily took up her

entire brain capacity. It was strong, but not overpowering, just earthy and pure male. She had the sudden urge to wrap that scent around her and never let go.

The muscles and hot male scent had her brain back to thinking about how long it'd been since she'd had sex. Too long.

Jo stepped back and looked up—way up, into the hottest face and most stunning green eyes she'd ever seen.

If only she didn't have to get back to find an ancient magic book.

SIMON DIDN'T HAVE a chance to respond to Ben as he was already headed toward the restrooms. By the time Simon glanced toward the front of the coffee shop and back to the restrooms, Ben had disappeared.

Simon knew instantly who Ben had been referring to. A woman stood at the counter waiting for her coffee and Simon wished he was in Lucas's form. He would saunter up to her and flirt, having the confidence that she, like any woman Lucas approached, would swoon at his feet. She would be putty in his hands.

She wasn't Lucas's normal type, but that didn't matter. She was striking in a way that called to Simon. Not tall in stature, he guessed five-foot-one or five-foot-two, with a small frame, and something about her spoke to him. His magic essence stirred, pulling him toward her like an invisible tether tugging on his soul. He wanted to touch her, see if her skin was as soft as it looked. Cradle his hand around the back of her neck and bring her curves flush against his hard body. He couldn't remember the last time just looking at a woman had affected him that way.

She had a short pixie haircut, dyed a mauve purple, and she carried it off, radiating a rare confidence. Her bangs were long and fell down over the side of one eye, an eyebrow piercing peeking through, accentuating her small nose and its light dusting of freckles. The morning sun streamed in through the large shop windows as if spotlighting her, shining a beacon on her beauty.

He wasn't normally a romantic, but he could have sworn she was there just for him. Her lipstick was a few shades darker than her hair, showcasing plump, succulent lips. They would likely be seen as too full on her small triangular face for her to be considered traditionally beautiful, but to him, she was arresting. He could imagine what those beautiful lips would look like trailing down his naked chest and then moving lower.

His body heated up just from watching her and he felt compelled to move closer. He needed to know what she smelled like and made a vow to himself right there that one day soon he'd learn what she tasted like, as well. As Simon or Lucas, he didn't know, but he wished it could be as Simon.

He pulled himself out of his trance and watched her for a few more moments before deciding what to do. Ben had told him not to engage, but Ben was gone, and talking to a woman in a coffee shop wasn't a crime.

Simon didn't have to look around to know that many eyes were drawn to her, just as his were. Maybe it was pheromones or something else, but whatever it was, some people just had that thing that drew people in. She had it in spades.

She joked with the barista, an obvious familiarity between them. The university kid was smitten, but the woman teased without being flirtatious. His magic essence stirred again, telling him she was a magic person.

After saying goodbye to the barista, she turned away from

the counter like she owned the space around her. She possessed a natural swagger he would have said was impossible for someone who probably weighed 110 pounds soaking wet with clothes on.

He internally groaned, mentally kicking himself for putting that image in his head. A vivid picture of what she'd look like if he stripped those proverbial soaking wet clothes off her petite, sporty frame was now front and center in his brain.

Giving his head a mental shake before his jeans became too tight and he embarrassed himself, he watched her head toward the door. Pulling his phone out of his pocket, he put his head down and walked directly toward her.

"Sorry," he said after he'd purposely bumped into her.

"Shit," she said at the same time, holding her coffee out to the side with quick reflexes, not spilling a drop, as her face pressed against his chest.

He held her upper arms to steady her, but he wanted to wrap his arms completely around her and pull her entire body flush against his.

Pulling in a deep breath, he forced his magic essence to calm. Never in his thirty-four years had it pulled at him as it did now. His first thought had been pheromones. Then maybe his magic was just reacting to her natural scent because it was unfamiliar, but that had never happened before either. No, this was all the birds and the bees. He was attracted to her on a level he'd never experienced.

Taking a step back, she looked up at him. Her bold stare captured his and he stared down into the biggest, bluest eyes he'd ever seen. Her skin looked like satin and except for the lipstick, she didn't seem to be wearing any other makeup. She didn't have to—she was beautiful.

She was dressed similarly to him, with dark, skinny jeans, running shoes, and a plain T-shirt. Overtop, she wore an open-zippered hoodie that partially covered her fit frame. Her T-shirt was taut across her breasts and nipped in as it tucked into the low rise of her jeans, showcasing her small waist and the flare of her hips.

"It's okay," she said, appearing completely confident in her own skin, not once giving off any embarrassment or shyness. She had to tilt her head back to look up at him and took another step back, probably to avoid craning her neck.

"Sorry for not paying attention. Thankfully, you had quick reflexes," he said with a smile.

"No worries, I'm good." She shot him a shit-eating grin and a wink, and just like that, she turned and headed for the door.

"Wait. Jo?" The words were out of his mouth before he even knew what he was doing.

Jo stopped just as she reached the door to the shop and turned around.

"How'd you know my name?"

Mr. Green Eyes smiled and took a step toward her, pointing at her coffee. "Your cup."

"Oh, right," she said with a laugh.

He took another step but didn't crowd her. "I know this is forward, but would you like to sit and have your coffee with me?"

"You don't have a coffee."

His grin touched his eyes in a way that made them seem even brighter. "I'll remedy that if you'll sit with me."

She looked over her shoulder at the door as if it had the answers she needed and then turned back to face Mr. Green Eyes. As Viktor had said, everything would still be there when she got back, and Reece would want her to take a break. "I'd like that."

Mr. Green Eyes gestured to a free table, and they walked toward it. "I'll just get my coffee and be right back."

Once he had his order, he sat across from her and extended his hand. "I'm Simon Hughes."

"Jo Williams." She returned the shake and felt a connection, like her magic was reaching out to him. There was still so much she didn't know about her magic; maybe that was normal when meeting another magic person. She'd have to remember to ask Viktor about it.

Simon was tall and athletically built. Not overly broad, but perfect for her. *Oh my god, get a grip.* Her first thought had been sex as tension relief. Not everything was about fulfilling her list.

He was dressed in dark jeans that fit his ass perfectly—she'd noticed when he went to get his coffee—and a long-sleeved shirt with the sleeves pushed up, exposing tattooed forearms. The shirt stretched across his shoulders, highlighting his muscles as if just for her. If she had her way, she'd have the most delicious dilemma in front of her—use her hands or her mouth to explore every part of his glorious chest, or trace each of his tattoos up his powerful-looking arms. She wondered how far up the tattoos went. The images caused her to do a mental check to ensure her mouth wasn't hanging open.

"So... do you come here often?" she asked him and grinned at her cheesy line. She'd never been nervous talking to someone new before, but there was something about this man that had butterflies dancing in her stomach.

He returned her smile, and it did something to his eyes. They were mesmerizing, with tiny flakes of gold, and he looked at her with an intensity that made her feel like she was the only woman in the world. His jaw was strong and the five o'clock shadow he was sporting made her want to feel it against her skin. He had to be the hottest man she'd ever seen.

He grinned back. "Not often, but I'm glad I came here today. What about you?"

Unconsciously, she rubbed the small tattoo on her own wrist, feeling the calm laughter flow through her. She dropped her shoulders and sat back before loosely grasping her coffee cup in both hands. She didn't want him to see the effect he had on her. "I haven't seen you here before," she said, hoping her voice didn't sound as breathless as she felt.

She met his intense gaze and he looked at her as if he didn't want to miss anything she said.

"I travel a lot for my job, so I've been gone a lot lately. What is it you do?"

Jo noticed the quick shift of focus to her and wasn't sure if he wanted to avoid talking about himself, or if he was more interested in learning about her, but she wouldn't push. She sensed something coming from him, but as always with magic, she couldn't tell what it was. She used to be so sure of herself and could tell in a split second if someone was lying, but not since her magic had been restored. "I'm a historian and professor, but I've taken a leave of absence from the university. I'm studying some old books and writing a paper."

"We're in complementary fields then," he said, giving her a breathtaking smile before leaning back and taking a sip of his coffee.

His smile could actually be her undoing. He was extremely hot, but when he smiled, it lit up his whole face, like his pure joy was being broadcast just for her.

"Oh?" she asked, even more curious about him. Now she wished more than ever that she had time to relieve some tension with a sexy stranger.

SIMON COULDN'T HOLD back the smile that spread across his face. He was fascinated by this woman in front of him and wanted to know everything about her. He wanted to stay here for days and keep talking to her.

"Oh?" she asked.

Simon had to bring his concentration back to Jo's question, hoping she didn't think he was staring at her. Which he was. "I'm an appraiser. I started out in antiquities, but I prefer antiques."

They talked about their jobs and old pieces of art that they both appreciated. The conversation was easy and before he knew it, almost an hour had passed.

Reaching forward, Jo circled his wrist with her fingers. "I didn't want to grab my phone to check the time," she said with a grin, and like before, appeared completely confident in her actions. She glanced down at his watch. "Oh shit, I should get back."

She seemed as reluctant to leave as he did. He couldn't remember the last time he'd enjoyed a conversation this much. He wasn't even itchy to get back to being Lucas.

"Holy shit. Is that Superman?"

Simon looked down to where Jo was checking out his ink after pushing his sleeves up higher. The tattoos on his arms disappeared when he took on another person's identity, his own identity ceasing to exist in every way but one—his memorial tattoo. Only inside was he still that shy boy looking for approval. "Yeah, I love Superman," he said, almost shyly.

Both his arms were covered in tattoo sleeves and he had no regrets. He got his first ink when he left the group home at eighteen. The iconic Superman shield was a no-brainer for the first one, high up on his right shoulder and coming down his biceps.

"Why Superman?"

He couldn't tell her the real reason he related to Super-man, but he wanted to be more authentically Simon around her and didn't want lies between them if he could avoid them. He didn't know why and wasn't going to do any self-reflection, just tell her how he felt. "I love that he's an amazing superhero, but also hiding in plain sight."

She chuckled. "Yes, those glasses are quite the disguise. Are you hiding in plain sight too, Simon?" There was a teasing tone in her voice; if only she knew how close to the truth her question actually was.

"No, this is all Simon," he said, holding out his arms. "But..." He paused as he tucked his hand into his pants pocket, out of sight under the table, and conjured some dark, thick-rimmed glasses. "How's this?" he asked as he put the glasses on and struck a Superman pose.

"Oh my god. I love it." She puffed out her chest and although he couldn't see her hands with the table in the way, he expected she'd adopted the Superman pose of hands on hips. "It doesn't take x-ray vision to see you are up to no good," she said and then laughed.

His cheeks might hurt tomorrow from all the smiling he had done. "I'm impressed. You can quote Superman."

"I like Superman too. But my favorite is Wonder Woman."

He wished she would per hand on him again—he missed her touch, even as brief as it had been. A thought of stripping down and showing her all his tats popped into his head. He accompanied the mental image with the thought of stripping her down as well and checking her fair skin for ink. Thoroughly.

Simon raised his eyebrows as he looked at Jo. "Any tattoos of the Amazon Warrior Princess?" he asked.

She stood and grinned down at him, gathering her things. "Nope, no tattoo showing on the first date."

"Ah, so you admit there is one?"

"Nuh uh, I'm not falling for that." Jo let out a laugh so playful, Simon felt it seep right into his soul. It warmed a spot inside of him he hadn't even realized was cold.

Simon sobered as he remembered why he was out as himself and not Lucas. He had a job to do, and he couldn't do it as Simon—except for his meetings with Ben. For almost ten years, the FBI had been his sole focus—be the best agent and someone else he could be. But just this once Simon wanted something for himself, though he wouldn't take it. His life was too complicated. He didn't even have his own place to take a woman to after a date. He'd cherish the hour he'd already had with Jo.

She moved to the garbage to throw away her cup and he followed right behind her. "Thanks, Simon. That was just the break I needed. Hey, how about—" She stopped when her phone rang. "Just a minute." She answered her phone and turned her eyes away. "What?... Okay, I'm on my way."

She turned back to Simon, and he saw regret in her eyes. The look probably matched his own.

"I gotta go… uh… thanks, bye." She turned and rushed out of the coffee shop without looking back.

Simon threw away his own cup and left the coffee shop. He headed to the back of the building to find a place to flash and wondered what Jo stood for. Perhaps Joanne or Jody or Joan. No, she definitely wasn't a Joan. She was far too feisty for that. Too bad he'd never find out.

"What happened?" Jo asked before her feet were even firmly on the kitchen floor. "Where is he?"

"He's fine. I'm sorry. I didn't mean to worry you, I just thought you'd want to know." Morgana bit her bottom lip and looked around, as if expecting someone to jump out.

Jo's shoulders deflated and she flopped on the stool at the kitchen island across from Morgana. "It's okay. I guess I overreacted. I was at a coffee shop when you called and didn't want to ask too many questions while there were others around."

"I'm sorry," Morgana said, looking at her hands in her lap.

"Hey, Mo, you already said that, and it wasn't needed the first time. It's fine. You didn't interrupt anything." Jo pictured Simon and his bright green eyes and knew she could have gotten lost looking in them for days. He was exactly the kind of man she was attracted to. Maybe it was a good thing Morgana called. Jo couldn't afford to get distracted right now. "So… where's Reece?"

Morgana looked up. "He's sleeping. I was at the bakery

helping out when he got dizzy. His part-timer had just arrived, so she took over and I came back with him."

"I know he's getting worse." Jo felt guilt descend on her like a load of bricks. She had been having fun with a man while her brother was getting worse. She needed to buckle down and focus. It didn't matter what Viktor said, she had to put in more hours to find the book. Maybe she could ask Meredith or Jack to give her more energy, like they did with Reece, so she could work harder.

"Maybe worse than when I got here six months ago, but in the last month or so he's just had good days and bad."

"Wow, you've been here six months already?" Jo stood, getting ready to leave when she saw the expression on Morgana's face and realized what she'd said. "No, Mo, that's not what I meant. We love having you here. I just can't believe how fast time is flying by."

"It's okay. You don't have to say anything. I get it since I've had my whole life fly by."

Jo sat back on the stool and looked at Morgana. She wanted to give her a hug, but Morgana didn't like to be touched, something Jo hoped would pass in time. "I haven't been a good friend. How are you? How are the migraines?"

"I'm okay. You don't have to stay and chat. I know you probably want to get back to the library."

"No, it's okay. I've got a few minutes. Please talk to me?"

"I'm like Reece. I've got good days and bad."

"What about your magic? Any improvement?"

Morgana shook her head. "I still don't have much magic, and no one knows why."

"Not even the Emissary? Did you finally get to talk to her?"

"Yes, but she couldn't figure it out either. She and the other council leaders are speculating that maybe I was born without much magic. But they said that's a bit unusual, unless my family line had started turning away from magic generations ago."

"But then why would someone have kidnapped you as a child?"

"Good question. That's another thing no one can figure out. I've been this way for as long as I can remember; the problem is there's just so much I don't remember."

"Nothing's come back to you? Where you're from? Who your family is?"

"Not much. Sometimes I'll see a young girl in my dreams, but I don't know who she is."

"I'm sorry, Mo. I wish I could say something that would help." She couldn't imagine what Morgana was going through. Jo had lost a lot of people in her life, but at least she knew who she was and she still had her brother and cousins. "Just know that I'm here if you want to talk."

"Thanks. Don't worry about me, I'm fine for now."

Meredith had given Morgana one of the empty condos in the building they all lived in so she wouldn't be alone. Jo just wished they could do more for her. "You're like family. We'll help you however we can."

Morgana's lips lifted in a small smile. "I'll stay here with Reece so you can get back to work."

"Thanks. I'll just check on him and then go." She got up and walked toward the hall before turning back. "Mo? We do like having you here and we'll figure out where you're from. I promise."

Morgana nodded and looked down at her hands.

Jo blew out a breath, her bangs fluttering and settling back on her forehead as she walked down the hall. She couldn't seem to help anyone lately.

Reece was flat on his back and snoring softly when she looked in his room. The little sister in her wanted to wake him up just to hear his voice. She'd loved it when he'd read stories to her when she was little. At eight years old he'd become the man of the family. Not that her mother had asked that of him, but he'd naturally assumed the role after the death of their father and older brother.

He'd done so much for her, and she couldn't even find one stupid book to save his life. She flashed back to the alley behind the library, determined to succeed. She didn't have time for coffee shops and a tattooed Superman.

SIMON GLANCED at Lucas's Patel Phillipe watch, noting the time, and pulled down his shirt cuff. Go time. The moment Simon had been working toward for almost a year was here. He wasn't given any details of the meeting, just that he would be given a task. If all went well, it would get him the names of the people who were looking for the magic box and had been working with Louis Copeland. But more than that, he wanted to figure out the identity of the FBI mole.

Simon looked into the large gold-framed mirror on the wall, and Lucas's reflection stared back. He checked out his hair, ensuring his dark blond locks gave the impression of just the right combination of mess and structure. The first time he'd had to style Lucas's hair, he'd ended up with a stiff and greasy-looking mess and had to take another shower.

Fortunately, problem solving was Simon's forte. He could look at any situation and figure out a solution. This one had been easy. He'd had Lucas's assistant book him a hair appointment at his usual salon. Not only did he learn who his stylist was, he watched what she did, and he could now replicate it. So many things made up a person and he had to learn everything that was Lucas Jenkins.

Turning away from the mirror, he surveyed his surroundings. The Jenkins Gallery's offices were no less posh than the gallery showrooms. They took up the entire second floor of an old historic building in the downtown core.

When researching Lucas, he'd learned that the Jenkins family had bought the building when it was built just after the turn of the twentieth century. Upgrades throughout the decades had modernized it, and they had turned the upper floors into condos and homes. The gallery was the last of the Jenkins's physical businesses; the rest of their vast financial holdings were investments, handled by various firms.

Lucas had been entrusted with the gallery several years ago after his father's death. In typical Lucas-fashion, he'd used the gallery as his personal playground. He'd let his assistants handle the running of the gallery while he entertained himself. Lucas had liked extravagance. The more expensive and lavish something was, the better.

During his first several months as Lucas, he'd made minor mistakes here and there—nothing big enough to have raised suspicion. Except for the time Simon had been too kind to his assistants, and he'd made the colossal mistake of doing business work, acquiring a piece of art as an art dealer would. The move sent shockwaves through the company until he laughed it off, explaining his actions as an opportunity with a down-on-her-luck hookup. After that, he'd perfected the part of the shallow and callous playboy everyone expected.

He looked at his watch again. His contact was now five minutes late. But if he reached out, he'd look desperate.

Since he had time to waste, he sat back at his desk and pulled up the gallery's latest acquisition report. No one expected, or even wanted, Lucas to be involved, but Simon kept on top of what was happening in the gallery anyway. It made him feel like part of the happenings around him.

The computer screen blurred in front of his eyes as a

picture of Jo laughing and touching his arm came to his mind. It had been two days since he'd met her in the coffee shop and he couldn't count the number of times he'd thought of her in the last twenty-four hours.

Last night in the shower he was soaping himself up when he imagined her there with him, her purple hair wet and pushed back from her face. She slowly dropped to her knees while she looked up at him, then gripped his hips and pulled him forward, her small mouth taking as much of him as she could. His own hand gripped tighter as he imagined Jo sucking him off. He leaned forward, one hand on the shower wall, and jerked faster. He came harder than he could remember coming in a long time, his cum hitting the tiles in front of him, his breathing short and fast.

Simon knew it wouldn't be the last time he'd use Jo's image to pleasure himself, but if that was all he'd have of her, he wouldn't feel guilty about it.

He looked down at his hand on the keyboard as the memory faded and saw Lucas's hands and watch. Looking at his hand was a habit he'd started years ago. A reminder that he was someone else and he had a job to do. He shook off the thoughts of Jo and got back to work.

When his phone pinged, he glanced at the time; he'd been working for an hour.

Eddie: Library @ 7

That was the only message. Too fucking cryptic for Simon's tastes, but then, he wasn't a thug.

Lucas made it to the library just before seven, giving him time to casually walk around, casing his surroundings. When he didn't see anyone suspicious, he leaned against a tree in the green space outside the library and pretended to scroll through his phone.

He kept his head down but was aware the moment his contact pulled up on the other side of the street and exited his vehicle. Simon had spent the last year observing the few contacts Lucas had made and decided from the get-go to let Lucas's true personality shine—arrogant and completely internally focused. It gave him an advantage when dealing with his contacts as they never expected very much from him.

When his contact, Eddie, was only a few feet away, Lucas looked up. "What's up with the change of location?"

Eddie was shorter than Lucas by about five inches and younger, maybe in his late twenties. He was Lucas's main contact, but Simon still didn't know as much as he'd like about the young man. He'd been able to piece together that Eddie was born in California, spoke Spanish fluently, loved wrestling, and worked out every chance he got, but not much else.

"Don't worry about it. Just go where you're told."

"Where's Rocky?"

"Stop with the fucking questions. If you want to help, do what I say."

Lucas stuffed his phone into his pocket and leaned back against the tree, presenting a casual air. "Yeah, man, no problem. What are we doing?"

"Fuck! Another question."

Simon worried he'd pushed too far this time.

"We're going to introduce ourselves to someone," Eddie said.

"Who?"

"You don't need to know that yet." Eddie shifted on his feet and looked over at the front of the library.

Simon watched as Eddie looked around, his head moving

left and right, then left again. Eddie's behavior had Simon on alert, but he didn't show it, continuing to lean against the tree.

"I can't figure you out," Eddie said, turning away from the library.

"What's there to figure out?"

"Why you're here."

"You told me to meet you," Lucas said, continuing with the dumb playboy act.

Eddie shook his head. "No, asshole, I meant why you're working with us."

Simon was surprised it'd taken someone this long to ask him. Lucas had only been working with them a couple months before his death, and Simon didn't know if they'd already posed the question, but he had a vague answer ready. "I've heard rumors about what you're doing, and I want in on it."

"But why? I mean, look at you." Eddie sneered and waved his hand up and down in front of Lucas. "You've got looks and money. You drive a sick car and your job is cushy as fuck. You can probably get as much pussy as you want. You don't need anything else."

"Right, but I still have to hide my magic, just like you do. Money won't change that."

"You want to be out in the open?"

"Don't you?"

Eddie shrugged. "I guess, but I don't have a choice. I'm in this whether I want to be or not."

"What do you mean?"

"Fuck, just forget it." Eddie's phone pinged. He glanced at it and then up at the library doors. "She should be coming out soon."

"You've got someone on the inside?"

"Just a piece I met a few days ago who was willing to do me a favor."

"You ready to tell me what we're doing?"

Eddie kept his gaze on the library doors. "There's a woman looking for a book and we're going to put a bit of pressure on her."

Simon had been leery about coming to the library to begin with and now all his internal warning bells were going off. Jo had said she was doing a research project at the library, and he knew from Ben that Jack had tasked someone with looking for an ancient book. It didn't take a genius to put two and two together. As an FBI agent, he didn't like to rough people up, but he'd do it for the job. Roughing up an innocent woman, especially Jo, was a completely different ball game and not one he wanted to play. He pulled away from the tree and faced Eddie head-on. "Why rough her up?"

"She's not working fast enough, and we need her to find the book."

"Didn't your mother ever tell you that you can catch more flies with honey than vinegar?"

"Don't mention my fucking mother, and what the fuck are you talking about? Flies and honey?"

"It's an express… never mind. I just think we'll get more out of her by charming her. If you rough her up, she's going to go on the defensive and be wary of everyone around her and she'll tell someone about us. But if we charm her, she'll never know what we want. That gives us an advantage."

"How the hell do you expect us to do that?"

Good question. Simon was thinking on his feet, but he had to think fast. Eddie still hadn't confirmed that Jo was the woman they were talking about, but Simon wasn't going to let Eddie hurt an innocent woman, no matter who she was. He had to find a way to keep her safe and keep his cover.

"You can pretend to mug her, and I'll stop you. Then she'll be thankful, and I can get close to her."

"Fuck that. You want the Latino to be the mugger and your white ass is going to save her?"

They didn't have time to fight over this if Jo was about to walk out of the library. "Don't be stupid. You said yourself that I could get any pussy I wanted. You think you have the money to charm her?" He stared Eddie down and hoped Jo never learned that he'd referred to her as pussy.

"Asshole. Okay, we'll do it your way. I'll follow her and you be ready to step in. She'll probably go somewhere she can flash home."

"What's the woman's name?"

"Josephine."

Well, that answered Simon's question. That meant the woman was definitely Jo—he knew she couldn't have been a Joan. Josephine was nice, but he preferred Jo; it suited her.

Lucas moved around behind the tree out of sight of the doors, and waited for Eddie to make his move.

8

Jo waved at the security guard as she left the library. Viktor had left a little while ago and she'd promised him that she wouldn't stay too late. It was an easy promise to keep tonight because she was exhausted after working almost all day and night for weeks.

She hadn't even gone back to the coffee shop since meeting Simon two days ago. The thought of going back this morning had entered her mind, but she'd resisted in case he was there. Simon was a temptation she couldn't afford right now.

The sun was starting to go down, but there were still people enjoying the tables on the lawn outside the library when she stepped into the cool spring night. She was just turning the corner into the alley beside the library before she bothered to look up to make sure no one was around. Entering alleys was becoming such a habit she sometimes forgot to make sure she was alone. And nothing had happened in months, so it didn't seem as dangerous as she'd first expected it would be.

Today she'd thought she'd found a clue that would lead

74

her to another book, but it was a dead end. Disappointment had flooded her. She was running out of time and didn't know what else to do. Viktor had been a godsend, finding book after book for her to comb through, and he was convinced she'd soon find what she needed, but Jo wasn't so sure. What if she found a clue and didn't recognize it for what it was? What if the clues they needed weren't even in the library?

She was walking on autopilot because she was so in her head. Her frustrations with the book were mounting and she didn't know what to do.

Someone yanked Jo's bag, threatening to pull her off her feet. "Hey!" She wobbled backward, but kicked out and spun around, regaining her footing. She kicked out at her attacker and yelled again, holding onto her bag's strap with both hands.

"Stop!" someone yelled from a distance.

Jo was in a game of tug-of-war with her opponent but looked up at the call just in time to see a man flash in front of her attacker. The man was tall and dressed in a suit, but his refined clothing didn't seem to hinder him. The man's hands curled into fists on the front of the attacker's shirt, pushing him back and forcing him to let go of the strap.

The sudden release of the bag sent Jo backward, and she landed on her butt on the cold, hard ground.

"Let me help you."

Jo looked up to see a hand held out near her face. Holding her bag in one hand, she grasped the stranger's hand with her free one. She let out a small gasp at the connection as her fingers tingled like her magic was reaching out, jut like it had with Simon. Since it had now happened twice, maybe it was normal. She'd forgotten to ask Viktor about it. "Ah, thanks."

"Are you okay?"

"Yeah, thanks." Jo looked up at her suited rescuer and then scanned the alley. "Where'd he go?"

"He ran off as soon as he dropped your bag." The man turned around as if to check and then looked back at Jo. "I'm guessing you were headed to the back of the building to flash?"

Jo stood back and focused on the man in front of her. She'd been right; he was about a foot taller than her. Probably about the same height as Simon. But his hair was a dark blond, whereas Simon's had been a deep chestnut brown, like dark chocolate. And Simon's eyes had been green, but even in the fading light, she could tell this man's eyes were a light blue.

She gave herself an internal slap. She needed to stop thinking about Simon and focus. What had he asked? "How'd you know I was going to fl—" She gave her forehead a face-palm. "Duh. I keep forgetting that magics can recognize that I'm magic too."

"How could you forget that?"

"I'm new to this. It's a long story. My mugger wasn't magic?"

"No." He held out his hand again. "I'm Lucas."

"Jo."

"Nice to meet you, Jo, although I wish it hadn't been under these circumstances."

Jo chuckled. "Yeah, me too."

Still holding her hand, Lucas turned it over. "You're scraped."

Before Jo could say anything, Lucas conjured a wet cloth and wiped her hand, removing any dirt. He disappeared the cloth and gently sandwiched her hand in both of his and Jo felt a slight sting.

"That should do it," he said, releasing her.

"Oh." Jo stared down at her palm. She'd seen magics heal

others in the last year, but this was the first time anyone had healed her. She didn't know if she should be impressed or ashamed that she couldn't have done it herself. She stepped back and looked up at Lucas. "Uh, thanks."

"My pleasure. Why don't I follow you around to the back so you can flash from there? Just to make sure you're safe."

It probably wasn't the best idea to go to the back of the building with a stranger, but she figured it couldn't hurt since he'd already saved her and healed her.

She flung her bag on her shoulder. "Thanks again."

"You're welcome, Jo. But before you go, two questions."

She stepped back and looked up at him. "Okay, but I don't guarantee answers."

"Fair enough," he said with a charming smile. "Why didn't you flash back there? When the guy came at you?"

"Like I said earlier, this magic thing is still new to me, so I think my non-magic instincts kicked in instead. What's your second question?"

"I'm guessing you were at the library. Are you there often?"

"Maybe. Bye, Lucas." She flashed home before she could do something stupid like ask Lucas out for coffee.

9

Jo reached back with both hands and rubbed her neck. Using her magic, she heated her hands and continued to massage her aching muscles. She dropped her chin to hide her grin, hoping no one saw her smiling to herself like a lunatic. Every time she learned a new trick with her magic, it expanded her world. Rowena had taught her this latest one.

A picture popped into her head of her mom teaching her how to use her magic to boil water as a child, and the smile dropped from her face. After the unbinding ceremony last year, random memories that had been taken away would come to her now and then. The usual anger from her mom and aunts taking away her magic and the following twenty years of lies threatened to overwhelm her as they usually did. She dropped her hands to her laptop on the desk and took a deep, calming breath, closing her eyes. There was no point in thinking about the lies they had told since her mom and aunts were gone now.

"Good morning, Jo."

She opened her eyes and found Lucas standing beside

her. She'd been so lost in her memory that she hadn't noticed him. That seemed to be happening more often lately, like last night. "Morning. What are you doing here?"

"May I?" he asked, gesturing to the chair across from her. She nodded. "Sure."

"I wanted to make sure you were alright after last night."

"How'd you know I'd be here?"

Lucas shrugged; the expensive material of his pinstriped suit flowed with his movement. "A lucky guess. You didn't answer when I asked you if you came here often. If you didn't, you probably would have told me that." He grinned and sat in the chair.

"Right. I'll have to remember that." She was able to get a better look at Lucas in the bright lights of the library than she had in the dim alley last night. He was just as good looking as she'd suspected. His blond hair was tussled to look messy, but it probably took him some time each morning to achieve the style. She looked at Lucas's wrists. No tattoos. At least, none that she could see at the edge of his shirt and jacket cuffs. It shouldn't matter, but she wished he was like Simon. It was ridiculous considering she'd only met Simon once.

"So… how are you? No pain from your fall last night?"

"Nope. I'm good." Jo didn't know what to say next and an awkward silence hung between them for a moment. "Thanks for dropping by."

"Do you work here?" Lucas asked, either not picking up on or ignoring her hint of dismissal.

"I'm a professor at the university, but I'm on sabbatical as I do some research."

"Sounds intriguing. What kind of research?"

She'd been asked that same question dozens of times in the last few months, but it almost seemed more than casual coming from Lucas. "Looking into ancient books."

"Magic ones?" he asked, his voice low.

"Why would you ask that?"

"It makes sense since this library has a large selection of magic books. The general public doesn't know that of course, but I think it's pretty common knowledge among magics."

"I hadn't thought about that."

"The long story you mentioned last night?"

"Something like that."

Lucas sat forward, his forearms resting on the table. "I get it. I won't pry." He paused but kept his eyes looking directly at hers. "Jo, can I take you to lunch?"

"That's really nice of you to offer, but I need to work."

"Another time?"

"Lucas, you seem nice, but I'm on a deadline and I don't have much time for anything else."

He stood. "I understand, but I'm a very persistent man. I'll see you around, Jo."

Jo watched Lucas walk away. If she wasn't so busy, would she have taken him up on his offer? An image of Simon came to her mind again and she realized that even though Lucas and Simon were so different on the surface, she was attracted to them both.

When she swung back to her laptop, she saw Viktor watching and got up, walking over to him.

Viktor stopped stacking books to smile at Jo. "Who was that?"

"His name is Lucas—I forgot to ask him his last name. Oh, but that reminds me. There was something I meant to ask you last week."

"What's that, *kicsim*?" Viktor ran his hands through his thick mop of dark hair with just a smattering of silver at his temples. It gave him a distinguished look, like he planned it that way. It was a frequent gesture she had come to recognize. She had learned all his gestures over the last couple of months. His hands in his hair meant he was thinking and weighing his words carefully.

She looked around to make sure no one was within hearing distance. "I had a strange reaction to someone I met a few days ago and I had the same reaction to Lucas when I met him last night. I wondered if it was because we're both magic."

"You sure the person you met the other day was magic?"

"Yes, and so is Lucas."

"What did this strange reaction feel like?"

"It was more intense the other day than with Lucas, but I got really hot, like I was flushed, and almost didn't know what to say. That never happens to me."

He just stared at her; his eyes crinkled more than usual at the corners.

"What?"

"Jo, your magic was blocked for twenty years, but otherwise your upbringing and education was normal, yes?"

"What do you mean?"

"Your mom or your aunts taught you about the birds and the bees, yes?"

"Birds… birds and the bees?" She felt her jaw drop as his words sunk in and then slammed her mouth shut.

He broke out in a grin. The shine of his straight, white teeth contrasted with his salt-and-pepper beard and mustache when he couldn't keep a straight face anymore. "Yes, Jo. When a girl likes a boy, she…"

"No. Just no, no, no." She cut him off, but he couldn't hold back his laughter. His full-on belly laugh echoed throughout the stacks of books, drawing the attention of several ladies on the other side of the room.

Jo leaned forward, getting as close to him as she could with the tall counter between them. She looked around and then lowered her voice. "You're wrong. I wasn't having that kind of a reaction to either man," she said, her words coming out almost in a hiss. "They're both magic, so it must have something to do with that."

"No, Jo. I don't think the reaction was anything but normal boy-likes-girl and girl-likes-boy-back."

If that was true, she was in big trouble.

"Lucas, is that you?" Catherine called out from the library.

"Yes," he said, walking into the room. Lucas's mother was sitting on the sofa with her tablet in her hands. She looked up as he walked over to her and bent down to kiss her cheek. "How was your day?"

"Lovely. Thank you for asking. I met with the ladies from one of my charity groups earlier today and now I'm trying to catch up on some of my reading before dinner. Will you be joining me?"

The hopeful, almost pleading look in her eyes cut right to that place inside of Simon where he felt too deeply every time he denied Catherine a request. Her husband had died years ago, and Lucas was her only child. Simon couldn't stand the thought of refusing her again, regardless of what her real son would have done. "Yes, I'd love to."

She beamed up at him, the laugh lines at the corners of her eyes showing more prominently on her beautiful face. She was an elegant woman and aging gracefully. Whether from genetics, the privileges that wealth could afford, or magic, he didn't know.

During dinner, the conversation flowed easily. Catherine talked about her different charities and events. She kept herself busy by serving on a couple of boards, volunteering with several organizations, and visiting with friends.

When Simon first became Lucas, he'd avoided Catherine as much as he could, which wasn't easy considering they lived in the same house. He wanted to learn more about the man he was portraying before he spent time with Catherine because if anyone could spot the lies, it would be Lucas's mother.

Simon knew he hadn't avoided her only because he was worried about being caught. Every time he was around her, he remembered his lack of a mother in his own life. He was more comfortable with Catherine now, but still on guard whenever they were together.

"Thank you, Cassandra," he said as the young staff member cleared his plate. In the early days, he'd realized his mistake too late when he was polite to the family's employees. His manners and kindness to the staff were so out of character for Lucas that it had raised eyebrows.

Simon had covered his mistake by saying he had forgotten his manners over the years and was trying to improve them. After a while those around him became used to the new, politer Lucas, but it put him on alert with other areas of Lucas's life, such as when he was with friends and something from Lucas's past could trip him up.

Regardless of how careful he had to be around some people, his time with Catherine was nice and relaxing.

They were enjoying a glass of wine after their dishes were cleared away when Catherine became quiet, staring down at her hands in her lap.

"What is it?" He usually avoided referring to her by name. In the early days he had to mentally stop himself from calling her Catherine after a slip. They had been out to lunch, and she'd raised her brows at him, but he'd just shrugged, hoping she'd chalk it up to being around others. He couldn't bring himself to call her mom and reverted to mother when he had to address her. "You seem nervous."

"Well…" She paused and then seemed to visibly shore herself up, raising her head to meet his gaze directly. "I have a favor to ask."

He chuckled, a grin teasing at the corners of his mouth. "Is that all? I thought you were going to kick me out or something."

"Since everything is in your name, hardly," she said with a small smile.

Well, that was news to him. Lucas didn't deserve anything from this family, but it was a moot point, really. Lucas no longer existed. Best to ignore her comment for now. "What do you need?"

"That charity ball I told you about, the one for children, is fast approaching and we have entertainment, but several board members brought up what you did in college."

She hesitated again, as if afraid to ask him something. Sometimes Simon really hated being Lucas. Lucas had been an ass and no matter how heartless it made him, Simon wasn't upset that Lucas was dead. He smiled, hoping it would encourage Catherine to continue.

"I was wondering if you and your usual buddies would help out again?"

Well, that certainly hadn't been in the Lucas Jenkins portfolio. "Christ, college, that was a long time ago," he said, hedging. "We did so many things, could you narrow it down?"

Catherine seemed almost excited, as if it was a good sign that he hadn't turned her down right away. As much as Simon was glad Lucas was dead, some days he wished the man was still alive so he could strangle him for how poorly he'd obviously treated his mother.

"Remember that time you and your friends went to a few country clubs and sang an acapella song and encouraged people to buy tickets to the event? You even promised you'd sing at the event if lots of people bought tickets." She laughed, as if remembering. "I think there must have been a lot of young women at the clubs, because you managed to sell us out."

"Sure. I'll ask them." Wow, Lucas had done something nice once. There must have been something in it for him. He'd talk to Lucas's buddies and see what he could pry out of them.

"Oh honey, thank you. That would be wonderful," she gushed as if he'd just given her the world. And maybe, as far as Lucas would have been concerned, he had. "I'll email you the details." She reached across the table and patted his hand, her eyes aglow with warmth, and that alone made it worth whatever Simon had to do.

They finished dinner a short time later and he walked around to give her a kiss on the cheek as she stood to greet him. She was an inch or two taller than average height with a trim figure and kept her dark blond hair in a classic bob, with long bangs crossing her forehead. Lucas got his looks from her, and she reminded him of a younger Helen Mirren, pure grace. He would miss her when he left.

They said their goodnights and he headed to his rooms.

Entering his wing of the mansion, he shut the large double doors to his section of the house. After turning the lock, he cast a strong spell that would give a subtle push to anyone who came to the door not to disturb him. The spell he used was detectable, but he didn't care who knew. No one here would question him.

Lucas had an entire wing of the mansion to himself and every toy imaginable. So much extravagance that it almost made Simon embarrassed.

He wasn't exactly a slouch when it came to money. He'd inherited money from his parents when he'd turned eighteen and he'd invested it wisely over the years, plus his expenses were low. But this house was on an entirely different level. During his first week as Lucas, Simon got lost twice and had to backtrack to figure out where he was. It wouldn't do for staff to figure out he was lost in the house they believed he grew up in.

He walked through a formal sitting room and into his bedroom—that room alone was the size of the main floor of a modest home. He stripped and tossed his clothes on the bed, then shed Lucas's persona as easily as he had his shirt and pants.

He took a deep breath and stretched his shoulders and neck as he walked to his bathroom naked. His footsteps were quiet on the marble floor as he made his way to the corner of the massive bathroom and turned on the shower heads.

Standing under the spray, he braced his arms against the wall in front of him. The water cascaded over his shoulders and back, his thoughts going to Jo and the assignment he'd been given. Or rather, the one he fabricated to avoid Jo being hurt.

Get close to Jo and charm her. He could do that, except it really wouldn't be him getting close, it would be Lucas.

Simon washed himself quickly and got out of the shower. It was one thing to jerk off to Jo's image when he thought he'd never see her again, but now it seemed disrespectful. He'd enjoyed chatting with Jo today, even though she'd turned him down as Lucas. Simon wasn't deterred; he'd just have to up Lucas's game.

He changed into shorts and a T-shirt that he grabbed from the enormous walk-in closet. Once he'd seen the house, the closet wasn't a surprise, and though it had been too ostentatious for his taste, he was used to it now.

He'd learned a long time ago that life was better when he was adaptable, so he had taken a lot of things over the years in stride. Like his living arrangements.

As soon as he'd reached eighteen, he left the foster care system and got his own place but hadn't kept it for long. He put his few possessions into storage when he'd joined the FBI because he was living in Quantico for his training.

When he'd got his first assignment with Ben's task force, he'd used the apartment of his new identity and he'd been doing that ever since. It had been almost ten years since the first time he took on an identity for the FBI, and in between assignments, it was easier to rent a furnished apartment by the month because he'd never be there long.

If he wanted a woman, he would either go to her place or take her back to his identity's place. It was convenient and made it difficult for him to be tracked. A win-win. When the assignment was over, he'd move on, and no one would ever be the wiser.

Lucas had been a man-whore and Simon had to keep up Lucas's reputation, but just being seen with the women was enough; most it didn't go further than that. Lucas's type had been tall, statuesque blonds, like himself, and preferably models. He'd been all about the eye candy and the attention. They could be fashion models or centerfold models; it hadn't mattered to Lucas as long as they'd kept up his image.

One of the hardest things about taking on someone's identity was figuring out how they fucked. It was a lot more difficult to figure out what an assignment was like in the sack than what kind of alcohol he drank. The only way around it had been to trust his instincts. He'd decided the real Lucas would have liked it hard and fast and only gave the woman enough to ensure she would gossip highly of him afterward. He'd rarely done repeats.

When Simon first became Lucas, he made the mistake of coming onto a woman Lucas had already fucked and dumped. It took some quick backpeddling to get out of that one.

After that, he'd spent one long night getting Lucas's friends drunk on some quality whisky and pumped them for information on stories about who he'd been with in the last year. He'd pushed enough alcohol on them to make it seem like he'd wanted to relive some of his glory days. It hadn't been perfect, but he'd learned enough. Now if he ran into anyone Lucas had been with more than a year before Simon came on the scene, he'd feign bad memory.

He shook his head at all the lies he'd told over the years and walked out of the closet. Picking up his tablet off the dresser, he caught his reflection in the mirror on the wall.

Simon stared at himself, trying to remember the last time he'd spent a significant amount of time in his own body, apart from when he wasn't sleeping. He could maintain another's form when sleeping but preferred not to, giving his body a chance to stretch out.

Except for the coffee date with Jo, he couldn't remember when he'd last been himself. Most days he didn't even know what *Simon* liked anymore, but he knew he liked Jo. Now Lucas had to woo her and then steal from her. It didn't matter what Simon wanted, and that was something he'd have to remember. He had a job to do—be the best Lucas he could be and charm Jo.

10

*J*o sat down after hugs and goodbyes when the older generation left The Magic Plate, the Williams's restaurant.

Jo, Meredith, Rowena, Morgana, Reece, Jack, and Damon were left. Sometimes, some of Jack's FBI colleagues and Damon's sister, Kate, stayed, but not tonight. Jo was the baby of their group, with Jack and Damon the eldest, and his sister Kate somewhere in the middle, like Reece.

Meredith had revived the weekly tradition of hosting a late-night dinner in their family's restaurant after their mothers died just over six months ago.

Some weeks the group was bigger than others, depending on who was around, but Jo tried to attend every week. She'd learned how short time with family could be and you never knew when someone was going to take their last breath, so she cherished each moment she had with them.

Jack conjured three bottles of wine and put them on the table in front of Jo before leaning over to give Meredith a kiss. "Since Jo is here, let me know if you need more."

"Ha ha, Jack, very funny. Wine is good for you, plus I've mastered conjuring my own."

Jack laughed. "I knew you would," he said, and turned to face Damon and Reece, probably filling them in on the latest magic council business. Jo usually liked to hear about it, but she didn't want Jack to ask about her search, so she faced her cousins and Morgana. "Meredith, picked a wedding date yet?"

"No, we're not in a rush. We might even just go to the courthouse."

"What? That's not like you, sweetie," Rowena said. "You've always wanted the big fairy-tale wedding."

"I don't need it now," she said quietly, and looked down at the table, folding a cloth napkin.

Jo looked at Meredith as if someone had taken over her cousin's body. Meredith had always made them play prince and princess when they were little—Jo hated it, but played along to please her cousin. "Mer, is it because of our moms?"

Meredith finished folding the napkin and cradled her wine glass with both hands before looking up and answering. "I'm not sure." She shrugged. "It just seems with everything going on that a big wedding is too decadent."

Jo walked over to Meredith and pulled her into a hug. "Our moms would have loved it. Do it for them and enjoy your day," she whispered in Meredith's ear.

When Jo pulled back, she could see tears shining in Meredith's eyes, ready to spill. Meredith waved her hand in front of her face and the tears disappeared, her eyes bright and clear. "I'll talk to Jack."

Jo nodded and went back to her seat, filling her wine glass. She thought back to when she'd walked into Reece's bakery a couple of weeks ago—thinking about her list of what a woman needed. She'd added fresh bread to the coffee, chocolate, wine, a good book, some great shoes, and an occasional good fuck. Well, six out of seven was pretty good. She had the opportunity to complete the list, but she was hesitating. Besides being busy, something was holding her back.

Lucas had dropped into the library every day since the night after the botched mugging. He was sweet and charming, and yet she hadn't accepted a date with him. If only she could find a clue. Maybe then she'd be okay with taking some time for herself.

"Have you seen that guy again?" Morgana asked, pulling Jo out of her thoughts.

"Wait, what guy?" Meredith asked, her wine glass halfway to her mouth. "You haven't mentioned anyone."

Morgana dropped her head, looking suddenly interested in the tablecloth. "Sorry, Jo. Didn't mean to spill the beans," she said quietly.

"It's okay, Mo. It's not a secret. I just haven't seen you lately, Mer, or Ro. You've both been busy."

"Right. Well, I'm here now. As Morgana said, spill the beans," Meredith said.

Jo didn't want to mention the attempted mugging and have everyone up in her face. Instead, she chose to keep things vague. "I met a guy outside the library last week and he's been coming in every day to say hi. He's asked me out each time, but I haven't said yes yet."

Rowena's brows furrowed in what Jo thought of as Rowena's psychologist-thinking face. "Why not? Are you interested?"

"Yes, he's nice and attractive. Really sweet, actually. But I'm busy. I need to find the book." Jo looked down the table at Reece and lowered her voice. "I'm worried I'm running out of time."

"You just told me to have my big wedding and not hold back because of what happened. Isn't this the same thing?" Meredith said with conviction while keeping her voice low.

"You need to date someone you're interested in because you never know what will happen tomorrow. And what if he's *The One?*"

Jo glanced at her brother again and saw he was still deep in conversation with Jack and Damon before she turned back to her cousin. "No, it's not the same. You're only getting married once so you shouldn't miss out on that. I've got a limited amount of time to find the book. If someone wants a date with me, he can wait."

Meredith nodded and talk turned to the continued renovations on the building.

"Now that Reece has one of the storefronts for his bakery and Isaac has the other for his tattoo shop, have you got anyone else lined up? There are three shops left, right?" Jo finished off the last of her wine.

"I've got a couple of prospects and the gym should be ready soon."

"Did you mention the gym?" Damon called from down the table.

Meredith chuckled. "Yes, Damon, soon."

Damon didn't need to lift weights and get any bigger. He was already as broad as a brick house, even bigger than Reece had been when he was healthy, but the man loved working out. There were a few minutes of teasing and then the group broke up. Everyone picked up something to take to the kitchen without anyone needing to be directed.

Jo and Morgana were both juggling multiple wine glasses when Damon walked over.

"Morgana, let me help you," Damon said as he lifted the glasses right out of Morgana's hands without asking her permission to take them.

"Dammit, Damon! I'm not helpless!" Morgana stalked away to the kitchen without looking Damon's way.

"Well, she told you, buddy," Reece joked.

Damon stormed off and Jo turned to her brother. "What's up with them?"

"Don't know. But I'm more concerned about you. How are things?"

She wrapped her arms around her brother's waist, and he hugged her back. Her throat tightened around a lump when she realized she could get her arms almost all the way around him. The last time she'd been able to do that was before they'd started high school. He felt even thinner than he had a couple of weeks ago.

He pulled back and looked down at her. "What's this I hear about you not accepting a date?"

She followed him into the kitchen. "You heard that?"

"I'm weak, not deaf."

Jo sat the wine glasses on the kitchen counter and wondered what to tell him. Her brother had never been weak a day in his life. Hearing him admit it was even worse because he usually brushed it off. She just hoped he hadn't given up. But even if he had, she wouldn't. "I'm just busy."

Reece put down the dishes he'd been carrying and used his finger to tilt Jo's chin up. "I know you're looking for the book, but you can't stop living. If you're interested in this guy, I want you to go out with him."

"I'll think about it, okay?"

"Don't think. Just say yes."

Jo wished it was that easy. Every minute she wasn't looking for the book, even while at family dinners, Reece was getting weaker, and she didn't know how much time she had left to find the clues.

*L*ucas was pleased with himself as he looked across the table at Jo and smiled. She'd finally agreed to go out on a date with him, and it had been a success. "You finished?"

"Yes, thanks."

He gathered up the items from their picnic, leaving out their bottles of water, and closed the picnic basket. "I was right, right? This was a good idea?"

She laughed and looked around her. "Yes, this was a good idea. I needed to get outside."

Lucas leaned back against the tree they'd had their picnic under. "We'll have to do it again soon." He'd dropped by the library every day for the last two weeks, but he'd made sure he never stayed too long, not wanting to come across as pushy.

He'd spotted his contacts a few times now, so Lucas needed to be seen with her. And it worked out for him too because she was becoming a compulsion to Simon—his day just wasn't right if he didn't get to see Jo.

When he stopped by, he'd ask how she was doing and a

couple of times he'd asked her out, but she'd continued to turn him down.

He made a show of looking at his watch and covertly glanced to the side. Eddie and Rocky, his two contacts, were sitting at an outside table at a restaurant across the street. They had become his constant shadows. So far, they hadn't put any pressure on him to do more with Jo, but he expected that wouldn't last forever.

"Thanks for lunch, but I have to get back to my research." Jo stood and picked up the blanket, folding it before passing it over.

"It's supposed to be another beautiful day tomorrow. Want to do this again?"

Jo ran one foot back and forth along the grass and glanced down at her Vans before looking back up. "I don't think so, Lucas. It's nice that you've dropped by every day, but I really need to work—I have a deadline."

Lucas was losing her, and Simon couldn't let that happen. Not only did he have a job to do, but his time with Jo was the highlight of his day. He didn't even mind that he had to be Lucas. He'd let go of Lucas's arrogance the very first day he'd dropped by and each time he saw her, a bit more of the real Simon slipped through. He wasn't always sure who Simon was anymore, but his time with Jo felt natural. "What if I can help you with your research?"

"What do you mean?"

"I'd like to introduce you to my mother and—"

Jo held up her hand like she needed to ward him off. "No, Lucas, that's way too soon. We're not even dating."

"Sorry, that's not what I meant. Please let me explain." He waited until Jo nodded. "My mother is a collector of old magical books. She must have hundreds in her collection, and probably has something that can help with your research. There's a charity event on Saturday for the children's hospital and my mother is a big supporter. Please come with me and I'll introduce you then. We can dance and you can ask my mother about her collection."

Simon could tell Jo was starting to waver and now was the time to close the deal. "Why don't you bring Viktor? I'm sure he would love it and then you'd have a chaperone." Lucas had met the older librarian the second day he dropped by to see Jo, and knew she had a soft spot for him.

"Can I think about it?"

Lucas gave her what he knew was a winning smile. "Sure, I'll drop by tomorrow and you can let me know. That'll give you a chance to talk to Viktor."

After Jo said goodbye and walked into the library, Lucas picked up the basket and blanket and headed to his car. He didn't need it, but it helped with his image around non-magics, plus the Alfa Romeo was fun to drive.

He put the items in the trunk and was reaching for the door when he felt a presence beside him. He dug deep and pulled up Lucas's arrogance. "Hello, gentlemen. What can I do for you today?"

Rocky hung back, but Eddie had no problem getting in Lucas's face. "You're a cocky bastard. It's been two weeks, where's the book?"

"These things take time. I'll have it soon."

"You better, or you might not like the consequences." When Eddie took a step back, Lucas got in his vehicle and pulled away from the curb.

He worried that if Jo didn't agree to go to the charity event with him, Eddie would go back to plan A—roughing up Jo to get what they wanted.

12

Jo walked into Morgana's apartment without knocking.

"Hey, Mo! Can you give me a hand?" Jo shouted from the large foyer.

"Just give me a minute," Morgana yelled from her bedroom.

Jo had been hesitant about accepting Lucas's invitation, but now she was starting to get excited. She hadn't had the instant attraction with Lucas that she'd had with Simon, but Lucas was slowly starting to win her over.

She glanced at her reflection in the floor-length mirror hanging near the front door. She was confident in her looks, but tonight she wanted to take things up a notch.

The sides of her hair were freshly trimmed and the longer hair on top swept over her forehead, with just enough height not to be laying flat. Her eye makeup was light to showcase her signature dark, pink lipstick, and she'd swapped out the rings in her eyebrow and ears for diamond studs.

Her light red, almost pink dress complemented her hair and hung to the floor with the material secured in dozens of tiny pleats, falling from her waist in graceful folds. The top was a panel of rich pleating held up by spaghetti straps, leaving her back completely bare, and connected to the skirt with leather-trimmed cut-outs at the waist in a dark shade of the same red, adding a touch of edge.

She turned, loving the way the material swayed, making her feel sexy. She finished the outfit with simple metallic high heel sandals that gave her an extra few inches in height.

"Wow," Morgana said as she walked out and took her first look at Jo's dress. "You look fabulous, darling!" Morgana drew out the last word and grinned at Jo. "You didn't use a glamour spell, did you? You know, to add a bit of extra shine?"

"No, baby, this is all me."

"You are so going to knock Lucas on his ass tonight!"

"Thanks." Jo chuckled. That was definitely the boost she needed. She turned her back to Morgana. "There's a clip at the top I can't fasten. Can you get it?"

"All done."

"Thanks." Jo gave herself one more look in the mirror to check her lipstick and turned back to Morgana. "I should have asked Lucas for a ticket for you. Sorry for not thinking of that."

Morgana shook her head. "It's okay. I don't think I'm ready for crowds like that."

"Maybe we can go someplace more low-key soon. Instead of always eating in the family restaurant."

"I'd like that."

The doorbell rang and Jo checked the time on her phone. "Are you expecting someone? I ordered a car for tonight, but it's picking up Viktor first, so it should still be a few minutes, and I was going to meet it downstairs."

Morgana frowned. She pulled the door open and took an abrupt step back. "Damon, what are you doing here?"

Damon strode into the apartment, forcing Morgana to step further back. "I came to check on you. Where are you going?" Damon asked, looking between Morgana and Jo.

Putting her hands on her hips, Morgan faced Damon down, even though she had to look up to do it. "Nowhere."

Morgana had been with them for almost seven months. She was lively with Jo, and she'd finally started to open up a bit more with her cousins too, but Damon made her shut down fast.

"You shouldn't be going out, Morgana. You're still suffering from headaches, and you don't know what's wrong with your magic. Something could happen and you wouldn't be able to protect yourself."

"Lots of people have headaches and no magic, Damon!" Morgana stomped her foot like a three-year-old, her sock-covered foot barely making a noise on the tiled floor.

"Hey, Damon. What's your problem? Morgana was just helping me." Jo had known Damon her entire life and although the guy could be intense, his caveman routine regarding Morgana was a bit much.

Jo's phone pinged so Morgana would have to stand up to Damon on her own, but she could handle it. "That's my ride. I've gotta go."

Morgana gave her a hug and held the door open for her. "Have fun, and Damon, don't let the door hit you on the way out."

"Morgana…"

Jo walked out and the door shut behind her, blocking the rest of Damon's sentence. She was going to love watching the journey between her two friends and her bets were on Damon. He was intense but she thought he really cared about Morgana. He'd just have to figure out how to tone it down. She chuckled and flashed downstairs to the waiting car.

Viktor stood waiting for her at the curb with the door

open and looked dashing in his tux. "Good evening, *kicsim*. You look beautiful." Jo's anticipation for the evening built as they made small talk on the ride to the Jenkins Gallery, where the event was being held.

As they showed their tickets and followed the streams of people into the gallery, Jo soaked up the excitement around her. She decided to push all worry aside for the night and go with the flow. This was a night for fun and there was a gorgeous man here waiting for her. Tonight, she'd focus on that and put the rest of her problems on the back burner for a few hours.

She'd lived in Blue Mountain her entire life, but she'd never been to the gallery. It was far larger than she'd been expecting, more like a luxury museum with several rooms branching off from the main one, each holding different collections.

Viktor took a glass of champagne from a passing waiter and handed it to Jo. "I am going to the bar. You will be fine?"

Jo gave his arm a squeeze. "I'm good." She watched him walk off and took a sip of the champagne while letting her gaze roam the room.

She spotted Lucas near the bar with a group of older couples and enjoyed watching him. He held the group riveted as he gestured with his hands, obviously telling a story. They seemed to hang on to his every word and then everyone burst into laughter when he finished. After shaking hands and kissing cheeks, he made a grand exit from the group.

He turned her way and their gazes met. A Cheshire cat smile took over his features as he stalked toward her.

"Good evening, Jo." He bent forward to kiss her cheek, displaying perfect gentlemanly manners, until he whispered in her ear, "You look ravishing tonight—good enough to eat."

Jo sucked in a small breath and tilted her head up to meet

his eyes as he stepped back. "Lucas," she said, a small smile lifting the corners of her mouth.

"Jo," he said, drawing out her short name, as if pondering it. "I've meant to ask... Joan? Jo-Anne? Jocelyn? Jodie?" he asked, one eyebrow raised.

"Josephine."

"Beautiful." He breathed the word almost in a whisper.

Over the past two weeks, she'd sometimes felt like Lucas was two different people—the quiet, introspective gallery owner, and the outgoing, sophisticated charmer. He was so smooth Jo wondered if it was natural or practiced. Her brother had been that way before the spell was cast on him. Reece could have charmed the pants off anyone. An ache for what her brother was going through squeezed her heart, and she swallowed against it. Tonight was a temporary reprieve from life and then she'd get back to searching for the book. She shook off the feeling and smiled at Lucas. "Thank you."

Jo watched as a beautiful, older woman walked toward them, coming up behind Lucas. She had to be Lucas's mother—the physical resemblance was unmistakable.

"Lucas," the woman said as she stepped to his side.

Another longing hit Jo like a splash of muddy rainwater from a passing car, drenching her in a feeling of sadness. Some days she could fool herself into thinking that her mom was still in her apartment and not gone forever. She closed her eyes for a moment, taking a small breath, and then focused on Lucas's mother, giving her a warm smile.

"Mother, I'd like you to meet Josephine Williams. Jo, this is my mother, Catherine Jenkins."

"Jo, please," she said, offering her hand to the older woman.

"Pleased to meet you," Catherine said, shaking her hand. "How did you two meet?" she asked, a wistful smile crinkling the corners of her eyes.

Jo held her breath, hoping Lucas would evade the truth, although she wouldn't want him to lie. After the first morning when Lucas came to check on her, they'd never talked about the botched mugging again.

"I met Jo when I was at the library."

He hadn't lied, or not completely.

"How lovely." Her smile appeared genuine as she turned to Jo. "Williams." She pondered the name the same way Lucas had, their mannerisms so similar. "Are you related to the Williams who own The Magic Plate?"

Jo's eyes rounded in shock. "Yes, how did you know?"

Catherine's eyes softened as she spoke. "I'm so sorry for your loss. I know it was years ago, so you would have been small when your family died. I'm sure I must have met you at the funeral. You look so much like the Williams men, especially Griffin. He and his brothers were friends of mine and my husband's in college."

"He was my father."

"He was a lovely man. I heard your aunt Lillian passed years ago, another tragedy. How are your mother and your aunt Elise?"

"They both died several months ago. My mother from an illness and my aunt in an accident."

"Oh my, I am so sorry. You have seen so much loss, you sweet girl."

"Thank you." Jo didn't know what more to say or how to change the subject. Catherine was so much softer spoken and different in personality than her son.

"Josephine," Viktor said as he came up beside Jo, like he was her personal lifesaver. "Please introduce me to your companion and this lovely woman."

Jo chuckled softly. Another charmer. "Viktor, this is Lucas Jenkins, the owner of the gallery, and his mother, Catherine.

Lucas, Catherine, this is Viktor Szabo. We work together at the library."

"It is nice to meet you." Viktor shook Lucas's hand and then Catherine's, giving her a slight bow.

"Nice to meet you as well," Lucas said.

"Viktor, let me introduce you to some people," Catherine said, and turned to her son. "Lucas, bring Josephine by the house for dinner one day soon." She kissed his cheek and turned to Jo. "It was nice meeting you, Josephine, and I look forward to seeing you again soon." She put her hand in the crook of Viktor's elbow when he extended his arm and they walked off.

Jo saw something pass across Lucas's features that she couldn't place as they walked away. When he turned back to her, he was grinning. She liked Lucas, but like over the last couple of weeks, she sensed something that told her to be cautious.

She hadn't dealt directly with a lot of magics since the unbinding ceremony, mostly just close friends and family, and now Viktor. Perhaps she was reading into his expression since she wasn't used to how people within this lifestyle acted, especially magics. She'd have to ask Viktor and hope it didn't lead to another *talk*. She couldn't hold back the small laugh as she thought of their conversation about the birds and the bees.

"I hope that's a good laugh," Lucas said, a question in his eyes.

"Yes, I was just remembering something." She pushed all thoughts from her mind, focusing on the man in front of her. She was drawn to Lucas so she didn't know why she kept thinking about Simon, a man she'd only spent an hour with and hadn't seen since. It was time to put him out of her mind. She smiled up at Lucas and decided to see where the chemistry between them led.

13

When Lucas had escorted his mother into the ballroom, Catherine was immediately caught up in the hoopla of the event. She gave him a wave as she left to join her usual circle of friends, grabbing a glass of champagne from a passing waiter as she moved into the fray.

Simon chuckled to himself, enjoying watching Lucas's mother excited at being out and about. She had everything money could buy, and yet she was alone. She didn't just sit in that big mausoleum of a house day after day—she had committees and lunches to keep her busy, as well as hobbies and friends—but at the end of the day, she went to her rooms alone.

He felt a connection to her in a way he was sure her selfish son never had since he was too busy looking out for himself and chasing power. Connecting with Catherine was two-sided. He liked the one-on-one conversations but they were also the hardest—he'd forget he was Lucas and just let out what came naturally. Being with Catherine made him long for his mother.

Simon was finding it harder and harder to stay in character the more he was around her. The same was happening when he was with Jo. It was a dangerous situation to be in. On the outside he was the gregarious and arrogant Lucas, but inside he would always be Simon, the young boy who didn't belong.

When Catherine had wandered off, he'd made his way to the bar, subtly scanning the room as he went. There were magics among the crowd, as there would be at any large event, but he hadn't sensed any threats.

His focus had been on looking for one particular magic person, and he'd sensed her before he saw her. When her gaze caught his, he'd felt something settle in him: an unexpected rightness.

She was uniquely beautiful. The bold dress and everything about Jo's outfit made a statement, just like the woman herself.

Lucas pulled his thoughts back to the present as he watched Catherine walk away with Viktor. Turning back to Jo, he watched her eyes light up with joy as she chuckled to herself.

"I hope that's a good laugh." He wanted in on the private thought that had crossed her mind.

"Yes, I was just remembering something," Jo said and smiled up at him.

Her smile lit something inside him, making him smile in return. Then he remembered she was smiling at Lucas.

Letting out a small breath, he straightened and projected the confident, charming Lucas. "Would you care to dance?" he asked with a small bow. Without waiting for an answer, he removed the glass she held and handed it to a passing waiter. He took her small hand in his much larger one, loving the feel of the contrast in their sizes, and escorted her to the dance floor.

Leading her in a waltz, he ignored decorum and held her

close. Regardless of upbringing, Lucas would have gone for what he wanted. But really, he knew he was telling himself that because he'd use any excuse to get close to Jo.

He'd learned to dance when he first joined the FBI magic task force. So many assignments put him in situations just like this one that it was a skill he needed. It had always just been part of the job. Until tonight. Tonight, he was thankful for a reason to pull Jo close.

"Enjoying yourself?" he asked. Her eyes sparkled in the low light, giving him ideas of what he would do with her if they were somewhere private.

He glanced at the watch on his wrist without being obvious. His reminder. Lucas's watch and hand. Jo was here with Lucas, and he had a job to do.

"Yes, it's exciting," she said. "I'm a bit more of a down-home girl, but who doesn't like to dress up once in a while?"

"I'm glad you came." He leaned down and kissed her forehead gently before he caught himself. Lucas wouldn't have done that.

He was about to make a teasing comment when the music stopped, and the MC took the mic, announcing Lucas and his friends.

"You're performing?"

"Yes." He gave Jo a quick kiss on the lips and winked. "You're in for a treat." He flashed her a hundred-watt smile and made his way to the stage.

Pulling up all the confidence and charm that he'd embraced over the last year, he took the mic from the MC and wowed the crowd. He teased and flirted with some of the older women standing in the front, complimenting them, but never crossing the line into inappropriateness. It was everything expected of someone born into a wealthy family, always knowing where he stood in life. Even if he was an arrogant ass.

He looked over at his friends, Lucas's friends, and counted down, then turned back to the front and focused on Jo.

The words were for her as he sang the first line of "Lady in Red."

He held her gaze through the entire song, not breaking eye contact as his friends joined him in the chorus.

The audience ate it up, women cheering for them as he and Lucas's friends played to the crowd, but he only saw one woman.

He sang the last line just for her.

They finished the song to a huge round of applause and flowed right into another one. By the time the MC took over, he was itching to get back to Jo.

He turned to his friends as they exited the stage. "I'll catch you later."

"No problem. I'd ditch us too if I had that woman waiting for me," one friend said. Lucas laughed and patted his buddy on the back. "Yeah, I'm a lucky bastard."

Some of the gallery's patrons greeted him as he made his way across the floor to Jo. He shook hands and accepted accolades but kept moving. Jo was only about ten feet away when someone walked across his path. "Excuse me," he said as he dodged to the right.

"Lucas."

"Yes?" Lucas focused on the man in front of him, taller than average height, maybe in his sixties, and wearing an expensive-looking tux. Only his bushy mustache seemed a bit out of place. Lucas extended his hand. "Have we met before?"

When the man returned Lucas's handshake, there was a dark tattoo showing under the end of his sleeve, like a swirl. "No, I've just heard great things about you and I wanted to introduce myself. My name is Andrew Smith. It's nice to meet you."

Lucas looked over at Jo as she waited patiently for him. "It's nice to meet you too. Thank you for your patronage."

"It is my pleasure, Lucas." Mr. Smith glanced over his shoulder, looking in Jo's direction. "She's a beautiful woman; I won't keep you any longer."

"Enjoy the event." Mr. Smith was already walking away by the time Lucas finished speaking. Something about the greeting didn't ring quite right. He'd have to talk to Ben later about Andrew Smith. Right now, he only wanted to focus on Jo.

When he reached her, she smiled up at him and his night got even better.

"You guys were fabulous. I didn't know you could sing."

He wrapped his arm around Jo's waist and gently guided her toward the back showroom. "We started singing for fun in college and my mother asked if we'd do it again tonight. I don't do it often, but this time it's for a good cause." He suspected Lucas had originally done it for the attention and the women, not to be charitable. Simon was just glad he could help Catherine's cause.

The noise level quieted the further they got from the main gallery. "It'll be easier to talk back here." He led her through large double glass doors that opened onto a stone patio, lined with pots of overflowing flowers.

Jo stepped further onto the patio and he dropped his hand. She looked around before her gaze focused back on Lucas. "It's beautiful out here."

"Not as beautiful as you."

"Oh, that's bad. So cheesy."

"No, just the truth. You are really beautiful." He looked into her eyes and knew he could get lost in them. He'd never felt like this for a woman before. In the last two weeks, he'd started to fall for Jo. But if she was feeling the same, it was Lucas she was falling for.

Simon wanted to kiss her, but not while she looked into Lucas's eyes. He unbuttoned his tux jacket and shoved his hands in his pant pockets to avoid reaching for her.

"What else do you do besides work at the gallery and hang around the library?" There was a lightness in her eyes as she teased him.

"I read." As soon as the words were out of his mouth, he wanted to kick himself. Jo made him want to be himself and answer as Simon would. Lucas didn't read. He hadn't had even a single book in his rooms when Simon had taken over his appearance.

"What types of books do you like to read?"

Good question. What would Lucas have read if he was so inclined? "A bit of this and that, but mostly action. An Ian Fleming book is always good."

Her smile widened as she looked up at him. "Right. I mean, who doesn't like James Bond?"

"So, what about you? What do you like to do when you're not at the library?"

"Normally, I teach and in the summers I go on excursions with students."

"No hobbies?" A funny look crossed her face—embarrassment maybe, but it was gone so quickly he wasn't sure.

"I like reading too."

"Action?" he asked, hoping to keep the mood light after the look he saw on her face.

"Yes, but also books about history and some biographies."

"Makes sense considering your career." He wondered if she wasn't going to mention the graphic novels she'd told him about in the coffee shop.

"Lucas, why me?"

"What do you mean?"

"I researched you."

Oh shit. He'd partied some since he'd become Lucas, but it had been pretty low-key compared to the real Lucas. If her search went back more than a year, she'd have found all kinds of pictures of Lucas with models and scantily clad women. Even pictures of him caught in compromising positions. All the pictures and articles had been great when he'd been researching Lucas to get a feel for the man, but probably not so great from Jo's perspective.

He leaned forward and grinned, bringing on the charm. "You Googled me? What did you find?"

"You date a lot, and the women didn't look to be five-foot-two professors. So… why me?"

"I like you, Jo. I was attracted to you from the first time I saw you in the alley." He took a step toward her and she stood her ground, her gaze never wavering from his. He loved that. She was strong and confident, something he found attractive.

"I like spending time with you," he said as he took another step closer until their bodies were almost touching. Placing his hands on her hips, he gave a small tug and closed the remaining distance between them. He smiled down at her with all of Lucas's cockiness. "Do you like spending time with me?"

"Yes, Lucas, I like spending time with you," she said with a laugh, like reassuring a child she was still friends with him. He wanted to kiss her so much.

He bent his head and moved his hands to cup her cheeks. The sight of Lucas's hand and watch was like a bucket of cold water in the face. He gave her a quick peck on the lips and pulled away, retreating a step. "We should get back to the event."

"Oh, right."

She turned from him, but not before he saw the look of disappointment on her face. Shit, he was such an ass.

They walked side by side, not touching as they made their way back into the gallery with its bright lights. Catherine waved them over as soon as they entered the large showroom.

Standing beside Jo as she spoke with Catherine and Viktor, he let his gaze wander the room. A man in a tux that looked a size or two too large stood in the shadows by the hallway to another showroom. Simon wasn't sure, but he thought it could be Eddie. Looking around, he didn't see any of Eddie's cohorts, but there were a lot of people mingling about.

He should have kissed Jo. It would have looked good if Eddie had been watching, but he hadn't wanted Jo to kiss Lucas. For the first time in over twenty-four years, Simon didn't want to be the best someone else. He wanted to be Simon and he wanted Jo for himself.

14

"Jo," Lucas said softly from where he sat across from her.

"Hmm?" Jo lifted her eyes from her computer and looked up at him. "When did you get here?"

"About five minutes ago. I was waiting for you to pause, but then I thought you might be falling asleep." He pushed a lid-covered coffee cup toward her.

She rubbed her eyes with her fists. "I'm exhausted."

"Can I help?"

He'd dropped by every day since the charity event a week ago, bringing her a coffee and asking if he could help each time. He needed to get close to her for his job, but he wanted to help because he was starting to care for her. Every day she'd said no, but today he thought she might be wavering. She still hadn't confessed what she was doing, but if she was closer to finding the book, she wouldn't look so forlorn.

"Thanks," she said, gesturing toward him with the coffee cup, and then took a sip of the coffee. "I'm not sure."

"I know you're researching and looking in ancient magic books, but you haven't said what the project is. You've also never explained why you're twenty-seven but only started using your magic a year ago." He reached around her laptop, capturing her free hand in his. "Jo, you're slowly working yourself to death. Please, let me help."

She opened her mouth to speak and then closed it again. Maybe she still didn't trust him.

She put down her coffee and rubbed a tattoo on her wrist, giving him an opening to break the tension. "Is that a memorial tattoo?"

Jo's eyes were wide as they met his. "How did you know?"

"It was just a guess. They're comforting, and I've seen you rub it whenever you're thinking hard."

She lowered her eyes, a self-conscious mannerism he hadn't seen from her before. A moment later, as if a switch had been flipped inside her, she lifted her chin with a determination that he thought of as pure Jo. It spoke volumes. He knew then that she was going to tell him what he needed to know to move forward with his task.

"It's in memory of my mother." She paused, rubbing the tattoo again. "I didn't know anything about memorial tattoos until this past year."

"I am for the loss of your mother." He paused for a moment, unsure how much of himself to give her. There was so much he couldn't say, but he'd open himself up to her as much as he could. "Losing my father was devastating." Guilt ate at him for not mentioning the loss of his mother as well, but he couldn't since Lucas still had his mother. "We move on, but I don't think we ever get over it. The ache never quite leaves you because you've lost pieces of yourself."

"Thank you," she said softly.

"Now, let's talk about ancient books." He grinned, flashing Lucas's most charming smile, hoping to lighten the mood.

He wanted the full story, to know more about Jo, but to get that he needed her trust. Common ground could help build that. "I have one as well, but I can't walk around rubbing my chest," he said and grinned. When she laughed, he got the reaction he'd hoped for.

"I'm guessing from your exhaustion that your work isn't going like you expected?"

"A couple weeks ago I thought I was making headway, but now I think it was a dead end. Almost three and half months in and I'm no further ahead than when I started."

"Well… like I said, I want to help. I've got a lot of experience with the arts, including literature. Tell me what you're working on, and I'll let you know what I can do." He held his breath, hoping he wasn't being too pushy, and that Lucas's ways hadn't rubbed off on him while still acting like Lucas. Fuck. Some days his life was too complicated.

"I'm looking for some ancient magic spellbooks."

"Looking? As in you don't know where they are?" He kept his voice casual, showing interest, but not too much. The thought of spending more time with her every day almost made him giddy, and not just so he could find the book and complete his task.

"Exactly. It is believed that there were seven spellbooks, or perhaps one book with seven volumes, created centuries ago. Maybe millennia. No one is sure. They are hidden and can only be found by unearthing clues, supposedly also hidden." Her eyes sparkled as she huffed out a snort. "Magic people sure like their secrets."

If only she knew. "Are all seven books here?"

"No and no one even knows if there really are seven books. Right now, it's just a guess. Two of the books were found in Europe over a century ago and rumor has it the rest are hidden here and somewhere in Hungary. I know a book was used in this city for a powerful spell almost twenty-one years ago, and then the book disappeared. Besides that, not much else is known."

That was more information than Eddie had given Lucas, but it still left some holes in the story. "If they've been lost for centuries, why look for them now? What prompted your search?"

Jo rubbed her wrist again and Simon recognized the gesture for the tell that it was. She did it when she was anxious or unsure about something.

"It's believed that the books hold a particular spell that can cure someone and I need it to help someone I know."

She closed her eyes briefly, then seemed to fortify herself. She took in a long slow breath before letting it out and meeting his eyes. He suspected that there was much more she wasn't saying, but at least she was opening up. That was enough for now.

Jo's fingers moved across her wrist for the third time in as many minutes and that movement telegraphed all the sadness she was feeling. "That's the only reason you're looking for the books?"

"No, but that's the biggest one as far as I'm concerned."

"And the other?"

"The new magic council that is forming needs the books. There are some..." she paused as if searching for the right word, "unsavory people also looking for them, so we need to find them first."

Lucas leaned forward, resting his forearms on the table. "I want to help you, Jo." He looked at her and waited. Tension ran through his entire body, but he forced himself to maintain his relaxed demeanor.

She was quiet for several moments as if weighing things in her mind. It took so much for him to be quiet and let her decide without any more pressure from him.

"Okay," she said. "I could use some help."

He smiled again and then looked down at his wrist. He

needed to remember she was asking Lucas for help and not Simon.

THEY'D BEEN RESEARCHING for six hours and only stopped once to quickly eat the sandwiches Lucas had conjured.

Jo leaned back in her chair and stretched her arms. "You find anything?" she asked him.

"Maybe."

About an hour ago Lucas had come across a reference in a 600-year-old text that talked about hidden binding spells and referenced another book. It wasn't much, but it was the first time they'd found a reference to an actual spell.

"Show me?" she asked.

He didn't look up from what he was scratching on a notepad. "Just give me a second, then we'll go find the book."

She watched him as he referenced some notes as if looking for something. He had on slacks with a button-up shirt, the sleeves rolled to mid-forearm. She liked the look and wondered what he'd look like with ink covering his arms.

It wasn't the first time she'd compared Lucas to Simon, which was strange. She'd only spent a short time with Simon, whereas she'd known Lucas for weeks now. Even rationalizing it, she couldn't help but compare the two men. They were so different, and yet at times they seemed so similar. Both smart and confident, both driven and outgoing, but Simon had a more natural way about him. Still, the more time she spent with Lucas, the more she realized he had a natural, soft way about him too, just not as likely to come out in public.

Her gaze dropped to his lips, and she wondered what

he'd kiss like. Most likely confident and a bit forceful. She'd been so sure he was going to kiss her last week at the gallery. Maybe she'd originally read Lucas all wrong, that his charm and arrogance were just an act and he was actually shy.

She looked up as he closed the laptop he'd magically retrieved from somewhere and stood. Her gaze tracked him as he walked around to stand in front of her.

"Come on, I'll show you what I found."

"Okay." She looked down at the hand he offered to help her up as she laid her hand in his. Such a simple gesture, putting her hand in someone else's. But it felt like more. His hand was large and warm as it engulfed hers, giving her a feeling of safety and something else. Comfort? Lust? Really like? She was attracted to Lucas in a way she never would have expected when she'd first met him.

She misjudged his strength, keeping her body too relaxed as he pulled her up. She lost her balance and fell into him.

She flattened her hands on his chest to steady herself, and her face was right up against him. He seemed so tall, but if he leaned his head forward, their lips would touch. Being short didn't usually bother her, but there were times, like now, where she'd give up wine forever for a few more inches in height.

He gripped her arms to steady her, and she had a brief flash of déjà vu. The smell of him, like a sexy man—woods, lust, and spice all blended together—wrapped in a beautiful package felt like it was made only for her.

Screw her wish for a few more inches. She tilted her head up to see what he would do.

When he let go and stepped back, disappointment pulsed through her. She'd felt the chemistry between them at the gallery, but he hadn't kissed her then either. His actions spoke loud and clear as he backed away. But then why had he been hanging around her for weeks? She schooled her features as her gaze met his.

"Ha, you seem to make it a habit of saving me," she said, trying to laugh off her reaction to him.

"No problem, I'll save you any day." He grinned down at her, but she was sure there was more than just humor written across his face. She saw the heat and knew he was as affected as she was. But then why didn't he do anything?

"I don't think what we're looking for is on any of the documents you've scanned so far, so we'll need to go look for it."

She followed as they walked to a sink Viktor had installed, thoroughly washing and drying their hands in preparation for touching the old books. Lucas was all business, showing none of his usual sexy flirtatiousness as she listened to him explain what they were looking for.

She breathed in a long breath through her nose and let it out in a small huff. Maybe Lucas wasn't as affected as she was, and she should follow his lead and get back to work. "I hope this is something more than just a clue to another book," she said.

"Yes, me too. I've only been at this for a day and already it's a bit discouraging."

"Tell me about it." It had definitely been a frustrating couple of months for her.

"Maybe what I've found will lead to something."

"What made you think it was a clue?"

"It wasn't really one thing, but several references to Adeodatus Fabricius. He was a magic historian."

The back room where Viktor held a good majority of the magic tomes was large, with shelves lining the walls from floor to ceiling. There was a table with chairs and several cradles for holding the books, some on the table and some on stands on the floor.

"I've come across his name too, but I hadn't found any connections to give context to who he was." Jesus, she'd been a historian for years and she'd never seen a single reference that spoke of magic people. It was amazing to her that magics had stayed hidden all this time. But duh... magic. "What did you find?"

"References to volumes of an apologia. Maybe that's what we're looking for."

"An apolo—Holy shit." A light bulb so big it felt like it could be seen from the moon lit inside her. Her mind raced as she put the pieces together. An apologia was a formal defense of an opinion, and if this Fabricius person was writing a history of magic people or defending magic as a whole... "Oh my god! You think these references are the actual volumes we're looking for?"

"Yes, I think we're on to something." There was excitement in his voice as he spoke. He paused for a second and then launched into an explanation of how he'd linked the pieces together.

His knowledge of ancient literature was so extensive she could listen to him for hours. In their first few meetings, he had come across as a playboy who only dabbled in his family's gallery, but it seemed as if she'd been wrong about him. He would make an amazing professor with his ability to make an otherwise boring subject come to life with tales and facts from the past, like weaving magic into his words.

Lucas walked over to one of the bookshelves. "Let me see if I can find the right reference."

His words pulled her from her thoughts, and she turned, watching as he carefully placed a large volume on a book cradle, adjusting it to make sure the spine was supported. Lucas stood back from the book and its old pages flipped quietly without his touch, like tiny whispers in the air.

"I don't want to touch the book any more than I have to.

Not only because it's old, but because I don't know what magic is hidden and I don't want to accidentally trigger a spell."

Jo leaned in to look at the book and noticed there weren't any page numbers, which wasn't unusual on a book this old. The pages continued to flip and then finally stopped on a page about two-thirds of the way through the book. "How did you know which page to turn to?"

"I didn't," he said, grinning at her. "I let the book decide for me."

"Holy shit, I didn't know that was a thing."

"It isn't. Usually. But I just had a feeling with this book. Look," he said, leaning forward and pointing to the page on the left. "I found a similar reference to this in the book that led me here. I don't know if it's the original, but it's written in Latin, so it's possible. I'm hoping it will give us a clue."

"You read Latin?"

Lucas's lips turned up in a small, almost devious smile. "No, but I have a neat little trick. A translation spell. Watch."

He waved his hand and as she watched, words appeared to float above the page. Words in English.

He read the passage aloud. *"Now I have undertaken the present work to provide for all magic peoples worthy of this gift; for it will contain all our antiquities, and the gifts of our people, as interpreted out of the magic world."*

As soon as Lucas dropped his hand, the English translation disappeared like mist. She looked below the first paragraph and saw more Latin. "It looks like a spell of some kind."

The words translated into English and appeared in the air like the previous passage. "Did you do that?" she asked, not turning to look at him.

"No," he said, close to her ear as he looked over her shoulder. She could feel the heat of his body snugged up against her back and forced herself to concentrate on the book.

The spell was only a few sentences long. "For all the magics seeking—"

"No, don't read it aloud," Lucas said, and pulled her away from the book so they faced each other. "We don't know what it will unleash. It might not be safe to read it now when the library is full of people and we don't have any backup."

"Oh, I never even thought of that. I was so excited I just wanted to jump in."

"I know, but we need to be cautious."

Lucas took a step closer to Jo and she froze, almost afraid to move for fear of him pulling away again. He cupped her face with his large hands, the warmth of his palms sinking into her cheeks, causing her body to tingle. This time she didn't need Viktor to translate the feeling. She knew.

"I can't hold back anymore. I'm going to kiss you, Jo." He looked in her eyes as if waiting for her to respond.

"It's about time." Her lids fluttered shut as his lips touched hers. His mouth was warm and firm, but the kiss wasn't aggressive. Instead, it was just right as his lips nudged hers open and they explored each other's mouths. He tasted like coffee and mint, a perfect blend.

"You taste exquisite," he said against her lips, his arms pulling her flush against his body.

She kissed him back with all the pent-up heat she'd been holding in for the last week. Lucas deepened the kiss and their tongues tangled and danced.

"Wait," he said, pulling away from her, but not letting her go completely. He spun them around, and lifted her by the waist, placing her on a desk, her legs dangling over the sides.

He tugged her to him again as he nestled himself between her knees and kissed her once more. "Much better. I didn't want to give you neck strain." Her lips curved against his and then she forgot all about smiling as his kiss devoured her again.

Her hands roamed up his back as if they had a mind of their own, kneading the muscles beneath his shirt. Her head fell back as he moved his lips down her throat and she groaned at the delicious scrape of his stubble against her neck.

They kissed for what felt like forever and yet also not long enough. The entire world had fallen away until it was only her and Lucas.

He pulled his lips away and leaned his forehead against hers. The touch was so intimate, she could practically feel her ovaries melt.

"I want you, Jo," he said quietly.

The door to the room was shut and there weren't any windows, but she understood his reason for whispering. Anything louder could have burst the little bubble that surrounded them.

"I want you too, Lucas," she whispered.

His body snapped up as if she'd slapped him and he lifted her, putting her back on her feet.

"We should figure out what to do next," he said, his tone formal. All the teasing and playfulness were gone like the words that hung in the air one second and had disappeared in the next.

She didn't know what she'd said that caused his sudden mood shift, but she knew Lucas was as attracted to her as she was to him. He'd said last week that she was special, and that he wanted to wait—maybe that's all it was. It was refreshing that someone liked her enough to honestly speak from his heart.

15

"It is done," Viktor said when he walked into the back room. "I spelled this door also."

Jo nodded and looked at Lucas. He was in charge of this little adventure. Jo stood several feet away from him and stuffed her hands into her hoodie pocket. Lucas standing so close to her was a temptation almost too difficult to resist. Now that she knew what it was like to kiss him, she thought about doing it constantly.

Lucas glanced at Viktor and told him thanks. Besides the door to this room, Lucas had asked Viktor to put a cloaking spell outside the room to gently repel anyone who happened to wander by.

After they found the spell, they'd talked to Viktor and decided not to wait until the next day. The library was empty for the night, except for the security guards patrolling. The guards on tonight were non-magics, but Viktor had explained to Jo that it was a balancing act when it came to cloaking and protection spells. Too strong a spell and it could alert magics to something happening, but not strong enough wouldn't repel non-magics.

There was so much Jo didn't know about spells. She'd always been one to study and research, and this not-knowing and feeling lost was such a new feeling for her. An uncomfortable one. Some days she had to push down the resentment that boiled up inside her. She should already be well experienced in all kinds of spells, but she wasn't because she'd been lied to. Since her mother and aunts were no longer around to defend themselves, Jo tried to let it go, but it wasn't easy. Lies could have repercussions for years; her life was proof of that.

She pushed the thoughts aside and rubbed the tattoo on her wrist. The feeling of her mother's laughter calmed a place deep inside her and focused her on the task at hand. Her mother had loved her, no matter what she'd done. This was one of those times she wished she could talk to her. Get advice and a reassuring hug that told her she was on the right track.

There was so much at stake, and they had no idea what the ancient spell they were about to perform would do.

"I will stay back here," Viktor said. "Ready to help."

Lucas chuckled as he looked over his shoulder at the older man. "Doesn't exactly give me a lot of confidence, but I get it."

Viktor shrugged and winked at Jo.

"Do you want to help with the spell or watch?" Lucas asked when he turned to her.

It gave her a warm feeling that he hadn't just taken over. Normally, she'd be all over helping, but in this case, she felt completely out of her element. "Maybe next time. I've never cast a strong spell before."

Lucas frowned. "What? Why not?"

Jo glanced a look at Viktor and the older man nodded in encouragement. Just one more way she felt off-kilter. She never looked to someone else for permission to do something, usually jumping in with both feet. "I didn't know I was magic until last summer. I'd been spellbound for twenty years."

Lucas looked at her as if he was trying to figure her out, but she didn't see any judgment on his face.

"I'm sure there's a big story there and I'd love to hear it someday. For now, just watch me." Lucas gestured for Jo to come closer to the book, then turned toward Viktor. "Before we begin, can you put a protection bubble around Jo and me?"

Lucas turned back to Jo. "If I do it, you might not be able to break it and get to us if we need help."

Jo let out a soundless laugh. "Now who's the one not instilling confidence? You're worried we could be hurt?"

"No. I'm more concerned about the books in the room. Powerful spells tend to whip up the wind and if we have a protection bubble around us, it will protect all the archived books in this room. It's not exactly a big space."

"Uh, Lucas. We're inside. How is it going to get windy?"

Lucas's face sobered. "Hopefully, it won't. But some spells come with enormous power."

"Ready," Viktor said from behind them, and then the lights dimmed. "If the book glows you will need the dark to see better," he said, nodding at Jo.

"Amazing. Wind and glowing books, let's go," Jo said, rubbing her hands together in excitement.

Lucas faced the book. He waved one hand over it and words floated in the air, like they were floating on an invisible cloud. "That's interesting. Without me providing the translation spell, the words are still appearing in English. Let's hope the translation from Latin is correct and I'm not going to turn us all into toads."

Lucas winked at Jo before focusing on the words.

"For all the magics seeking within be worthy of this book.
To know thine self to know that worth is the right look."

After two sentences, he paused, and Jo leaned forward, hoping to see something. So far, no wind and no glowing.

"For the spells of magic herein have been undertaken.
Only by the most rightful and honest will they awaken.
Evil that lies in wait be gone now, abate.
Reveal thyself to be true and end this wait."

When he finished, the words in the air disappeared like smoke in the wind, and he stepped back.

Nothing happened. Jo's shoulders fell. "That's it?"

"I dropped the protection," Viktor said as he brought the lights up to full strength.

Jo blinked at the brightness and looked between the two men. "What happened? Weren't we supposed to get another clue?"

Lucas shrugged. "I'm not sure. I think we're missing something."

"I don't understand. I thought a spell just worked."

"Not always. Sometimes ancient spells are protected, and they need something else. Almost like a key to unlock them."

"Great," Jo said, not holding in her sarcasm. "We're trying to find clues to an ancient book, but the clues need us to find a different ancient book for them to work."

"It will work. You just need to find another clue," Viktor said with one hand on the doorknob. "I know it will. I will go back to work, but let me know if you need my help." He nodded and left.

Jo ran her hands through her hair and gave the short strands a tug. "What do we do now?"

"I think we need more help. Willing to come to my place

tomorrow and talk to my mother? She might know something or have another book that will help."

Jo gave a small snort. "Sure, as long as it doesn't just lead to another book."

Lucas walked toward Jo, and she let her hands fall to her sides and looked up at him as he towered over her. He gently cupped her cheeks and placed a kiss on her forehead. Never before had she thought forehead kisses were sexy, until now that is. Lucas didn't seem like the type to give them, but it was intimate and stirred things in her. She just had to remember to stay focused on the task at hand. But a little kissing now and then couldn't possibly hurt.

Simon couldn't remember a time in his life when he'd been this conflicted. He loved being an FBI agent and wanted to put away the organization that was looking for the magic box. Yet, for the first time in too long to remember, he wanted to be Simon. He wanted Jo to look at him like she'd been looking at Lucas.

Lucas sat back and watched Jo and Catherine talk about books while he sipped his coffee. Catherine had had a lavish lunch prepared for them, and they'd taken their time. Afterward they'd moved into the library and had been looking at books for the last hour.

Catherine frowned. "It must be upstairs in Oliver's old office. I'll have to look for it and I'll get it to you as soon as I find it."

Jo shelved the book she had been looking through. "Just let me know when you find it and I'll pop over and get it."

"That'd be lovely, and perhaps you could stay for some tea."

Jo gave Catherine a quick hug. "I'd love to." She turned and gave Simon a grin. "Thanks for bringing me, and thanks for lunch and the tour," she said, turning back to Catherine.

"It was my pleasure, my dear. Now, why don't you have Lucas show you his wing of the house?"

Simon had a sinking feeling that Catherine had images of grandchildren dancing in her head. He'd taken on a lot of personas over the years and yet he'd never felt guilt like he had since becoming Lucas. Ironic, considering Lucas had been a selfish bastard and probably never felt guilty for a second in his life.

Jo and Catherine said their goodbyes and Lucas led Jo to his wing of the house. When she walked into his suite, she turned in a circle, taking everything in. He loved how expressive she was and that she never seemed to hold back what she thought or felt. Loved? Simon was falling for her; he'd made a career out of lying, but he couldn't lie to himself about his feelings.

Eventually, his time as Lucas would come to an end, and then what? If Jo fell for him, she'd be falling for Lucas, not Simon.

Lucas propped himself against a wall and watched as Jo snooped through the different rooms in this area of his wing. He laughed when he heard her joyfully cursing about his bathroom. There was a huge smile plastered on her face when she came toward him. "This space is massive, and I *love* your bathroom."

"It is pretty impressive."

He looked down when Jo grabbed Lucas's hand and tugged him toward the loveseat near the bed. "Come on, let's sit."

This was dangerous territory with the bed so close. "We could go into the sitting room." He was already moving toward it when Jo pushed him, and his ass hit the loveseat.

Her laughter bubbled over when she straddled him, their

pants no protection against the heat radiating off their bodies. His hands reached out as if of their own accord to steady her by her hips.

Her hands wound into his hair at the nape of his neck and she leaned forward, seductively kissing him. She teased his lips with her teeth and tongue and any resistance he had melted away.

Inhaling her fresh natural scent, he forgot all about Lucas and just let himself feel. He ran his hands up her back, bringing them around to her front, teasing the underside of one breast. She gasped into his mouth and he deepened the kiss.

After several minutes, she pulled back, her groin rubbing against his, the heat intensifying, their breathing loud in the quiet room. She reached for his shirt, undid the top button, and continued moving lower. "I want more, Lucas."

Hearing Lucas's name was like jumping into the Colorado River on a cold winter day. Without clothes. Simon didn't want to make love to Jo while in Lucas's body. And it would be making love when it happened, not just sex. He reached up to still her hands when Jo sucked in a breath.

"Oh, I forgot about your tattoo. You said it was a memorial for your father." Jo ran her finger over the ink, and he sucked in his own breath. Her palm felt almost cool on his heated flesh. "It's beautiful. I love the way the daisies are scattered around the old book—they look like they'll pop off your chest. What's the significance of the flowers and books?"

Simon closed his eyes for a moment. He couldn't tell Jo the truth and the guilt ate at him for telling one more lie. His mother had always loved the simplicity of daisies, saying they were the perfect flower. Every spring he and his mom would spend hours in the garden weeding and tending to the soil to nurture the daisies. He'd asked her once why she didn't just conjure the daisies and she'd told him that conjuring was too easy. She wanted to plant and nurture and watch them grow, knowing she'd had a hand in helping them bloom when she saw the beautiful colors spread across the garden like a rainbow coming from the earth.

The book represented the hundreds of hours his dad would read to him and eventually listen as he read to his dad. He swallowed the lump in his throat and looked at Jo. "My dad loved reading and flowers are lovely and simple." It was the truth, just not the complete one.

"That's beautiful." She rubbed her wrist and then looked up at him through her lashes before reaching for the next button on his shirt. "I want you. I want to lose myself in you."

He gripped her wrists softly, halting her movements. "No, not right now."

She dropped her hands and pulled back, a frown marring her face.

"Why not?" She pushed back and jumped off his lap, standing in front of him. "Do you not want me, Lucas? If you don't, just say so, but I'm getting sick of your mixed messages."

He reached for her, pulling her between his legs while he stayed on the loveseat. "Yes, I want you. But..." Simon struggled to come up with a convincing excuse, another lie.

"But what?"

He ran his hands along her back and down her ass and legs as he looked up into her eyes. "Jo, I care about you."

"Well, you don't—"

He put his finger gently on her lips, stilling her words. "Please, let me try and explain." She nodded and he brought his hand to her hip so he could hold her and look in her eyes. "I was a man-whore before, but you mean so much more to me, Jo. I want to cherish you. I want to take things slow with us. And you're under so much pressure right now, I don't want to be just a way for you to relieve stress. When we make love, I want it to mean something."

She put her hands on his cheeks and kissed his lips softly. "That has to be one of the most amazing things someone has ever said to me." She kissed him again. "Okay, we'll wait. But not too long."

He pulled her down on his lap and she lay her head on his shoulder. He wanted to hold her and cherish this moment, but he knew it wouldn't be long before his life blew up in his face. He just hoped he could find a way so they could both win, but he'd lived in a harsh reality for so long, he knew it was a naïve thought.

17

A staff person led Jo into the library where Catherine was waiting for her. It'd been two days since Catherine had said she'd look for the book and Jo was thankful she didn't have to wait any longer. Her worry for her brother increased each day as he continued to grow weaker.

"Jo, sweetheart, thanks so much for dropping by so quickly."

"No problem. I'm just so happy you found the book. I hope it's what I need." Jo took the book Catherine held out and slipped it in the protective sleeve she'd brought with her before she put it in her large bag.

"Will you stay for some tea?"

"I'd love to."

"That's wonderful. Lucas just got home a few minutes ago, so why don't you go up and see him while I get us some tea. See if you can convince him to join us."

"I will." She left Catherine and admired the artwork on the walls as she walked to Lucas's wing.

Since Catherine was expecting them to come back down,

Jo and Lucas couldn't be long, but perhaps afterward they could head back up to Lucas's wing. Lucas wanted to wait before they made love, and wanted their first time to be special, and it would be. Just having Lucas want to wait made it special.

Yes, having sex would be a great way to burn off some stress, but she wouldn't use Lucas like that. She wanted more with him, just as much as he did with her. He was unlike anyone she'd ever met before. Outgoing and charming, almost to the point of arrogance, but when they were alone, he was sweet and caring and she loved to listen to him talk about magic history. Intelligence had always been a huge turn-on for her.

She was falling for Lucas.

The doors to his wing were closed and she felt the protection spell Lucas had taught her, so she knocked and waited. After a few moments, when there was no response, she wondered if she should break the spell. Since Lucas had taught her how, she broke it quickly and pushed the door open, calling out, "Lucas?"

She walked further into the room and heard the shower running. They weren't at the point in their relationship where she could walk in and join him, but she wanted to. She'd never been shy before, so why was she holding back now?

This was the twenty-first century and so many before her had paved the way for her to go after what she wanted. Her hesitation to pursue a man was new, and not something she liked. She was brave and bold, and she wanted Lucas. If he didn't want her, so be it, but she didn't need to wait for him to make the next move.

Maybe this was exactly what Lucas needed to take their relationship to the next step.

Jo laid her bag on the loveseat by the bed and walked to

the bathroom. The door was slightly ajar, so she pushed it open with one hand as she walked in.

She gasped at the sight before her.

"Jo!"

"Simon, what are you doing in here? Are you friends with Lucas?"

She took three steps further into the bathroom as if her eyes were lying to her and she needed to get closer to see. The steam from the shower clung to her shirt as she watched Simon tighten the towel more securely around his waist.

He was a good-looking man and his looks had called to her from the moment they had met. Simon was so different from Lucas with his tattoo sleeves, dark chocolate-colored hair and bright green eyes. She knew she was gawking but couldn't make herself look away. Her eyes traveled from his face to his chest and she felt a tightness in her throat like all the air had suddenly been sucked from the room. "Simon, why do you have the same memorial tattoo as Lucas?"

Simon waved his hand, and he was suddenly dry and dressed in jeans and a short-sleeved T-shirt. He gestured to the door behind Jo. "Let's go out in the sitting room and I'll explain."

"No, explain right now." Her uneasiness was growing by the second.

"Jo, there isn't an easy explanation."

"There should be. I am so tired of people lying. Why, Simon?"

"Because the tattoo is mine. I got it to honor my parents when I turned eighteen and left my last group home."

"But why does Lucas have the same tattoo? He said it was to honor his father. And where is Lucas? Catherine said he was up here." She looked around as if expecting Lucas to jump out of a corner somewhere and join them in the bathroom.

"I am Lucas too."

"What? I don't understand."

Jo gasped as Simon transformed into Lucas in front of her eyes. Simon's dark hair and green eyes were replaced by Lucas's blond locks and light blue gaze. Simon had become Lucas. Only the clothes remained the same.

Jo walked up to Lucas and reached out to touch his arm where Simon's tattoos had been moments before. She grappled with what she was seeing. She tugged down the neck of Lucas's T-shirt and saw the same memorial tattoo that Simon had.

"Change back!"

"What?"

"Change back into Simon. I want to see it again. Do it!" Her words were rushed and her voice raised on the last word, but she didn't care. She knew many magics had different specialties, but she didn't understand how someone could be two people.

She watched as Lucas's blond hair and light blue eyes changed back into Simon's darker features. Extending her fingers slowly, as if afraid they might touch something distasteful, she ran them along Simon's arms where his Superman tattoo stood in stark contrast to Lucas's ink-free skin.

"No! No, no, no." She stumbled backward and Simon reached out to steady her. "No, don't touch me! This is wrong. I can't believe this."

Jo backed up again, staring at Simon, and then spun, and rushed out of the bathroom.

"Jo, wait, let me explain."

"No, Simon. Lucas. Whoever the fuck you are! There is no explaining. You lied!" Jo grabbed her bag from the loveseat and sprinted out the door.

She could hear Simon calling her name but didn't turn

around. Her shoulder bumped against the wall as she spun around a corner and raced down the stairs. She was almost at the front door when she stopped.

She had to stop thinking like a regular human. She had magic. Taking a deep breath, she steadied herself and flashed.

18

*S*imon called after Jo and followed, but she didn't stop. He saw her hit the staircase when he caught sight of his hand. Shit. He was still himself. He stopped and focused to change back into Lucas. It took precious moments he didn't have, but he couldn't reveal himself as Simon to Catherine or any of the household staff.

His T-shirt and jeans wouldn't do either, but he didn't have clothes ready to retrieve and conjuring them would take too much time. Racing back to his closet, all he could see was the horror on Jo's face when he'd changed.

Assessing the clothes in his closet, he magically grabbed some and dressed. It had taken him a minute, a minute he didn't have if he wanted to catch Jo. Not wanting to waste any more time, he flashed down to the front parlor. Jo wasn't there.

"Cath—Mother!" he called out as he walked to the library. He needed to get a grip on himself or he'd lose everything he'd worked the past ten years for. The FBI was his life and he was royally screwing up his role in it.

"Lucas? What's wrong?" Catherine was sitting on a high-backed chair with a tea service spread out before her on a small table.

"Have you seen Jo?" He felt breathless and his heart hammered like he'd just run a marathon instead of executing a simple flash.

"I saw her in the foyer and then she flashed away." Catherine grabbed the teapot and poured two cups. "Sit down, dear. She's gone for now, and I don't know where she went, so sit down and tell me what's wrong."

He didn't sit, instead walking to the window and looking out at the immaculate front lawn and gardens, his vision unfocused.

He'd fucked up with Jo and he had to fix it. Jo had awakened so many firsts in him. Since he'd met her, he had wanted to be himself for the first time in years. He didn't know what he wanted out of life anymore. And he was questioning whether he wanted to be the best someone else. Another first.

Simon turned away from the window and sat on a chair opposite Catherine. He took a sip of the tea but didn't taste it. His mind was in turmoil.

"Did Jo discover the truth? Is that why she left?"

Simon's head shot up as he looked at Lucas's mother. "What do you mean?"

"Did she figure out that you're not who you say you are?"

Simon hesitated before he answered. Blurting out the truth could get him in a bigger mess if Catherine meant something different than what he thought she did. Maybe her question was innocent, like she knew her son was working with some unsavory people and that was why he wasn't who he said he was. Not that he was Simon. "Mother, I don't know what you're talking about."

"Yes, you do." Catherine put down her cup and saucer and leveled him with a look only a mother could give. "A mother knows her own child. She'll always know. And you are not my son."

"Of course I'm your son. Mother, maybe we should get you to a doctor. I think you're hallucinating." He put his tea on the tray and stood, going over to Catherine and kneeling down in front of her. "I look like I've always looked. I'm your son." He stood and pulled his phone out of his pocket. "I'll call your doctor to meet us at the hospital and he'll figure out what's wrong."

"Put your phone away."

"No, we need someone to check you out."

Catherine snapped her hand toward him and the phone flew out of his hands, landing in the chair in front of him. "You and I both know there's nothing wrong with me. Drop the act."

Simon had worked a lot of cases in his years in the FBI, but never had he lived with someone's mother for this amount of time. Nor had he ever been discovered.

He walked over to the window again and then turned back. He felt like a lion in a cage, trapped, unable to get out. If he told her the truth, he'd destroy all his work over the last year. Work desperately needed to uncover who was behind kidnapping children to get enough power to obtain the magic box.

If he didn't tell her the truth, she could out him to powerful people in their circle of magic friends and colleagues.

"Lucas, come sit back down."

Like a recalcitrant young child, he went back to the chair in front of Catherine and picked up his tea before sitting.

"I need you to tell me one thing."

He looked Catherine in the eyes but didn't say anything. Without knowing what she wanted, he couldn't promise he'd tell her anything.

"Is my son dead?"

Simon kept the expression on his face, Lucas's face, neutral. He was telling a mother that her son was dead. Made stranger by the fact that for all intents and purposes, that son was sitting in front of her. He didn't know what emotion to offer. Should he be empathetic? Tell her he was sorry? In the end he decided to just be straight with her. "Yes, your son is dead."

"Did he suffer?"

"No. He was in a car accident and died instantly."

"That day you said you decided you wanted a new car? That you were tired of your old one?"

He nodded again and looked down at the cup and saucer in his hands when he heard a rattle. His hands were shaking. Carefully, he placed the cup and saucer back on the table.

"I knew," she said, so softly Simon only just made out her words. "I think I've known since that day."

"How?"

Catherine looked down at her hands and a tissue appeared. She twisted the tissue around her finger several times before looking up and meeting his eyes. "You were too polite. You made that comment to Cassandra, remember?"

Lucas nodded. "Yes. I said that I'd forgotten my manners over the years and was trying to improve them."

Catherine's eyes filled with tears and she lifted her hand holding the tissue but didn't use it, waving her hand in front of her eyes instead. Her tears disappeared. "I was happy at first, thinking you had decided to be kinder. I had tried to teach you manners, as you said, but you never cared."

"What made you realize it was something more?" Simon wanted to know where he'd slipped up, but it was more than that. He wanted to know how he had brought this beautiful, kind woman to tears.

"I loved my son, but he was arrogant and greedy. It didn't

matter what I tried to teach him. When his father died, he became worse. I still loved him, but that didn't mean I didn't recognize what he was." Catherine disappeared the torn tissue and rubbed her hands on her slacks. "You became more than just polite. You became kind, helping me and offering to do things you'd never offered before. Then some of the staff at the gallery commented on how you'd changed. People don't change that much. I knew then that magic was involved."

Simon didn't know what to say. He'd already admitted that he wasn't Lucas. "What do we do now?"

"We go forward."

"Just like that?"

"I might be a horrible mother for saying this, but I like this new improved version of my son. Did you take over his life because you could, or do you have an end goal in mind?"

"I'm working."

"And Lucas was your in?"

"Yes."

"Did you kill him?"

"No. I just took advantage of the situation."

She took in a shuddering breath, and her eyes welled with tears, but her gaze met his head on. "Then you won't be my son forever?" she whispered.

In that moment, Simon wished he could tell another lie, like so many lies he'd told in the service of doing his job. He wanted to say that yes, he'd be her son forever. But he couldn't lie to a mother about that. "No, when my job is done, I'll go."

She waved her hand in front of her face after the first tear fell and dried away all evidence of her crying. "And what about Jo, is she part of your job too?"

He let out a long sigh and slouched back in the chair. Simon couldn't tell her he was an FBI agent or why, but something in him yearned to tell her what he was going through. He could have used some motherly advice over the last twenty years. "Yes, but I met her when I wasn't Lucas and I liked her. Then I was tasked with helping her find the book she needs." It was close enough to the truth and right now the details didn't matter. He was going to leave Jo too.

"And now you love her."

"I'm not sure, but I think I might. Only she doesn't really love me. She loves the person I'm pretending to be. A kinder version of Lucas, I guess."

"Then you have to go get her."

"It's not that easy. She thinks the world is black and white and there's never a good reason to lie."

"Well, then you'll have to show her she's wrong. The world can be very gray." When she stood and picked up the tea service, Lucas jumped to his feet to assist her.

"Here, let me." He took the service from her and followed her out of the room.

"I think you should give her some time to cool down." She looked back over her shoulder. "Lucas, will you join me for dinner?"

"I'd love to, Mom," he said, and the smile on Catherine's face made some of his lies seem worth it. Now, he had to see if he could get Jo to smile at him again.

19

Jo's feet touched down in her apartment foyer and she fumbled forward, catching herself on the table by the wall. She'd been flashing for almost a year now and had never stumbled before.

She'd flashed out of Lucas's place so quickly she was surprised she even managed to make it home instead of flashing herself into the side of a mountain.

Dropping her bag by the door, she kicked her shoes off into the corner. Wine or change into comfy lounge pants first? Wine. Definitely wine.

After she conjured herself a large glass of wine, she curled up on the corner of the couch in her living room. Her mind raced with everything she'd seen. Lucas was Simon or Simon was Lucas. She didn't know which came first, like the chicken or the egg. She laughed out loud and then snorted to herself. Maybe she was losing it.

I'm coming up. Jo heard the thought Meredith threw into her mind but couldn't respond. She'd learned to throw thoughts, but could only do it short distances, like most magics. Meredith and her fiancé, Jack, weren't like normal magics anymore. They'd taken on more power when they'd become co-leaders of the new magic council they were setting up, and now could do things others couldn't, like throw thoughts long distances or between floors in an apartment building. Sometimes it was annoying.

"What's wrong?"

Jo jerked and sloshed wine over her hand as she looked up at Meredith standing in her living room. "Holy shit, Mer! Warn a person, why don't you?"

"I did. I told you I was coming up." Meredith conjured herself a glass of wine and burrowed into the opposite end of the couch. "Something's wrong. What is it?"

Jo dried her hand and eyed her cousin cautiously. "Why do you think something's wrong?"

"Because I felt it."

"You felt what?"

"I was going to reach out to ask you to come to our place for a drink when I felt you flash home. It was like you used more energy than you should have. I can't explain it. And I knew something must be wrong because I felt it."

"What's wrong?"

The question came from a second person and Jo whipped her head around and saw Rowena standing beside her. "Holy shit! You two need to stop doing that!"

"Meredith said something was wrong. So?" Rowena asked as she conjured a glass of wine and sat across from them.

Before Jo could say anything, there was a knock at the door and then it opened. Morgana peered inside. "Can I come in?"

"Sure, it's suddenly Grand Central Station in here."

Morgana took a seat on the loveseat beside the chair Rowena sat in. All her family had lots of seating in their living rooms for occasions just like this. Maybe she should rethink her seating arrangements.

"Morgana, would you like a glass of wine?" Rowena asked as she held a second glass and was already passing it to Morgana.

Jo gave Morgana a reassuring smile. Her friend's magic was weak—she couldn't flash and conjuring anything was difficult. They all tried not to make a big deal out of it when they were around her.

"Thanks," Morgana said with a small smile. "Jo, Meredith said something's wrong. What happened?"

Jo took a large gulp of wine and let her magic flow out, watching her glass refill. "I didn't say anything was wrong."

"You didn't have to," Meredith said. "I told you I could feel the extra energy you used to flash home and now you're guzzling wine."

"I wouldn't call it guzzling."

"Sweetie, stop stalling," Rowena said, her voice calm but stern. Probably part of what made her such a good psychologist.

Jo couldn't resist the prompting anymore. "Lucas is not Lucas and he lied." Jo spit out the words as fast as she could and took a gulp of wine, but this time it didn't soothe her. She could almost taste the bitterness of Lucas's lies.

"What do you mean Lucas isn't Lucas?" Morgana asked.

"I mean that he can change into someone else." She looked at the other women and steeled herself. "That doesn't matter. What matters is that he lied to me. He's not who he said he was."

"I've never heard of someone changing into someone else," Meredith said. "I'll have to ask Jack if he's heard of a magic person being able to change into another person before."

"No!" Jo almost lurched forward, putting her hand out as if she could stop her cousin from mentally communicating with her fiancé. "Please, not yet. Don't tell anyone that he's two people."

Meredith looked like she wanted to argue but nodded. "Okay, but I won't keep it a secret forever. It might be important that someone is two people or can change or whatever. I'm guessing it could have implications for other magics."

"I get it, I just need time."

"Did he say why he was two people?" Morgana asked.

"No, and it doesn't matter."

Rowena tsked at Jo like she was a child. "Of course it matters."

Jo glared at her cousin. "Not to me, at least not right now. I already told you, he lied."

"So? People lie all the time. I know you don't like it, but it's a fact of life," Meredith said.

"I won't tolerate having anyone around me who lies."

Meredith and Rowena both laughed and stood up. "I guess we better go then," Rowena said.

"Me too." Morgana stood, but none of the women flashed or moved toward the door.

"Okay, I get it. Don't be drama queens. Sit down." Jo put her wine down on the table and pushed some magazines off onto the floor. She needed room for chocolate and pulled on her magic while she thought about what kind of chocolate she wanted. Hershey Kisses and plain bars of milk chocolate soon littered the table. She grabbed a few kisses and stuffed herself back into the corner of the sofa.

"Oh, good idea," Meredith said when she sat down again and held out her hand, palm up. M&Ms appeared in her palm. "Morgana, you want anything?"

"The kisses are fine," Morgana said, reaching forward to grab a handful.

Jo looked over at Rowena, who had what looked like a chunk of plain chocolate in her hand.

"Okay, now that we've got a chocolate fix," Meredith said, "let's get back to the lying. Jo, you know why we stood up."

"Yes, I'm not dumb. You've all lied. But that's different. One," she said ticking her points off on her fingers, "it doesn't make it right, and two, telling someone a bad haircut looks nice isn't much of a lie. And three, you've never told a significant lie to someone you really care about."

"Yes, I have," Meredith said.

"What? When?" Jo looked at her cousin, surprised miss-rule-follower Meredith would have told a whopper to someone she loved. Jo paused. Love? Is that what she had started to feel for Lucas? Well, obviously he didn't feel the same way if he could lie to her like he did. She shrugged it off and looked at Meredith, waiting to hear her explanation.

"I lied when I said I didn't want my magic and then I waited too long to admit the truth. If I had taken it on earlier, my mom might still be alive."

No one said a word, letting Meredith's words soak in, but Jo hated seeing the grief on her cousin's face. "Mer, that's not true. You were scared and trying to protect your family. Lying to keep the people you love safe and outright deceiving someone aren't the same thing." Jo put down her wine and brushed chocolate crumbs off her legs so she could lean over and squeeze Meredith's hand. "You did what you thought was best at the time."

Meredith returned the squeeze and then let go, giving Jo a nod.

"Maybe Lucas was doing the same thing," Morgana said as Jo sat back down.

Jo looked over at Morgana. "How could he be? He's living in a mansion and hardly working. He's definitely living it up."

"Jo, I'm surprised at you," Rowena said. "You're the

researcher in the family. You usually dig until you have all the facts."

Once more Jo felt like a child from the recrimination in Rowena's voice, but she wasn't going to back down. "I have the facts. Lucas pretended to be someone else and lied to me. Regardless of his reason, he didn't tell me the truth. If he was lying for the greater good, to protect someone or whatever, I would have understood."

"Really?" Morgana asked.

"Of course. Why would you even ask that?"

"When your mom and aunts bound your magic, they did it because they thought they were protecting you. You haven't accepted that," Morgana said, but her words weren't unkind, just softly stating facts.

Jo's pulse sped up and she sent some cooling magic through her body. She didn't need her cheeks the same color as her hair. "That was different. They lied and because of that our mothers are dead, and we missed out on being our true selves for twenty years."

"Morgana is right, Jo. Our mothers lied because they thought they were protecting us. Maybe Lucas is protecting you too."

Jo was frustrated that no one could see what she could. "No, it's still not right. Our mothers' lies took our choices away and we don't truly know if what they did even protected us."

Rowena kneeled in front of Jo. "No, we don't. And we never will, but we have to accept that they believed they did." She gave Jo a quick hug.

Jo loved her cousins and was coming to deeply care for Morgana, but they were wrong. If the world was black and white, it would be a far better place.

"Did you hear that?" Rowena asked when she stood up beside Jo.

Jo looked up at her cousin, who looked almost frozen in place. "No. What did you hear?"

"It sounded like a voice." Rowena walked back to her chair, picked up her wine glass, and disappeared it. "I have to go. I'll see you all later." Rowena flashed away before Jo could say anything more.

Jo looked at Meredith. "That was weird."

Her cousin nodded. "Yes, I think she's been working too hard trying to set up her new practice. She said she's nervous about taking on only magic people as clients. It's taken a lot of networking, so maybe she's just tired. Thanks for this—" Meredith stopped as if listening to something. "Jack's home, so I'm going to go, but I hope you give Lucas a chance to explain. And let me know when I can tell Jack about the two people thing." Meredith waved goodbye and flashed away.

"You gotta go too?" Jo asked Morgana.

"No. Once the bakery is closed for the day, I'm free as a bird."

A frown briefly crossed Morgana's face, but then she smiled, so Jo let it go. "Want some pizza?"

"Yes! Should I call down to the restaurant?"

Jo laughed. "Oh ye of little faith." Jo moved the chocolate on the coffee table to one side and concentrated on what kind of pizza she wanted. Wine, chocolate, and pizza were her specialties when it came to conjuring.

While they were eating, Jo's phone had pinged several times. She'd wondered if it was Lucas but had refused to check, trying her best to ignore it.

After they'd both consumed their fill and chatted about the latest movies and gossip, Jo brought the conversation back around to Lucas's lying. "Mo, be honest with me, do you think I'm overreacting?"

Morgana didn't answer right away, which gave Jo a bad

feeling. How could her cousins and friend not see that what Lucas did was wrong?

"I don't think you're overreacting because your feelings are hurt."

"So you agree with me?"

"Not really… I mean, I understand that you're upset, but you don't know Lucas's side of the story. Don't you want to know?"

No, she didn't. She was still confused about who he was, but whether he looked like Lucas or Simon, he'd lied. And whatever the reason, she didn't want to ask so he could justify lying. It didn't change the fact that he had. "You think I should ask him?"

"Yes." Morgana opened her mouth to say something and then stopped.

"Just tell me. I can take it."

"I've lied my whole life."

"Mo, that's different. You did what you needed to in order to survive."

"But if I use your logic that all lying is bad, then what I did was wrong."

Jo couldn't imagine what Morgana had gone through—being taken from her family as a child and forced to lie or service someone just to survive. And now, even safe, she didn't know who she was.

Morgana and her cousins had given Jo situations where lies were considered okay. She didn't want to accept that. "Did you tell different lies or was it a recurring one?"

"I know what you're doing, Jo. You're trying to rationalize why my lies are different, but I get it. Okay… let me think."

Jo waited and waged an inner war—she wanted to hear Morgana's lie and know how it was different from Lucas's but hated that she was making this kind woman remember her horrible past.

"There is so much of my past that I can't remember, but when Zeus—I mean Louis Copeland… I keep forgetting not to use their code names…" She paused, as if stuck in her memories. "Anyway, the memories of the year Copeland brought me to Colorado, before Meredith and Jack rescued me, are clearer. I'm sure I lied a lot before that, but I can't pinpoint anything."

She huffed out a breath and looked at Jo. "Sorry, I'm a bit all over the place."

"It's okay. You don't have to continue if you don't want to."

"No, I need to. I haven't talked things out with Rowena yet, at least not much, because I'm not ready. But I do need to start remembering." Morgana took a deep breath and looked Jo in the eyes. "I lied and hurt someone."

"You were just trying to survive."

"No! Don't justify this, Jo. I was selfish." Morgana closed her eyes and pressed her fists to her forehead. "My headache is really bad."

"You don't have to tell me."

"Yes, I do." Morgana pressed on her forehead for a moment more, and then dropped her hands and looked Jo in the eye. "I had been with Copeland for several months and I was bored. I did chores for him, but a lot of the time I was kept in a room by myself. I wanted attention. Not totally crazy, I guess, but to get the attention, I yelled and screamed and said someone was hurting me."

"Was someone there with you?"

Morgana shook her head. "No, I was alone. When one of Copeland's guys came to check on me, I curled up on the floor and moaned like I was in pain. He brought Copeland's healer to me."

"Did he know you were lying?"

"Yes, but he didn't say anything. I don't know who he

was… or wait, I think maybe I did…" Morgana rubbed her forehead again. "I can't remember. I think I was supposed to know him, but I didn't. He was always kind to me."

"Did he pretend to heal you?"

A frown marred Morgana's suddenly ashen face. "That's the thing—I think they continually drained his power, leaving him weak, so he only ever had enough to heal people when needed. When he healed people, it drained him to the point of collapse. If he didn't heal me, they'd know."

Jo could see the internal struggle as plain as day on Morgana's face. She still believed lying was wrong, but Jo couldn't say she'd have done anything differently in the same situation. She was a natural extrovert and loved being around people. She couldn't say what she would have done to get attention if left alone day after day. Like Morgana had said she would, Jo was rationalizing the lie. She couldn't say if it was right or wrong. Only that Lucas-slash-Simon's lie had sliced through her like a sword blade, leaving behind a part of her on that bathroom floor. She didn't know if she'd ever be able to accept the lie as being necessary.

A moment later, Morgana looked at Jo with tears welling in her eyes. "The healer healed me, but I didn't need it. Essentially, he gave me his life's essence, making me feel healthier and stronger than I'd ever felt and in doing so it weakened him further."

"What happened to him?"

"He collapsed on the floor. At first I thought he was dead. That I'd killed him. But when a couple guys carried him out, he groaned. I never saw him again after that. And it's all because I lied."

Jo went over to her friend and squished beside her on the chair, pulling her into a hug. She ran her hand up and down Morgana's back as she cried silently. Only when she stopped shaking did Jo know Morgana's tears had stopped.

Not wanting to make things more awkward, Jo went back to her place on the sofa, and used her magic to refill her wine glass. "Mo, you didn't know what would happen."

Morgana looked up, her lashes still wet from her tears. "That's the thing, Jo—we never know what's going to happen when we lie. You can't justify what I did because there was no reason for it. I hurt someone because I was selfish. You don't know why Lucas lied. What if he's not selfish? What if he had a good reason?"

Nothing seemed to be as black and white as Jo wished it were.

Later that night when Jo was getting ready for bed, she was still thinking about Morgana's lie. About how many lies Jo had been told throughout her life. Had her mother and aunts been right to lie? The only people that lie had hurt was themselves, and they didn't know if it had even saved their children. They'd never know.

She plugged in her phone on the bedside table and checked for messages. There were six texts from Lucas. Each one just asked her to let him explain.

If he regretted lying, could she forgive him? Was Morgana right that she still hadn't forgiven her mother and aunts for lying? If that was true, that she couldn't forgive a twenty-year lie, how could she forgive a two-month one?

Lucas wiped his damp palms on his trousers, thankful they were dark, before pulling open the library door. Guilt ate at him for what he'd put Jo through, but also for letting things get out of hand and threatening his operation with the FBI. It was a no-win situation, but he was determined to fix it.

When Catherine had told him to give Jo space, he knew it was good advice, but he'd only been able to wait so long. And for every text he sent, he wanted to pick up the phone and call. Explaining why he'd lied was a priority, but he'd also just wanted to hear her voice.

"Good morning," he said quietly to several people who greeted him as he walked through the library. He wasn't loud and didn't wink at the pretty girl who eyed him when he walked by. He still looked like Lucas on the outside, but inside he was the same scared little boy who had been rejected time and again. But whether he was that shy, nerdy little boy or not, he had to face Jo. He had to make her listen.

He was on a mission, but in his mind, he was in a battle. Go for the girl or do the job? In the past, he'd reveled at being someone else and doing the right thing. He took joy from pleasing people, being who they wanted and what they needed.

Not this time. The question of how much to tell her weighed heavily on him. He still had to get her to work with Lucas, but if he said too much, he could push her further away.

He scanned his surroundings as he moved further into the library. As a kid, he'd loved libraries with their endless supply of comics and graphic novels. There were also books about the canon of comics, and he devoured them like a starving man at a buffet, eating his fill of facts until he was a walking dictionary of comics and superheroes. His tattooed sleeves were a testament to his love of the genre.

Just as he rounded the corner to the section where Jo worked, a baseball hat with a popular sports team's logo caught his attention. The person wearing it was standing in a corner near a group of shelves. The person's face was hidden, and they were too far away to tell if they were magic, but he'd seen that baseball cap before. Eddie had a similar one, and even though thousands of people probably had the same cap, he'd been in the job too long to believe in coincidences. Lucas was being watched. If he approached Eddie, he'd be letting him know that Lucas was too aware of his surroundings. It was better to let it go.

He spotted Jo at the counter with Viktor. She was turned away from him as she spoke to Viktor, a laptop open in front of her and papers scattered all over the counter's surface. Simon watched as she moved her hands when she spoke, her passion a beacon that drew him in. There was a vibrancy about her that was breathtaking. It sucked in those around her, making them want to get to know her, to be a part of her passion.

Viktor saw Lucas first, but his expression gave nothing

away. He was magic, but it was more than that. His eyes spoke of a power and wisdom that so belied his relaxed, almost grandfatherly appearance.

"Jo." Viktor tilted his head in Lucas's direction as he reached the counter.

"What?" Jo turned around and Simon knew the minute she spotted Lucas. The smile fell from her face and her eyes narrowed. "Go away, Lucas… or Simon, or whoever you are."

She wasn't exactly rude, just abrupt, but the room's temperature felt like it dropped several degrees with her frosty comment.

"Jo, I want to explain. Can we go somewhere and talk?"

"No, there's nothing to say."

"You know there is."

"No, Lucas, I don't. You lied to me, and you know I detest lies. End of story."

"Life isn't always that clear-cut."

"In my world it is."

Her gaze seemed fierce as she stood up straight, all five-foot-two of her, and perched her hands on her hips.

"In mine it's not," he said.

"Too bad for you. Please leave."

She was being stubborn, but he had too much on the line to give up so easily. He tried another tactic. "My mother said she gave you her book—did it help unlock the spell we found?"

Jo's eyes flicked away for a moment before she met Lucas's gaze. "No, it didn't work."

"Do you know why?"

"Because it didn't. I'll keep looking, and speaking of which, I need to get back to work." She turned away from him in a clear sign of dismissal.

"Jo, I might be able to figure out why the spell didn't work."

She turned back to face him. "No, Lucas. I don't want your help. I can't trust you." She put her hands on the counter and leaned forward. "Please leave."

Her voice was a soft plea this time and it cut straight to his gut. "Okay, I'll leave for now."

Giving Viktor a nod, Lucas turned and left, but he'd be back.

Jo CONJURED MORE coffee in her cup and took a tentative sip. Her eyes drooped and she'd drunk half the brew before she put the cup down, hoping the caffeine would kick in quickly. It had been a long week and she was beyond exhausted.

She looked around the library and realized that it was empty except for her and Viktor. Most of the lights were off. Another late night, like the week of late nights she'd had since she found out the truth about Lucas.

Lucas had dropped by every day, and she'd refused to see him. After the fourth day, she'd started hiding in the back, having Viktor run interference. It was cowardly, but it hurt too much to see him.

"Maybe you should put the coffee in an IV. It would be more efficient," Viktor said.

"So funny," Jo said, sarcasm dripping from her words. "I might have to ask Jack or Meredith to give me some extra energy, like they were doing for Reece." The thought of her brother brought a lump to her throat.

"That will not help."

"Why not? It helped Reece. At least for a while."

"His magic was weakened and yours is not. Your healthy body will not accept extra magic without a consequence."

Maybe it would be worth it. "What kind of consequences?"

"Headaches, racing heart—like a heart attack, if it isn't too much and doesn't kill you."

That definitely didn't sound worth it, but she was becoming more exhausted by the day. "Well, then I'll stick with caffeine because I need more energy if I'm going to find the book."

Viktor pulled out the chair in front of Jo and sat down. "There is a way."

Jo's head snapped up. "What? You know how to find the book and haven't told me?"

"No, *kicsim*, I did not say that. I do not know where the book is, but there is a way to find it."

"How?"

"Lucas."

Jo shook her head. "No. Just no. He lied and I can't trust him."

"You trusted him when you didn't know he was lying."

"That's different."

"Have you asked him why he lied?"

"No, and I won't."

Viktor shook his head. "So stubborn. He might have a valid reason."

"There isn't a valid reason for pretending to be two people."

Viktor frowned, his big eyebrows narrowing. "Did I tell you the story about why I came to Blue Mountain?"

She huffed out a laugh. "You've told me a lot of stories, but no, I don't remember that one. So, tell me, why did you come here?"

"When I left my home country and came to America, I lived with some Hungarian magics in Oregon. We were a community." He closed his eyes as if remembering and then took a breath before looking at Jo. "I fell in love."

"What was her name?"

"Léna. She was ten years younger than me and the most beautiful woman I had ever seen. I tried to resist her at first, thinking I was too old for her, but she wore me down." He chuckled to himself, and then the smile fell from his face. "When I gave in and let myself be with her, we were inseparable. She was a schoolteacher and loved children. There wasn't a person who didn't like Léna. She was kind and giving and…"

He paused and his eyes glazed over as if lost in memory before he visibly shook himself and looked back at Jo. "I was going to ask her to marry me and then I caught her in a lie."

Jo sat forward, caught up in the story. "What was the lie?"

He leaned back in his chair and captured Jo with his piercing gaze. "She was betrothed to someone back home."

"Did she tell you why she lied?"

Viktor's shoulders sagged as he shook his head. "No. I did not give her a chance. I told her that I would not be with her if she was bound to someone else. I thought I was doing the honorable thing by letting her go. She begged me to listen, but I wouldn't. I thought maybe she just had cold feet and once she saw her betrothed again, she would change her mind. I contacted her brother and had him come and get her."

"Did she marry him?"

"No."

Jo ground her teeth together. Getting the story out of Viktor was like pulling teeth. "Why not?"

"Because she refused to marry someone she did not love. She did not love the man she was betrothed to, she loved me. That is why she hadn't told me about him."

"So she came back?"

"No. The magic she was betrothed to was from another strong bloodline and a promise had been made between the families. Her family killed her for breaking the promise and dishonoring them."

"What? And they got away with it?"

"Yes, of course. They're magic and from a family connected to the old council. They made her body and magic disappear as if she had never existed." Viktor stood and pushed in his chair. "Come, *kicsim*, it is late."

Jo packed up her things, too stunned by Viktor's story to say anything. He'd been through so much because of a lie. Or maybe it wasn't the lie that made him suffer. Maybe it was because he didn't listen. She knew what Viktor was telling her, that she didn't have all the information. Yes, Lucas had lied, but Viktor was right, she needed to find out why.

Jo waited while Viktor cleaned up the library, using his magic to push in chairs and tidy bookshelves. She'd seen a lot of magic in the last year, but it was still a thrill to see chairs snugging up to tables and books flying neatly onto shelves all by themselves like something out of a magical movie.

"I'll get the lights." She pulled on her magic and lifted one hand toward the bank of light switches. She grinned when the library went dark except for the running lights.

They walked out of the library together, waving at the security guard on duty. Her energy level was drained, and it felt like every step was an effort. All she wanted to do was flash from inside the library, but they couldn't. The majority of the security guards were non-magic as there were always a mix of magics and non-magics working in most places. They would suspect something if she and Viktor were never seen leaving the library at night.

When she and Viktor were in the back alley, he put a hand on her arm and stopped her. "*Kicsim*, you are like a daughter to me. One I could never have because of the mistakes I made."

Jo felt an ache in her throat and her eyes became itchy at the thought of the pain Viktor had held in all these years. She knew what he wanted without him having to say it. "I'll think about it."

"Good. Now, go straight home."

She grabbed Viktor in a spontaneous hug, then stood back and nodded at him. "See you tomorrow."

When her feet hit the tile in her apartment foyer, she mentally went through the ingredients in her fridge, Viktor's story playing over and over again in the back of her mind.

"Jo." Rowena's voice came from the living room.

She looked up as she kicked her shoes into the corner. Rowena, Meredith, and Morgana were in her living room.

All three of their faces were somber. They weren't here for a girls' get-together. "What's wrong?"

Rowena came forward. "It's Reece."

*L*ucas checked his watch for the fifth time in as many minutes and shuffled his feet, feigning impatience for anyone who might be watching. Eddie had texted him two hours ago with an address for a condo on Court Street in downtown Blue Mountain and told Lucas to meet him there.

He'd arrived at the building and was escorted up to the penthouse suite, where he was told to wait in the spacious room. Lucas leaned back into the couch cushions and draped his arm over its back.

He aimed for relaxed and cocky with a bit of impatience thrown in. Lucas looked around at the opulence of the room. It was decorated in neutrals with dark drapes bracketing the floor-to-ceiling windows that captured a view of the setting sun. It looked professionally decorated, lacking even a single memento of someone who lived there.

By the time Lucas would be able to leave, it'd be too late to meet Jo at the library before she left for the day. He'd dropped by every day since she'd discovered his lie a week ago, but he hadn't made any headway. She was definitely stubborn, and it was ironic because her stubbornness was one of the things he most liked about her. She didn't waver on her principles.

Lucas checked his watch again. He'd been waiting fifteen minutes and he still didn't know why Eddie had asked to meet him here. And except for it being a new apartment building, he didn't know the significance of the place. It wasn't the same building Copeland had been in when he'd been killed months ago. The rent would be too high for someone of Eddie's means, so this could be a good sign Lucas was being introduced to someone higher in the food chain.

As he waited, he should have been thinking about possible strategies in case things went south, but he had no room in his thoughts for a game plan. Thoughts of Jo had consumed him, both while awake and in his dreams.

When he saw her yesterday, it was only from a distance because he couldn't get past Viktor without making a scene. The old man had become Jo's watchdog. If Jo didn't give in soon, Simon was going to have to think of what to report to Ben.

That was another first brought on by Jo. In the past, Simon only ever reported the truth. He'd never deviated from the plan before. Not only was this operation at risk, but so was his job as an agent. He'd revealed himself to Jo, and unlike Catherine, Jo knew his real identity. She could endanger his position within the FBI if she chose to divulge who he really was.

Twenty minutes later, he was ready to crawl out of his skin. He looked up when he heard someone and saw Eddie finally walk in from a hallway off to the right, shuffling his Chucks on the hardwood floor.

Lucas stood. "It's about time," he said with what he hoped

was just enough impatience and cockiness to be true to Lucas, but not enough to piss Eddie off.

"You'll wait as long as I need you to," Eddie said, stopping in front of Lucas. "We're ready for you now."

"Ready for what?" Simon saw Rocky circle around behind him, but he kept his gaze on Eddie, pretending to be oblivious. There were times these guys were such a joke that Simon sometimes had to act dumber than he expected Lucas ever was.

It took all his training to keep himself from blocking Rocky as he came up behind Lucas with a syringe. When he felt the needle plunge into the side of his neck, he figured he could finally react.

"Hey, what'd you do?" he asked, spinning around and grabbing his neck as he confronted Rocky. Whatever they'd given him, probably Propofol, it had already started to act.

Rocky looked nervous and backed up a step as Lucas dropped to his knees. Simon still had enough energy and wits about him, due to years of experience, that he could have flashed out of the building, but he chose not to. He was in this until the end, so he would keep his cover. He let the darkness take over.

SIMON CAME AWAKE QUICKLY but kept his eyes closed as he listened. He remembered Rocky coming up behind him with a syringe, but nothing afterward.

Lucas! His eyes flew open, and he pulled at his arm to see his hand, but his hands wouldn't move. Looking down, he could see Lucas's wrists strapped to a chair. He let out his breath slowly, wishing he could send some magic through his system to slow his heart rate.

During training with Ben, Simon had been drugged several times while transformed into someone else to see if he'd change back while unconscious. Each time he'd remained as he was, but there was a first time for everything.

"That was fast. I thought you'd be out for longer."

Lucas saw Eddie's black Chucks, the white scuffed and gray, before he raised his head to look the man in the eyes. Eddie wasn't a big man, about five foot nine, so he didn't tower over Lucas, even while he was sitting down.

"Can't keep me down for long." Lucas lowered his eyes to the rope around his wrist before sending a pointed stare to Eddie. "You going to explain why you drugged me and tied me up?" he said, hoping he projected just the right amount of sneer. He sent a small amount of magic through his arms to test the ropes. His magic bounced back, like a rubber ball hitting a brick wall. Lucas cursed under his breath when he realized the rope was spelled, making it resistant to his magic.

"You're not working fast enough to get the book."

"So, tying me up is going to get me to work faster?"

Eddie cuffed Lucas on the side of the head. "*Hijo de puta.*"

Lucas righted his head and stared down Eddie again. "You can just say motherfucker, I get it."

"Not only a tough guy, but a stupid one." Eddie jerked his head, gesturing with his chin to Rocky. "He's all yours."

Rocky didn't move. "I have to?"

"Yeah, Snake said to teach him a lesson."

Simon wanted to smile inside at the new information. He'd already figured out everyone went by codenames, but that was the first time he'd heard someone in this group referred to by Snake. When Ben had interviewed Morgana after her rescue, she'd mentioned the name. She knew the man had been working with Copeland, whose codename had been Zeus. He would laugh at having some of the pieces finally coming together if he wasn't tied to a chair.

Ben and Jack believed that Snake could be one of the two council members that went missing with Copeland over twenty years ago. Snake. Something was pinging in his memory, but his thoughts were a bit foggy from the drug. It would come to him.

Rocky held his left fist in the palm of his right hand and cracked his knuckles, the noise loud in the room. Then he cracked the knuckles of his other hand. The move was so cliché Simon wanted to laugh out loud, despite the thought of the pain that was soon coming his way.

At just under six feet tall, Rocky was broad and muscular, but not as confident and cocky as Eddie. When Simon had first met the two cohorts, they'd almost been glued at the hip, but Rocky hadn't been around much while Lucas had been with Jo. Eddie had been the one watching him from the shadows. It was another piece of the puzzle that Simon had to figure out. Rocky's absence had meant something, but he didn't know what yet.

The first punch came at Lucas from his left and spun his head to the side, the pain radiating up his cheek, forcing his eyes closed. Dizziness threatened to envelop him, but he shook it off. He'd just righted his head when Rocky hit him again in the same spot.

Simon could see stars behind his eyes and breathed deeply. Bad move. Rocky sent a blow to Lucas's gut, knocking the wind out of him, but there was no time to catch his breath. The chair wobbled backward, and he braced himself for the fall, but suddenly the chair was righted and Rocky came at him again and again. The first blows landed in the middle of his gut, and Lucas clenched his abs against the hits. He was in pain but holding his own until he saw

Rocky shift and the next fist landed on Lucas's liver. The impact would have sent him backward if the chair hadn't been secured. A burning pain radiated through Simon as he struggled to suck in enough oxygen.

"Eddie, that's enough."

Rocky didn't sound winded, but Simon could hear the anguish in the man's voice. He didn't like inflicting pain.

"Not yet, Rock. Our boy Lucas here needs to learn that when we give him a job to do, he needs to get it done, pronto."

"Sorry," Rocky whispered.

Lucas didn't have a chance to reply before he was hit again. And then again. His gut, his face, and his liver.

"Oh no. No blacking out," Eddie said.

Simon didn't think he'd have a choice until the smell of acrid bleach wafted into his nostrils. He reared his head back without thinking.

Eddie laughed as he gripped a tight handful of Lucas's hair, forcing him to look into Eddie's eyes. "Smelling salts work every time. Not so cocky now, are you, motherfucker?" he said, enunciating the curse. Eddie tilted his chin toward Rocky. "Go get the healer."

Simon heard Eddie's order at the same time that Eddie let go of Lucas's hair, and his head fell forward. He didn't have the strength to hold it up. Sending some magic through his body, he checked for internal injuries. Healing was never his strong suit, but he could tell that several organs were swelling.

He worked to cool his body and decrease the inflammation, but that was all he could do. He was fucked.

"Make sure he doesn't die, and get rid of any physical signs that he was hurt, but leave the pain."

Lucas lifted his head at Eddie's directions, looking for who he was talking to. Rocky had one meaty fist around the arm of a man he dragged into the room. Lucas's eyes were swelling shut as he squinted against the room's light and the pain to make out the newcomer. He was thin to the point of being gaunt, and his dirty blond hair stuck out of a baseball cap. He had a long scar on the left side of his face that cut through his eyebrow and ran down his cheek, ending in several days' worth of scruff.

"Untie him," the scarred man said, his voice rusty as if he didn't speak often.

The ropes on Lucas's arms disappeared and without time to brace himself, he fell forward. His knees hit the hard wooden floor as he rolled to his side, unable to stifle a groan.

"Rocky, watch 'em both. I'll let Snake know that we won't have a problem with our friend Lucas from now on. Right, Lucas?" Eddie kicked Lucas in the thigh hard enough to jerk him to the right.

Simon couldn't hold back the small cry that erupted from him as he rolled onto his right, putting more pressure on his liver. He took in small breaths, unable to rally the energy to send more soothing magic through his system.

The scarred man laid his hand on Lucas's shoulder, gently forcing him down onto his back. "Easy. I'll help you."

The man moved his hands to Lucas's face, cupping his cheeks like a lover or a parent might do. A warmth started at Lucas's temples and spread down into his cheeks. He sucked in his breath as the tiny pinprick sensation started to heal his face. It wasn't a fun feeling—magical healing never was— but it was better than looking and feeling like a punching bag.

Just as Simon settled into the sensations, they stopped. He opened his eyes to look at the scarred man above him, and almost gasped. The man looked gaunter than he had a few minutes ago. His face was pale and sweat dripped from his forehead, but it was his pinched lips and hollow cheeks that were most telling. The healing was sucking the life from this man.

Lucas pushed himself up to his elbows. "Hey, you don't have to continue."

The healer put his hand on Lucas's shoulder and gently pushed him back. "Yes, I do." He looked over his shoulder at Rocky. "I need your help."

Rocky's eyes darted to the hallway Eddie had walked down before he put his hand on the healer's shoulder. "Take just what you need, or they'll know."

The healer nodded and his hands scanned down Lucas's torso, healing as they went. He sucked in a breath at the pricks of pain that intensified as the man healed his liver. "Rocky gave you energy, didn't he?"

The man only nodded and continued to heal. After several minutes, he put his hands on the floor beside Lucas, his head falling forward as if he had no more strength to hold it up. Simon could still feel pain, but he doubted he was in danger from internal bleeding now, and his face no longer felt like he'd gone a few rounds with Rocky Balboa. Steadying himself, he got to his feet to help the healer stand. The man wobbled and his arms flailed, trying to find purchase in the air, and he would have fallen if Lucas didn't have hold of both his arms.

Rocky put one arm at the healer's back, bent to put his other arm behind the man's legs, then stood, the healer cradled in his arms like a child. "I'll take him back."

"Thank you..." Simon hoped for a name, even a code name, but the man didn't look at him as Rocky carried him down the hallway.

Simon was about to follow them when Eddie came forward, passing them in the narrow corridor. "Feeling better, Lucas?" he asked with a shit-eating grin on his face. "Not too much better, I hope?"

"I'm fine."

"Good. Next time will be worse, and we'd hate for something to happen to Josephine. You've got five days to find the book."

Even if Jo was talking to him, Simon didn't think five days would be enough. With the cold shoulder she was giving him? They were both fucked.

"It's Reece," her cousin said again.

"No. No, no, no." Jo dropped to her knees as her world shattered.

Rowena knelt in front of Jo and held her by the arms, forcing Jo to look up. "He's alive," Rowena whispered, "but the council leaders had to put him in a coma."

"Like a medically-induced coma? I don't understand." Jo's eyes flicked from Rowena to where Meredith stood a few feet away.

Rowena stood and pulled Jo up with her, wrapping her arm around Jo as she guided them into the living room. Morgana stood by, wringing her hands in front of her. Jo lifted a corner of her mouth, trying to give Morgana a reassuring smile but knew she failed.

Meredith pulled Jo into a hug and held tighter when Jo refused to melt. When Meredith let go, her expression was stark. "Reece was dying. His body was too weak to accept any more energy from us. We called Mary and three other council leaders and they decided the best thing was to put

Reece in a magic coma. It put the spell on him in stasis and prevented it from killing him."

"Will his body heal itself while the spell is in stasis?"

Meredith briefly closed her eyes. "No, we don't think so. All it will do is buy us some time."

"How much time?"

"We don't know. A week or two maybe."

"I need to see him. Where is he?"

"In my apartment so Jack and I can watch—" Jo flashed to Meredith's before her cousin finished her sentence.

"Jo?" Jo looked up at Jack. "I felt your energy and thought you were Meredith. It's radiating off you."

"I need to see him."

"He's fine for now. Resting. He's in our spare bedroom."

Jo nodded and walked down the hallway leading to the bedrooms. The door to the spare room was ajar and a light shone from the adjoining bathroom. Reece was on the bed, the blankets folded back at his chest. Her brother had always been big and broad, but the man lying in the bed looked like a shadow of his former self.

She reached for Reece's hand lying limp by his side and brought it up to her lips. "I'll fix this," she whispered. "Don't die on me, Reece. You can't. You're all I have left."

Not letting go of Reece's hand, she reached behind her and dragged the single chair closer, the scraping sound jarring in the quiet room. She sat on the edge of the chair and kept her brother's bony hand in between her two smaller ones. "Hey Reece's Pieces, you have to hold on." Jo's throat tightened and she swallowed around the lump. "More of my memories are coming back now that we're unbound..." She hesitated. Should she talk about her magic when his was still bound?

Yes, Reece would want her to. Regardless of what he was

going through, he was her brother and would be happy for her.

"Now that we're unbound…" She took another deep breath and forced herself to keep going. "…I remember new things… well, I guess they're old things. Do you remember that time before the fire when Dylan wanted to turn the neighbor's dog into a dragon?" She chuckled at the memory, one of the few she had of her older brother. "I think he was about ten, I would have been six and you eight. Anyway, remember he convinced us what a good idea it was? He thought if he just gave the dog some fire before he cast a spell, it would help." She chuckled at the memory. "The poor dog, at least you had the hose ready and put out the fire and his fur was only a bit singed. I remember Dad being so mad and we were grounded for forever. It was probably only a few days, but it felt like forever. I don't know if I ever told you, but later that night, I slipped out of bed for a snack and heard Dad telling Dylan how proud he was of him for taking some initiative to do something different but warned him not to use live subjects in the future." Jo smiled at the memory. So bitter-sweet. Both her parents and her oldest brother were no longer with them.

"Let me see what else I can remember." Jo spoke to Reece for hours, telling him story after story. Partway through she conjured water and drank several glasses to soothe her throat so she could keep talking. She still couldn't tell if he could hear her, but she rubbed his hand and kept talking.

"Jo, you need some rest."

Jo didn't take her eyes off her brother when Meredith walked up behind her. "I've failed him," she said quietly.

"No, you haven't. You'll find the book; I believe that."

Meredith draped her arms around Jo, and using her free hand, Jo gripped Meredith's arm tightly. "I haven't let Lucas help me," Jo whispered again, afraid to speak too loudly for fear it would further disrupt the peace.

"Then listen to him," Meredith said, resting her chin on Jo's shoulder and speaking just as softly as Jo.

"How do I trust him?"

"You'll know when it's time."

"I hope you're right, Mer."

Jo LOOKED around the gallery's wide-open space, seeing it for the first time in daylight. Her Vans were quiet on the polished tile floor as she made her way to a reception desk off to the side.

A woman came around the desk with a welcoming smile. "Good morning, how may I help you?"

"I'm here to see Lucas."

"Is he expecting you?"

"No, but he'll see me." At least Jo hoped he would and if he wouldn't, she'd beg.

"I'll call up to the offices."

Jo nodded and turned around, looking at the art on the walls, though she didn't take it in. She could still see her brother's nearly lifeless form on the bed as she spoke to him for hours last night.

"Josephine. Good morning. How fabulous of you to drop by."

Jo looked up as Lucas walked toward her, his smile as loud and broad as his greeting. Confidence dripped from the man, but then, why shouldn't it? He owned this gallery and had the world at his fingertips. The sight of him made her ache for the time when she could just be attracted to him and didn't yet know he'd lied.

But he had lied, and now she needed his help. She wanted the world to still be black and white, like she'd always viewed it, but she suspected that was seeing the world through the eyes of the child she'd once been. If she chose to view the world through shades of gray, like her family told her she should, how would she know what to accept? She gave herself an internal shake—that was a quandary for another day. Right now, she needed to convince Lucas to help her. "I need to talk to you."

"Of course. Come up to my office."

Lucas escorted Jo up the plush carpeted stairway with his hand at the small of her back. His touch was light, yet she swore she could feel his heat seeping into her, warming her down to her bones. That was crazy; maybe it was magic.

"Can I get you a coffee or tea?" he asked once they were in his office.

"No, thank you." She took a seat on one of the chairs in a small sitting area he gestured to and watched him as he closed the door.

An immediate change came over him, though not a transformation—he was still Lucas. His shoulders dropped and his posture relaxed, even his smile wasn't quite the same when he turned to face her.

He sat on a loveseat facing her and rested one foot on the other knee and stretched his arm over the back of the sofa. She thought she saw him wince when he extended his arm. The smile he turned on her this time would have made any dentist proud—big, confident, and all teeth, with a touch of cockiness.

Holy shit. She was seeing both Lucas and Simon and how he changed between the two. She'd never noticed it before, but then she hadn't known he was two different people. Lucas was an act, but then how much of what he'd done with her had been real? Who had he been when he'd kissed her?

"What can I do for you, Jo?"

His question brought her back to reality. It didn't matter who had kissed her as long as he helped her. "I need your help to find the book."

"Last week you said that you hadn't managed to find a clue with my mother's book—have you found any answers in the last few days?"

Jo was fascinated, wanting to analyze every expression and gesture Lucas made, but she had to stay on track. "No. I'm stuck. I think my inexperience with my magic might be holding me back. When I first started looking for the book, I thought it would be simple research, putting the pieces together, but the magic brings in too many nuances. I just don't know enough yet to recognize them."

Lucas smiled. "I'd be happy to help you, but why now? You wouldn't even talk to me last week."

"Reece has gotten worse."

"I'm sorry to hear that. I'll help any way I can."

She kept watching him to see if she could see any of Simon in him. It was stupid, but she couldn't seem to help herself. His smile dimmed only slightly when he uncrossed his legs and took his arm off the loveseat. He might have winced again. "Are you okay?" she asked him.

His smile brightened again. "Yes, why wouldn't I be? I have a beautiful woman here asking for my help."

That was all Lucas. She was starting to notice subtle differences in his actions when he put on his Lucas façade. Fascinating. "I have some questions."

"I'm surprised you've waited this long. Ask away."

"Who's real? Simon or Lucas?"

Lucas sat back and stretched his arm over the sofa again. His wince was barely noticeable this time, but Jo had been watching for it. She expected that she was going to see full-on Lucas now. She wanted to whip out her phone and jot down some notes, but instead mentally cataloged his movements.

His smile was breathtaking and lit up his light blue eyes. The way his blond hair looked both styled and carefree topped off the package. "They're both real. Simon's birthday is June twenty-ninth and Lucas's birthday is April fifteenth. Simon is thirty-four and Lucas is thirty-six. They were both born in Blue Mountain."

He was stalling, but Jo wanted to see where this would go.

"Why do they have the same memorial tattoo?"

Lucas dropped his arm again and looked down at his watch before focusing his attention on Jo. She wanted to fist pump because she was starting to figure them out. She'd bet money that the memorial tattoo belonged to Simon. Looking at his watch was a mannerism she'd noticed before, but many people did that. Though he did it too often for him just to be checking the time. She was sure it was a tell, she'd just have to pay closer attention to figure out for what.

"Memorial tattoos can be embedded with the memory of a loved one, as you know." Lucas looked over Jo's shoulder, as if deep in thought for a moment, before looking her in the eyes again. "It's the only thing that stays when I transform into someone else. I know there is a spell that people can use to transform, but it comes at a great cost. However, I don't know any other magics who can do what I do. I'd appreciate it if you kept that to yourself."

She nodded. "That's why all of Simon's other tattoos disappear." She didn't need an answer, but Lucas nodded. "Is the tattoo really in memory of Simon's father?" He hadn't confirmed that the tattoo was Simon's, not Lucas's, but he didn't need to; she already knew.

"For both Simon's mother and father."

"Ah... but since Catherine is still alive you had to adjust

the story." Holy shit—Catherine. He was living with Lucas's mother. "Does Catherine know about Simon?"

"Not Simon, specifically, but she knows there is someone," he said quietly. That was all Simon.

"Why?" Viktor's story about finding out the truth behind the lie had hit her hard and she knew she had to ask. Plus, it was a part of her. She'd spent her entire adult career looking for the truth, and yet in this one instance she wasn't sure she really wanted to know.

"I'm working. Lucas has access to people that I need to… associate with."

She noticed the pause but didn't question him about it. "Are you doing anything illegal?"

"Except for being two people, which no one can prove? No."

"Okay. I'll accept that for now because I need your help."

Lucas grinned, all teeth, and she knew the cocky man was back. "Perfect. When would you like to start? This afternoon?"

"Sure, I just have one request."

"What's that?"

"You can't be Lucas."

*L*ucas sat back and looked at Jo, not letting the surprise of her declaration show on his face. He forced a laugh. "I am Lucas."

"No, you're Simon, and that's who I want to work with."

Another first. Jo wanted to work with Simon when most people didn't even know he existed. He should be jumping up and down for joy, but all he could think was that if he worked with her as Simon, he was throwing his career away. For the past ten years his career had defined him—a job that required him to be the best someone else. Could he really be Simon when he had a job to do?

Yesterday's warning that he wasn't doing his job was still quick to come to the forefront whenever he moved the wrong way, even after the healer did his thing. "I can't, Jo."

"Yes, you can."

She didn't flinch, just sat back in the chair with a smug smile on her face. A smile so like the many that Lucas sported. She knew she'd won before they even started the game.

"I wish I could, but I can't reveal myself."

"Yes, you can. I saw you in the coffee shop as Simon, so we can just say I met you that day and bumped into you again and now you're helping me."

She was right, but what would he do about Lucas? He leaned forward and rested his forearms on his knees. "I really want to help you, but there is more at stake here than you know. I'm working and I can't jeopardize the mission I've been tasked with. A lot of people are depending on me."

She leaned forward as well, and if he moved a fraction more, he could kiss her. He'd never wanted a kiss so badly in his entire life. Jo did something to him. He glanced at her lips and then forced himself to look her in the eyes.

"I understand high stakes. My brother is dying." She was dry-eyed as she stared at him, but he could clearly see the anguish written on her face. "I wouldn't ask you, Lucas… Simon, if there wasn't a life at stake."

He wanted to chuckle at the two names, but there wasn't anything funny about what she was asking. It also hadn't escaped his notice that if her brother wasn't dying, she wouldn't have come to him.

He would have loved to have had a brother or a sister. Maybe he wouldn't have always felt so lonely, but was he willing to risk leaving her an only child too? She'd already lost so many of her loved ones, he would do what he could so she didn't lose one more. "Okay, I'll help, but there will be times I'll need to be Lucas."

She stood and rubbed her palms on her jeans. "Fine, just be Simon when you're with me. How's one this afternoon?"

"That works." He stood and watched Jo turn and walk out of his office. She knew as well as he did that he wouldn't let her down. He would just be letting down everyone else in his life, even himself.

It HAD BEEN three days since Jo asked Lucas, or rather Simon, for help and they still hadn't gotten anywhere. She'd introduced Simon to Viktor, saying he was someone she'd met at the coffee shop who was an expert in ancient books and was going to help her. Viktor hadn't asked about Lucas and she'd only volunteered that she'd listened to what he'd had to say and they were fine.

"Still nothing?" she asked Simon as she closed the book she'd been looking through and rubbed the back of her neck to ease the tension radiating across her shoulders.

"Not really. But I want to check the book Catherine gave you. I think it's the key and we're missing something."

"You sure it's not a waste of time? We've gone over it several times." She watched Simon as he reached across the table for the book. The muscles in his forearms rippled, moving his tattoos in a way that made Jo want to run her finger down them and trace the images.

Simon was dressed in dark jeans and a Henley, with the sleeves pushed up almost to his elbows. Jo blinked several times to refocus on the task at hand and take her eyes off Simon's ink.

They were in the back room where they'd worked before and didn't have to worry about prying eyes.

"It could be a waste of time, but it would be worse if we missed something." He laid the book on the cradle stand they'd used before and stepped back. The pages flipped back and forth until finally settling about a quarter of the way through. Simon flicked his hand toward the book and English words appeared in the air.

Simon read the words aloud.

"The present work we seek to know and see.
Beastly desires we cast aside and speak the truth.
Hear thy word and know thine heart."

"That seems familiar. Isn't this one of the spells that we looked at already and ruled out?" Jo gestured to the book. "I mean, nothing happened then or now."

"Yes, but I think that's because it's been divided."

She raised an eyebrow, feeling her piercing move her bangs to the side. "You mean like a spell being purposely split in two pieces?"

"Exactly." Simon waved his hand and the words of the spell solidified in a bubble in the air.

"Wow, that's cool. Better than writing it down."

He grinned down at her and then looked back to the book and waved his hand at it again. "*See these words; a spell once broken. Find the words lost and make the spell whole.*" The pages continued to flip until they stopped near the end of the book.

"How did you know what spell to say?"

"I didn't, not really, but words don't really matter for our magic to work, except for specific spells. In this case, I just needed something to guide my magic so the book knew what I was looking for."

Jo watched Simon close his eyes for a moment, as if concentrating, before waving his hand at the open book. English words floated up in a bubble similar to the first one.

Honest hearts and open souls have we.
Reveal thyself for those worthy to know.
A pledge for good and do no harm.

She looked at both bubbles, back and forth, and sighed. "They don't make sense. I've read the first bubble first and then the second, and then the second bubble first and then the first. Wow, that sounded something like that game 'Who's On First,' but you know what I mean, right?"

Simon chuckled. "Funnily enough, I do. But I think it's not as straightforward as that."

Simon read the first sentence from the first bubble, followed by the first from the second bubble, and continued to alternate. Still nothing.

"I think we need to rearrange the sentences."

Jo did a quick calculation in her head. "Woah, with six sentences, that's over forty-five thousand possible combinations."

"Yes, but we've got a little magic on our side."

"What do we need to do?"

"First, let's type them out."

Jo pulled up her laptop and copied the paragraphs and then sat back and watched as Simon focused on the words on the screen. The words moved and rearranged themselves again and again, moving too fast for Jo's eyes to see the details, until it was all a blur.

After twenty minutes, the words stopped moving and a combination appeared. Simon flicked his fingers toward the two word bubbles still suspended in the air and rearranged the sentences to match what was on the computer.

The lights dimmed and Jo looked up at Simon.

Simon looked sheepish. "Ah, I probably should have dimmed the lights and protected the books in the room before we started all this, but better late than never. I put a spell around the word bubbles." He turned, facing the bubbles, and read the words aloud.

> *"The present work we seek to know and see.*
> *Beastly desires we cast aside and speak the truth.*
> *Honest hearts and open souls have we.*
> *Hear thy word and know thine heart.*

*A pledge for good and do no harm.
Reveal thyself for those worthy to know."*

"Oh my god!" She pointed at the bubbles. "Do you see that?"

"Yes," he said with awe in his voice.

She stood beside Simon and watched as the sentences rearranged themselves until there was only one bubble and the words glowed. "Now what?"

"Look," Simon said, pointing to a book on the shelf that was glowing too. He walked to the shelf and very gently extracted the glowing volume. The light in the room seemed to dim as both the book and the words stopped glowing and the bubble disappeared.

Jo closed the first book and placed it on the table while Simon laid the new book open on the cradle.

He turned to Jo and gently cupped her face with one hand. "I don't think this is the book we're looking for, but another clue. If it was the book, I don't think it would have been here in plain sight all along."

His words barely registered with Jo as she focused on the feel of his hand. It was the first time he'd touched her since she found out about his lie, but she didn't pull away.

His hand felt warm as he looked into her eyes. "Don't get discouraged. We're getting close"

She breathed in deep and turned into his hand. "I know. But it feels like a wild goose chase and we're running out of time."

Simon leaned forward, his lips only inches from hers. Her tongue shot out to wet her lips as she kept her eyes on his. She wanted the kiss so badly, but there were still so many unanswered questions between them. She pulled back, and Simon dropped his hand. "Whatever this book reveals... thank you."

He nodded and turned back to the book. "We've still got work to do."

Jo didn't play games and she felt horrible for pulling away, but they needed to focus on the book. She'd figure her feelings out later when Reece was healthy.

Simon looked over at Jo and the corners of his lips twitched at what he saw. Jo had her head resting on her arms and was sound asleep beside her laptop. They'd been working almost non-stop during the two days since they'd found the clue and the new book.

They'd only left the library to get a few hours of sleep each night, but even the extra hours of work hadn't helped. They were still no closer to figuring out this new book than they'd been when they'd started.

It also meant that Simon's time was up. Eddie had given him five days and that meant he had to have results tonight. Not only did he not have results, he hadn't shown Lucas around Jo in the entire five days.

When they got to the library early this morning, just as the sun was coming up, it had been closed to the public. The security guards let them in because Viktor had arranged it.

Simon had flashed to the alley at the back of the library first and waited for Jo to arrive. When they walked to the front of the building, he saw Eddie and another of his cohorts, someone he didn't know by name, leaning against a tree out on the library's lawns. Simon had moved to block Jo's view of the grounds and ushered her quickly into the library.

Eddie didn't know who Simon was, but that didn't matter. Simon and Jo had been in the library all day and now it was closed again and dark outside. Hopefully Eddie had left.

He walked over to Jo and crouched down beside her chair. He wanted to pull her into his arms and make love to her, but she still didn't completely trust him. Nor had she asked any more questions about his job or his transformation into Lucas. Their conversations mostly consisted of work, except when they ate and she let her guard down. They'd talked about comics and movies and music. Just normal getting-to-know-you topics.

Simon would cherish those moments for as long as he remained on this earth. He didn't know what the future held, but he knew he was falling in love with Jo.

He put his hand gently on her back and rubbed in slow circles. "Jo, sweetheart, time to wake up and go home."

"Hmmm?" she mumbled and slowly lifted her head. Her eyes were glazed with sleep when she turned to look at him. "I fell asleep?"

"You did." He got to his feet and pulled her up with him. "Let's pack up for the night."

Jo shook her head. "No. I got some sleep so I can keep going. But… it's okay if you want to go."

Simon chuckled. "That fifteen minutes of sleep you just got wasn't enough. Let's go home and get some real sleep and we can get back at it again bright and early tomorrow."

Jo yawned and gave Simon a sheepish look. "You're right."

They packed up in silence and waved to the night guard when they left the building, but Simon's focus was already on the outside. He magically scanned the area in front of the building, but it was only eleven p.m. on a weekend in a popular area and there were too many people outside for him to know if one of them was Eddie.

They were halfway down the alley toward the back of the building when Simon heard something. He turned to look over his shoulder but was too late. Eddie and his crony had flashed to Jo and were flanking her on either side.

Simon had to play innocent because he wasn't supposed to know who Eddie was. "Hey, leave her alone."

"No, man, you fuck off. We just want to talk to the lady. Right, babe?" Eddie said while turning to Jo, as if anyone would believe that was a friendly gesture. She wiggled to pull her arm free, but Eddie's grip was obviously too tight.

"Get your hands off me!" Jo stamped her foot down hard on Eddie's instep, but her Vans didn't have an impact on Eddie's combat boots.

Simon lunged for Eddie's goon, knocking the guy off his feet. He swung hard, punching the man in the face, knocking him out.

When Simon jumped to his feet and spun, Jo was facing him and still fighting with Eddie, but he had a grip on both her upper arms.

Simon pulled deep on his magic and rubbed his hands together, creating a ball of energy. He'd have one shot to hit Eddie, hopefully not killing him.

He raised his hand just as Jo looked over Eddie's shoulder and saw Simon's intent. She looked left and Simon hoped that meant she would move left so he took aim.

The ball of energy hit Eddie square in the back, causing him to fall forward just as Simon spun further to the right.

He didn't wait to see the results and grabbed Jo's hand, tugging her toward the back of the library. "Flash to my house," he said and then she was gone.

He flashed home, hoping Jo would be there. As soon as his feet hit the foyer, he looked around for Jo.

"Simon," she whispered.

When he told her to flash, his only concern was getting her to safety, not whose body he was in. Everything with Jo had melded into one huge blur. In the last couple of weeks, he was Simon more and more when he was with her, regardless of whose body he was in.

Pulling on his magic, he transformed into Lucas. Gone were his dark hair and green eyes, replaced with a shag of blond hair and light blue eyes. He didn't worry about his clothes, which were a little too casual for Lucas.

Jo's lips curved up as he looked at her. "That's still amazing." Her expression sobered. "And sometimes I forget."

He chose to ignore that comment and took Jo's hand, guiding her up to Lucas's wing of the house.

"Lucas, is that you? Oh, Josephine, so good to see you," Catherine said, coming out of the library.

He leaned down and kissed Catherine on the cheek. "I didn't expect you to be up so late."

Catherine glanced at the slim watch on her wrist. "I hadn't realized the time, I just got lost in a good book." She looked Lucas up and down but didn't comment on his attire. "Can I get either of you a late-night snack?"

He was about to refuse when Jo spoke first.

"That'd be lovely, Catherine, if it's not too late."

"No, I'm a bit of a night owl anyway."

Lucas smiled and followed Catherine and Jo back into the library. Catherine conjured some tea in china cups and saucers, along with some tiny finger sandwiches. So like Catherine, even at midnight, that he smiled at her in thanks.

They ate the sandwiches and chatted for a half hour, Catherine filling Jo in on the money the gallery had raised for the children's charity, and then the conversation turned to the latest books they'd read.

He sat back and watched the two women who he hadn't known a year ago, but who had both come to mean so much to him. A year from now could be an entirely different story —they might both be out of his life. He could have an entirely new life, if he managed to figure out who he was after they found the book to open the magic box. He'd turn everything over to Ben and move on to another assignment. The thought was depressing—another first brought on by Jo.

"Thank you both for sitting with me," Catherine said as she disappeared the tray along with the cups and saucers and stood. "I'll retire to my room now."

They said their goodnights and Catherine left him and Jo alone in the library. "Why didn't she flash to her rooms?"

"Not all the house staff are magic, and even if they were, I think there might be a certain etiquette to flashing out of a room, as far as Catherine is concerned."

"Well, that shit in the back alley woke me up." Jo laughed and kicked her shoes off, tucking her feet under her on the sofa.

She froze and then dropped her feet to the floor, the mirthful expression falling from her face. "Sorry, that was presumptuous of me. Did you want to stay up and talk?"

"I'd love nothing more," he said. Reaching down, Lucas pulled Jo's feet onto his lap and she settled back into the cushions the way he'd hoped. It would have been better if he wasn't in Lucas's form, but he'd take it. "What would you like to talk about?"

She groaned as he rubbed her sock-covered instep with his knuckle. They were silent for several minutes as he massaged first one foot and then the other.

"Thanks." She pulled her feet out of his lap and curled them underneath her.

She was fortifying her walls and back to not trusting him, but he was determined to someday see those walls in crumbled ruins. He'd take what Jo would give of herself and hope that eventually she would trust him so that maybe they'd have a future together. He knew in that moment that he wanted one with her. He wanted her to love Simon.

He pushed the thought from his mind for now. "Ask away."

"Ask what?"

"I know you're dying to ask me something." He grinned at her and waited.

"I guess I am, but I'm not sure what to ask." She conjured a glass of water and held it in her hands like it could protect her. "You said you were Lucas for work. What kind of work?"

"I'm undercover, trying to get in with some…" He chuckled. "What did you call them before… Oh, right. Some unsavory people."

"The same people who want the book I'm looking for?"

"Yes."

Jo disappeared her water glass and jumped to her feet. "You're working against me." She put her hands on her hips and glared at him. "You were going to take the book all along," she hissed the accusation.

Lucas stayed relaxed on the couch as Simon tried to figure out what to say. He was so tired of lying and telling only half-truths that he decided to be honest. "I was tasked with taking the book, but I hadn't decided what to do yet. We don't want the book in the hands of those I'm currently working with."

Telling the truth must have earned him some more trust because Jo sat on the sofa again, curling into the corner. "You said 'we.' Who is we? It can't be the council Jack Knight is setting up, or he would have told me."

"No, it's not Jack, at least not directly. It's the FBI."

"You work for the FBI? With Jack and Ben?"

"I work *for* Ben, and I've never met Jack or most of the other agents. That's Ben's doing. The more people who know about what I can do, the more dangerous it would be for me."

"How long have you worked for the FBI?"

"Almost eleven years, and I've worked directly for Ben for all but one of those."

"Ben must have recruited you about the same time he recruited Jack."

"A couple of years before, I think, but close enough." Simon paused. It was strange talking to Jo about Simon when he looked like Lucas. He turned his head and used his magic to close the door to the library and cast a small protection spell.

"Why'd you do that?"

"Because I don't want to talk about myself when I look like Lucas." He pulled on his magic again and shed Lucas's appearance. Moving his head side to side, he stretched his neck and shoulders.

"Does it hurt transforming back and forth?"

"No, but I'm taller than Lucas." He gave her a small smile as he shrugged. "Lucas wasn't as tall or broad as me and making him broader was easy to explain—weightlifting—but the height was a bit trickier. I've grown Lucas a bit in the last year, but I'm still taller."

Jo blinked at him and then laughed. The sound was music to his ears and one he hadn't heard much of during the last week. "Well, that's not something you hear everyday. Sometimes I wish I could grow taller."

"You're perfect the way you are." The smile fell from her face as soon as he said the words and he could have kicked himself for breaking their easy comfort.

"How'd you come to be Lucas?"

Simon told her what he could without going into too

much depth and giving away classified information, glossing over some of the details. He entertained her with a few stories about some of the mistakes he made when he'd been other people and when he first became Lucas, just to hear her laugh.

Jo stood. "I should go. Would it be alright if I flash home from here?"

It was two thirty in the morning when he looked at his watch, but he didn't want the night to end.

Simon stood and closed the short distance between them. He cupped her face in his palm, like he'd done earlier, and leaned forward. The kiss was the barest touch of his lips against hers before he pulled away. "Thanks for tonight, Jo."

She touched her lips with her fingers and then flashed away.

Simon transformed back into Lucas before unlocking the library door and removing the spell. He made his way slowly to his rooms, not in a rush to be alone in Lucas's space.

For just a couple of hours, Simon had been himself in a bubble with Jo, but dawn was only hours away and then he'd have to face Eddie.

His biggest problem at the moment was figuring out how to approach the situation and what to tell Ben.

25

*L*ucas strode into the library the next morning with all the confidence that Simon could muster. Going on only a few hours of sleep, and lousy sleep at that, he still needed to check on Jo. He was under no illusion that she got a full night's sleep and was sleeping in. She'd probably been here for awhile already.

He waved at Viktor as he approached the desk and the man motioned to the back room where Simon and Jo had been doing most of their research. If the older man thought it strange that today Lucas showed up when sometimes Simon did, he didn't give any indication.

Jo had her head in a book when he walked into the room. "Good morning, beautiful!" He shut the door behind him and took a seat at the table across from Jo.

Her head popped up and the look on her face wasn't a welcome one. "Lucas, what are you doing here? And I mean *Lucas*." She sat back and crossed her arms over her chest. A chest Simon still wanted to see when he could worship every inch of her body. How ironic, considering Lucas could have had sex with her already but had turned her down. "Well?" she asked, pulling him out of his thoughts, forcing him to raise his eyes to look at hers.

"I'm worried about what happened last night."

Jo's arms dropped to the table with a small thud. "You mean in the alley?"

"Yes. I haven't been doing my job and Lucas needs to be seen."

"Do your job? Like steal the book from me, you mean?"

Simon sighed and dropped Lucas's cocky pretense, regardless of what he looked like on the outside at the moment. "I didn't know you when I agreed to steal the book. I was doing my job and not for just one person, but for all magic people." The words were out of his mouth before it registered with him what he'd said. "Jo, that's not—"

Jo pushed back from the desk and stood, the chair toppling onto the carpet behind her. "Oh, you don't have to explain, I get it. You wouldn't help me for just *one person*— like my brother! One individual doesn't matter to you." She stood tall, even with her small stature, her hands resting on her hips, and it struck him that she looked like a purple-haired goddess ready to take on the world.

He wanted her to be *his* purple-haired goddess. But he doubted that would ever happen. His job aside, she had just proved she didn't trust him.

He stayed seated, not wanting to tower over her or move into her space. "Jo, please sit down and talk about this."

"This? You mean talk about your lies?" Her voice rose higher, and he waved his hand toward the door, throwing a light protection and sound-dampening spell at it.

She threw her arms in the air and energy swirled around her; papers lifted off the table and fluttered to the ground. "What did you do now? Lock us in?" she almost shouted as she glared at him.

"I put a small spell on the door so hopefully no one will hear us. Regardless of what you think of me, we are still magic and have to be careful."

Jo's head snapped to the door and then she glanced at the papers on the floor, probably realizing for the first time what she'd done. She flopped into her chair like a deflated balloon. "I'm sorry for the outburst." She ran a hand through her short hair, pushing the bangs out of her eyes. "I think I'm just tired and frustrated."

"I get it. You love your brother and you're working your ass off day and night to help him." He conjured her favorite coffee and pushed the to-go cup across the table.

"Thank you. For understanding and the coffee, but I shouldn't have put us in danger by almost revealing what we are."

He shrugged. She wasn't the first magic to do so and wouldn't be the last. There was a reason they could wipe some memories and magically change evidence if needed. He'd had to doctor a photo more than once to show himself looking like he'd been somewhere he hadn't. "Jo, I wanted to make sure you were okay today and apologize for you getting attacked last night. It was my fault."

"But I thought the people you were working with don't know you're Simon."

"They don't, but they haven't seen Lucas around, so they know he's not doing his job. They gave Lucas five days to find the book and that pumpkin shattered last night."

"You think that's why they attacked last night—they've given up on you and are going to take the book from me directly?"

That was Simon's worst nightmare. He wished he could wrap her up and protect her. "That's my guess, but I'm hoping that if I show myself... as Lucas... they'll back off."

"Even without the book?"

"I doubt it, but we just have to hold them off long enough to find the book and come up with a plan."

Jo raised an eyebrow. "That easy, huh?"

He knew it wasn't, but then nothing had been going as planned since he took on Lucas's life. He was going to try and fix things but Jo would still be in danger unless she trusted him enough to follow his lead.

The only way to gain more of her trust was to be more himself. He took a deep breath and looked her in the eyes. "My parents died when I was ten and ever since then I've been trying to fit in." He conjured a coffee for something to occupy his hands as he spoke, his voice barely above a whisper.

"When I was sixteen, I realized I could transform into someone else, and about a year after I joined the FBI, Ben figured it out." He huffed out a laugh. "I guess I wasn't as careful as I thought. Anyway, ever since then I've been trying to be the best someone else I could be."

The corner of her lip lifted as she returned his gaze. "At some point, we all have to choose between what the world wants you to be, and who you are."

"Wonder Woman?"

She laughed. "No, Natasha Romanoff, from the Black Widow movie."

He didn't laugh in return. "I thought I knew until I met you." The tension between them felt charged, but he didn't regret being honest for once. Disappearing his coffee, he stood and looked down at Jo. "I'm worried about you."

"I'll be fine."

"They want the book, and they don't care who they have to hurt to get it."

"Like they hurt you? I saw you wince the day I came to your office to ask for help."

"Yes, like that." He didn't bother to hide that he'd been injured since she'd noticed. Maybe it would make her more cautious. "Can you make sure you're never alone when you leave here? Have Viktor escort you out?"

"I'll try."

"Jo, I…" He wanted to say more, tell her how he felt, but he wouldn't do it while he looked like Lucas.

"I know," she whispered.

He nodded, and then turned and left. He wasn't sure what she knew, if she knew he was falling for her, but he couldn't stay. It was time to be full-on Lucas. He'd head to the gallery and see if he could fix this mess he'd made. Then he'd have to tell Ben. That was a conversation he wasn't looking forward to.

Jo packed up her laptop and used her magic to turn off the lights in the back room when she left to head out for the night.

The place was as quiet as a morgue when she headed into the main section of the library. It was far later than she had originally wanted to leave and Viktor wasn't around. She had been going to ask him to walk her out. Checking her phone, she noticed what day it was and groaned. Viktor would be at the university teaching his class.

She was so tired she was getting sloppy and careless.

"Leaving now, Jo?"

Jo whipped around and plastered a smile on her face for the night security guard. So much for going into the back room and flashing from there. "Yes, I'm just heading out. Have a good night."

"Yeah, you too. I'll make sure the door is locked behind you."

Oh great. "Thanks." She couldn't delay any longer and she hadn't learned how to scan for threats yet anyway, so there was nothing she could do. She'd have to put threat scanning on her list of things to do.

She walked out into the warm night and took a deep breath of the fresh spring air. The sun had long set, even for this late in May, but the street lamps gave her plenty of light to see by. She did a visual scan of the grounds and street and didn't see anyone. Walking briskly, she headed to the alley and decided she'd flash from there instead of going all the way to the back of the building.

Stopping just inside the alley, she cinched her bag onto her right shoulder and drew on her magic to flash. A tug on her left wrist pulled her back and she stumbled to stay upright. "The fuck?" Looking down, she saw a rope encircling her wrist.

"Hello again."

Jo whipped around and came face to face with the man from the alley last night. She thought he might have been the mugger that Lucas had stopped, as well, but she wasn't positive. Lucas had said that man had been non-magic, but now she didn't know, since Lucas hadn't really been her rescuer.

Ignoring the man, she pulled on her magic again and tried to flash. Nothing.

The man tugged on the rope, pulling her arm forward as he laughed. "You can't flash. The rope prevents you from using your magic."

She faced him and stood as tall as she could, refusing to cower. "What do you want?"

He stepped closer, only about a foot away now, his cologne overpowering, fighting with the putrid scents in the alley. "My boss wants to have a little talk with you, Josephine."

"I'm at the library most days. He can talk to me then."

"Oh, a sassy one, aren't ya. No problem."

The man moved so quickly she didn't see his fist before he hit her in the face. She fell to her side with no time to brace herself, landing on her hip. A cry burst from her as her free hand skidded along the pavement. She sucked in a breath as her face, hip, and hand were all in a sudden competition for causing her the most pain.

"Get up." The man tugged on the rope again, yanking her arm high, forcing her to stand. She shook her injured hand, hoping to ease some of the pain, and stood on shaky legs. "I'm up," she said when he tugged on the rope again.

The man laughed. "Good, just checking."

She flinched when he moved his arm toward her again, ready to duck out of the way, but he didn't hit her. Grabbing her shoulder, he squeezed, keeping her in place, even as she squirmed and tried to free herself. "Hey!"

"This won't hurt. Much."

"What—" Jo felt the pinch in her neck and her knees buckled.

"WAKE UP!" The yell in Jo's ear registered seconds before a fist slammed into her already battered cheek, swinging her head to the side. "Hey, boss, she's awake."

Jo righted her head and roamed the room with her eyes, careful not to move too much. She was tied to a chair in what looked like a condo, if the view of the city out of the floor-to-ceiling window was any indication.

"Josephine Williams, how nice of you to join us."

"Is that a fucking joke?" She couldn't help the sarcasm that dripped from her words. Her biting sarcasm was a bad habit she should probably curb… but not today.

The slap to the injured side of her face came hard and fast. She suspected the guy who greeted her hadn't liked her response. Her face throbbed as she once more righted her head and looked in front of her.

A well-dressed man, probably in his early sixties and with a bushy mustache, stood only a few feet away. His hands were clasped in front of him as if he was enjoying watching some form of entertainment. "I expect you to be more respectful from now on, Josephine, since we'll be working together."

Jo bit the inside of her cheek to avoid telling Mr. Mustache to fuck off. Another thing she should add to her to-do list—don't piss off the bad guys. Angering the man probably wasn't in her best interests.

He seemed to take her silence as acquiescence and smiled. "My name is Andrew Smith and I want the book you're looking for."

"I haven't found it."

"No, but you will, and I'd like it once you do."

She looked up at him but couldn't see him clearly. Her head pounded, and it felt like a hammer was slamming into the back of her eyelids, trying to beat her eyes out of her skull. The bright sun streaming in through the windows hurt her eyes and her cheeks pulsed with pain. "Why would I give you the book?"

He leaned down and squeezed her chin, forcing her to look directly in his eyes. "I've been looking for that book for a long time and I want it. You're going to find it and give it to me, or you'll know pain like you've never known before."

"I can't give it to you."

"Yes, you can, and you will. I know all about Jack Knight

and his new council looking for the book, but I am no match for them. If you want to keep your cousins Meredith and Rowena safe, you'll give me the book." He dropped her chin and she closed her eyes, moving her jaw from side to side to ease the pain.

Jo didn't know how he knew all about her, but her family had a public restaurant, so they weren't exactly private.

"Oh, and about your brother, Reece…"

Her eyes flung open as much as they could and she gasped, looking up at him.

"Yes, I know all about the horrible spell that was cast on him when you underwent the unbinding ceremony to remove the spell from your mother. So unfortunate." He shook his head and tsked, like he was talking about something as mundane as a broken fingernail. "I have been a patient man for far too long. You now have three days to find the book. I will help all magics when I find it and non-magics will never dictate to us again."

He walked away and Jo followed him with her eyes. When he reached the entrance to a hallway, he turned back. "And Jo, I'll have someone watching, so we'll know when you find the book. You wouldn't want to cross me."

Her eyes burned and she blinked, staving off any tears. She hadn't cried in over twenty years, and she wasn't about to start now. She'd find the book and she'd save her brother and then this asshole and Jack could fight it out. She didn't care what they did as long as Reece was safe.

Simon had been right. She'd been in over her head and hadn't even realized it. She didn't know how long they'd keep her here, but she couldn't find the book if they didn't let her go. Going to Jack and Meredith for help was definitely out now. Jack would probably lock her and her cousins behind closed doors and send someone else to look for the book. They'd have to familiarize themselves with everything she'd already learned and that could take more time than Reece had. Plus, where did that leave Simon?

Her fingers tingled, going numb from being tied up for so long. Her arms were raw from where she tugged on the ropes, and she tried to flash again, but to no avail. She couldn't even conjure so much as a tissue. So much for her magic.

Footsteps sounded behind her and she twisted to see if it was Mr. Smith, but the person was in her blind spot. A hand clamped over her mouth and she struggled to break free.

"Quiet," someone whispered in her ear. "I'm here to help you."

Jo stopped moving because there was no harm in hearing him out. She obviously wasn't going to get free on her own anyway.

"You can't see me, so I'm going to put a blindfold on you. I'll take my hand off your mouth, but don't scream. Do you understand?"

She nodded, the hand on her mouth moving up and down with her head.

"Okay, I'm going to remove my hand now. I'm the only one here who will help you, so don't scream."

Jo didn't trust the man, but she didn't have anything to lose, so she nodded again. The hand lifted off her mouth and she sucked in a large gulp of air as something that felt like a silk scarf went around her head. "This is for your safety and mine," he whispered in her ear.

His safety? Maybe he wasn't supposed to help her. She nodded again; it seemed to be the only response she could give at the moment.

She felt him crouch down beside her but didn't try to look. "I'm going to cut the rope on both your arms and then I want you to flash. Don't stop and don't look at me. Got it?" She didn't recognize the man's deep and rough voice.

The wrist of her injured hand was freed and she gasped as blood flowed back into it, causing pinpricks of pain.

"Okay, as soon as I free your next wrist, you flash. Yeah?"

She nodded and took in a deep breath, pulling on her magic. As soon as she felt her other wrist freed, she flashed home.

fter Lucas left Jo yesterday morning, he'd hung out in the gallery's showrooms all day to be visible and accessible, not leaving until after closing. Eddie didn't show or send him a message, and he began to worry that he'd fucked up so badly by helping Jo as himself that they'd written Lucas off. The problem was he knew better than to think they'd leave Lucas as a loose end.

He'd been at the gallery for three hours this morning, pretending to flirt and schmooze, when Eddie and Rocky arrived. Lucas escorted them up to his office and closed the door behind them.

"May I offer you gentlemen a drink?" He purposely stretched out the word gentlemen, letting them know exactly what he thought of them. He was still Lucas, after all.

"No, but we've got something for you." Eddie sneered and got up in his face, and Lucas let him, backing up until his ass hit the wall. Looking over his shoulder at Rocky, Eddie gestured with his head toward Lucas. "Rock, show him what we've got."

Lucas looked over at Rocky and moved to the left just as a

punch came toward his face. Rocky's right fist hit the wall behind Lucas's head, but his left caught Lucas in his still sore liver. Lucas doubled over, trying to breathe through the pain and catch his breath. He had to give it to the man, Rocky was ambidextrous. Too bad for Lucas. He took in another breath and straightened as Rocky hit him again, one fist after another landing direct hits on Lucas's gut.

His knees buckled and he dropped, his arms catching his fall on the soft carpet.

Rocky crouched down in front of Lucas and grabbed him by the hair, twisting his head to the side. Simon didn't fight or use his magic, letting Eddie think he had Lucas beat. "Now, Lucas my boy, you listening?"

Lucas nodded and fell to his side when Eddie let go of his hair.

"We warned you last week, but it didn't seem to do the job. This is your last warning. You've got three days to find the book. Mr. Smith is tired of being patient."

Smith? That was a new one. Not Snake, but perhaps one and the same. The Mr. Smith he'd met at the gallery had sported a tattoo with a swirl that could have been a snake. Smith was a common last name, but what were the chances that the one who introduced himself to Lucas out of the blue when Eddie had been in the background was not this same Mr. Smith? Probably slim to none.

"Get up." Eddie nudged his foot into Lucas's side. Hefting himself up and using the corner of his desk as leverage, Lucas stood and faced him.

"I hear you. I'll look for the book."

"Good. Because, like I said, Mr. Smith has run out of patience. He's already had a talk with Josephine, and your mother is next." Eddie jerked his head to Rocky and they both flashed away.

There were some non-magic employees in the gallery, but

Simon didn't have the strength to care that some non-magics might wonder where the men went. He pulled in another breath and stood up straight, testing his stomach, when his phone beeped.

"Just what I need," he said to the empty office. Ben had texted asking for an update. He wanted to meet him tomorrow. He was just about to text Ben back when something Eddie said registered. The threat to Catherine and Jo had come in loud and clear, but he'd also said he'd talked to Jo. Was she hurt?

Lucas glanced in the mirror on the wall to make sure he still looked like put-together Lucas, and for once was thankful Rocky had hit him in the gut and not the face. Screw the non-magics in the building; he flashed to the back room of the library.

Jo put her head down on the table to rest for a moment and flinched. She traced her cheekbone lightly with her fingers and could still feel some bruising but knew that at least it wasn't visible.

Being so new to her magic, she wasn't a great healer, but in the last year she'd learned how to do a glamour spell. It had been enough to fool Morgana when she'd dropped in for coffee this morning, but she kept her distance across the kitchen island. Jo also dimmed the kitchen lights, knowing it would be easier on Morgana's migraines, which had become worse over the last month.

Jo hated the thought of Morgana suffering, but at least lowering the lights worked in both their favors—a win-win. She'd gotten to the library early enough that she'd avoided Viktor until he'd come in to check on her. Again, she used dim lights in her favor and hoped the glamour spell was enough.

She hadn't learned how to glamour her arms, so she wore a long-sleeved T-shirt. Glamouring arms was another thing to add to her magic learning list. Her to-do list was getting longer by the day.

The energy in the room shifted and she looked up to see Lucas standing in front of her. "You flashed in here?"

He came to her chair and crouched down by her side. She didn't miss his wince. "What's wrong?" she asked, putting her hand on his arm.

"Are you hurt?" he asked, ignoring her question.

"Stand up, Lucas. You're hurting, I can see it."

Grasping the back of her chair, Lucas hoisted himself up and she saw him wince again. When he stood straight, he softly cupped her cheeks in his hands and looked down into her eyes. "I'm more worried about you. Your cheeks are hot." He flicked his hand in front of her face, and she felt cool air, knowing he'd removed her glamour and now her black eyes and bruised cheeks were on full display. "Oh, fuck. They beat you." Still cupping her cheeks, he touched his forehead to hers.

"I'm okay." But now she had another thing to add to her list—learn how to do a spell so someone else couldn't undo it.

"No, you're not." His hands warmed and she felt little pinpricks in her cheeks, not unlike when the blood was flowing back to her wrists after being bound. Lucas held her cheeks more firmly when she wiggled so she couldn't pull away. "Shhh, don't fight me. I'm healing you."

She leaned into him and let him heal her. After several moments, he dropped his hands and she reached up, grazing her fingers over her cheek. No more pain and her eyes felt like she could open them fully for the first time in over twelve hours.

He kissed her forehead and took a step back. "Are you hurt anywhere else?"

"No, but what about you?"

"I'm okay," he said and sat in the chair across from her laptop.

"No, you're not. Why didn't you heal yourself?"

He huffed out a derisive laugh. "I'm better at healing others than myself."

She yanked on her chair and pulled it beside his. Sitting down, she took his hand in hers. "Teach me how."

He moved his chair to face her, putting his legs on either side of hers, and placed her hands on his abs.

His muscles rippled beneath her fingers when he moved, and she also felt heat radiating off him. "Do you have a fever?" She lifted her hand to his forehead to check.

"No, I'm fine. I've been trying to heal myself, so you're feeling the heat of the swelling and the healing." He placed his hands over hers on his stomach. "Close your eyes and concentrate on your magic.

She did as he said and nodded.

"Now open your mind's eye to see through your hands into me."

Her magic was swirling inside her, a feeling that still sometimes caught her off guard. Pulling in a large breath, she let it out slowly and closed herself off to everything but pushing her magic into Lucas and seeing where it led her. She gasped when a picture of his insides formed in her mind. She'd taken one anatomy course in college to fulfill a science requirement and what she saw now looked just like the illustrations in her textbook. Except... "Everything looks red and swollen."

Lucas sucked in a shallow breath. "Right. So now push your magic to cool the inflamed areas."

Once more, she did as he instructed and watched the redness disappear and the tissue reduce in size. "Holy shit, it's working!"

Lucas chuckled. "Oh, ow, don't make me laugh."

She worked for a few more minutes before Lucas gripped her wrists and pulled her hands away. "That's enough, Jo. I'm not in any danger and it's draining you."

Jo lifted her head to look up at him and swayed, a sudden dizziness overtaking her. "Wow."

Pushing her head down between her knees, Lucas held her there for a minute before helping her up. "Better?"

"Much." She grinned at him. "I'm sorry you were hurt, but that was fucking cool."

Her grin made him feel like the Grinch when his heart swelled three sizes larger. Her cheeks were flushed, and her blue eyes were bright with her laughter. He wanted to kiss her. It was becoming a need he was having a harder and harder time fighting.

She gripped his biceps and leaned in. "I want to kiss you too."

He hadn't spoken out loud, but the attraction between them was so strong, anyone could likely see it. Her lips were soft when they touched his and her tongue darted out, seeking an invitation. Bringing his hands up to cup her face, he caught sight of his wrist and watch. An unwelcome reminder. He kissed her once more, hard, and then pulled back.

Her grip on his biceps eased. "What's wrong?"

"I don't want Lucas to kiss you."

She chuckled. "That's funny. You're talking about yourself in third person."

"Jo." He tried for a stern face but failed as the corners of his mouth twitched upward.

"Okay, I get it." She gripped his biceps again and leaned in as her expression sobered. "I don't care. I like who you are on the inside, and I want to kiss you no matter what you look like."

Not bothering to look, he flicked his hand over his head and aimed a locking spell at the door. When he brought his hand back, he slipped it around her neck, gently pulling her toward him. With his other hand, he ran a finger down her cheek, watching her eyes close as she let out a small breath. Everything about her spoke to him. He licked his lips and leaned forward, softly kissing her.

Even with them both sitting down, the height difference between them was vast. Gripping her around the hips, he hauled her onto his lap. She let out a laugh and he captured it with his mouth as she wrapped her arms around his shoulders.

He wound his hand into her short purple hair and tugged back, exposing her neck to his lips. She groaned as he trailed his lips and tongue across her neck and nipped at her ear lobe. "You are intoxicating," he whispered in her ear before capturing her mouth once more.

A sound from outside captured his attention, and he pulled back. He wanted to bury himself inside her, but a quickie in the library when he looked like Lucas wasn't how he wanted to be with Jo for the first time. He kissed her and then looked into her eyes. "I want you, but not here and not like this," he said, looking down at his appearance.

Jo scooted off his lap and straightened her shirt. "I guess I got carried away."

He tugged on her hips and pulled her back between his legs. "No, you didn't. Please don't pull away. When we make love for the first time, I don't want to be in the library and I don't want to look like Lucas. I care about you, Jo."

She nodded and pushed off from his shoulders, going back to the other side of the table. He was quiet for a moment while she shuffled papers, and then she stared him in the eyes. "Who would I be making love to?"

"Simon." He didn't hesitate when he answered. His life was still complicated, but he knew with certainty that he wanted Jo for himself. He wanted to only be himself with her. It was what came after that was unclear.

*L*ater that night Jo sat at a table in The Magic Plate, finishing off a glass of wine. They'd had their usual weekly family dinner and the place had been packed. So many of their friends and family had been there, but not Reece, and she'd felt his absence like a gaping hole in her chest.

Before dinner she'd sat for an hour at his bedside, holding his hand and telling him stories, and then Fiona had relieved her. Fiona and Stella were spending a lot of time watching over Reece; they'd truly become surrogate mothers to Jo and her cousins.

She sat back and looked around the tables. Now just her core group of cousins remained, along with Stella and Ben. She'd always considered Jack, Damon, and Kate like cousins since they'd all grown up together, and some time in the last several months, she had lumped Morgana into that category as well.

Rowena sat beside Jo and bumped her shoulder. "Any more details to spill about the guy?"

"Oh, that's right," Meredith said. "I've been so busy I

forgot to get an update about the lie. So… you changed your mind about him?" Meredith looked down the table at the others, and then leaned in closer to Jo. "What about the two-person thing?" she whispered.

"I told him that he had to be himself if he wanted to help me."

"And he was?"

"For a while, but then something happened." Jo hadn't mentioned the mugging and so she certainly wasn't about to mention her most recent brushes with Lucas's unsavory colleagues.

She skipped the parts about the incidents and told them about finding a clue instead.

Morgana stood and walked to Jo, placing a hand on her shoulder. "I'm going to head upstairs," she said as she squinted.

Jo stood and turned around to give her friend a hug. "Are your migraines worse?"

Morgana just shrugged and said her goodbyes.

She'd just sat back down when Damon walked by with a concerned look on his face, heading after Morgana. Jo chuckled; that girl didn't stand a chance. Damon was big and overbearing and damn persuasive, and he seemed to have a thing for Morgana. Knowing him, eventually he'd wear her down.

The others moved down the table, all congregating at one end. Meredith moved to the other side of the table to sit by Jack, and they laughed. It was great to see the two of them so in love, but that didn't mean they couldn't be teased about it.

"So, Jo," Kate said from where she sat beside Rowena, "what's this I hear about you dating two guys?"

"What?" Jo's head flicked up and she managed not to spill her wine.

Just as Ben and Stella got up to say their goodbyes, Kate

leaned forward to look around Jack and grinned at Jo. "I heard you were dating two guys and they're both mysterious."

Jo didn't know who had said something, but after the 'spill the beans' conversation at dinner a couple of weeks earlier, she knew it would come out eventually.

"Jo, you didn't say you were dating anyone, that's fabulous," Stella said.

Jo didn't know how much she could say. Maybe it would be fine if she didn't link the two men together. "Ah, yeah. A gallery owner and an antiquities collector."

Ben stopped and walked back over to Jo, staring down at her. Uh oh.

Kate seemed oblivious to Jo's discomfort. "Awesome. Perhaps I can talk to one of them about a sword I'm working on that's similar to an ancient one. I've seen pictures of the sword, but I haven't been able to trace its full ancestry."

Jo held onto her wine glass and tried to look relaxed. "I'll talk to them and see what I can do."

"Fantastic. Please give them my number."

Jo nodded and stood, hoping to end the conversation. The others stood as well, and everyone started clearing the tables.

"Oh, Jo," Kate called out as she was leaving. "What are their names, just in case they call?"

There was no turning back now, and she refused to lie. "The gallery owner is Lucas, and the antiquities dealer is Simon."

Soon after that the tables were clear and Jo was about to flash to her apartment, Jack and Ben cornered her by the kitchen door.

Ben put his hand on her arm. "Jo, can you please stay a moment?"

"I need to go see Reece."

"He's fine. Stella just went to go check on him." Ben gestured toward the table and chairs they'd just vacated. She walked over, feeling like a kid walking to the principal's office after being caught cheating on a test.

She sat down and Ben and Jack took the chairs across from her.

Jack leveled her with a stare worse than a principal's. "How's the search for the book going?"

"Good. We found a clue and I think we're close."

This felt like a case of good cop, bad cop, and Ben was taking up the mantle of bad cop. "Who is *we*, Jo?"

"Lucas."

"And Simon?" Ben asked.

Jo wanted to hang her head, but she looked Ben in the eyes. "Yes. I figured out that Lucas was Simon, but I wouldn't let him work with me unless he was himself."

"You forced him to give up his cover, you mean?"

Jo straightened and pushed out her chest, feeling the need to defend herself. "Hey, it wasn't like that, Ben. I didn't know he was two people until I caught him at Lucas's house."

"Did he tell you he was FBI?"

She shook her head. "Not at first. He just said he was working, and he kept coming around as Lucas, but then Reece got worse. I knew I needed his help, but I hated that he lied, so I told him I wouldn't work with him unless he was Simon." Jo forced the words out in one long breath and looked between Ben and Jack. "Is he in trouble?"

Ben sat back in his chair and sighed. "This isn't some high school game, Jo, where Simon can do something wrong and he'll get detention or a reprimand. This could mean his life if the wrong people find out what he can do. Or if they start to distrust Lucas. They could kill him."

"I know," Jo whispered. She already knew too well what could happen and who they were dealing with.

Jack conjured a scotch and leaned back, his posture relaxed. "What do you know?"

It must be time for the good cop now, but Jo didn't find the situation amusing. "The guys that Lucas is working for got impatient when he wasn't hanging out with me, so they gave us a warning."

"Did Simon heal you?" Ben asked. Jo nodded and he seemed satisfied with her answer. "Did you see them? Get any names?"

"I think the guy who took me was named Eddie. He was the same guy who approached us before."

Ben ran his hand through his hair, causing some of the ends to stick up. "You've been approached more than once?"

Jo figured things couldn't get any worse, so she told Ben and Jack everything that happened, minus the intimate moments between her and Simon. They didn't need to know about those.

"Okay, I'll talk to Simon about this, and we'll have to think about the repercussions of the memorial tattoo in the future. I didn't know that he had one and that it wouldn't transform with him if he did." Ben stood and turned to Jack. "See you at the office at zero seven hundred?"

As soon as Jack nodded, Ben disappeared.

Jo flopped back in her chair and let out a long breath. "Wow."

"Wow, exactly. Do you know what you've done, forcing Simon to forego his role as Lucas?"

"I just didn't want him to lie to me anymore."

Jack disappeared his drink and stood. "Jo, I know you hate lying, but it's naïve to think people won't ever do it. Especially when undercover. You've put both your life and Simon's at risk."

Jo nodded but didn't respond. She already felt like shit.

"Can you please flash in and out of the library from now on so you're safe?"

Jo looked him in the eyes and nodded again.

"Would you like me to assign someone to protect you?"

"No, that could raise eyebrows, and I've already got enough people watching me. I promise I'll be okay."

Jack nodded. "I'll accept that for now, but if something else happens, you need to tell me."

"I will."

Jack said goodbye and flashed away.

Jo slowly got to her feet and rubbed the back of her neck. Simon had healed all her injuries from yesterday, but she was exhausted and now felt defeated.

She wanted to go back to when the world was black and white. She wanted Simon to be the tattooed, comic hero-loving guy she'd met at the coffee shop, not a spy. As for Lucas, she wanted him too. She feared she wouldn't get anything she wanted.

SIMON WAS NEARING the end of his second loop of the three-mile trail through Blue Mountain's largest park on the edge of the city when he spotted a runner stretching against a park bench up ahead.

Stopping at the other end of the bench, he nodded at the runner and held one of the armrests to support him as he pulled one foot behind him to stretch his thighs.

"A bit clandestine, don't you think," he said dryly, looking at his boss.

Ben groaned as he pulled his leg off the bench and sat down, giving up all pretext of stretching. "No, just efficient, and I wanted to make sure we didn't bump into anyone, like it appears you have. You've been avoiding me."

Simon knew what was coming but continued to stretch.

"I spoke with Jo last night. You should have told me. I've been texting you for an update."

"Jo caught me off guard."

"That's all you've got to say for yourself?"

Out of the corner of his eye, Simon could just make out Ben's gaze focused on the trees ahead of him, but the tension in his voice was unmistakable.

He moved around to the front of the bench and placed his foot on the worn boards, stretching his hamstring as he leaned over. "There wasn't much else to say. She came to the house to pick up a book from Catherine and came to my rooms. She saw me as I was getting out of the shower. She zeroed in on my memorial tattoo right away—the same one she saw on Lucas that I said was for his father."

Simon took his leg off the bench and forced himself to meet Ben's gaze and not shuffle his feet like a recalcitrant teenager.

Ben stood and faced him. "The tattoo couldn't be helped, but then you met with her as yourself and not Lucas? What the hell were you thinking? We've kept you secluded for almost a decade and you're going to throw that all away?" Ben didn't wait for an answer. He paced in front of the bench and ran his hands through his hair. He stopped and whirled around, his piercing glare directed at Simon. "Were you thinking with your dick?"

"No, I uh…" Simon shut his mouth. Ben had never spoken to him that way before.

"I get it, Jo is a young, attractive woman. She's spunky, intelligent, and kind, but you can't fuck this up for her. There's too much at stake."

"I've been struggling. You know that! We spoke about it at

the cemetery." His voice had risen and he took a deep breath to steady himself. "I like her. And I'm not sure that constantly lying and being someone else is the right thing for me anymore. I want a life that's not someone else's."

Ben let out a huge breath and dropped his head for a moment. The anger had drained from his features when he looked back at Simon. "I get that, but not in the middle of a job. You need to focus. Jo is like a daughter to me, but she has a job to do, the same as you. We've worked so hard for this. Between what Morgana has told us and what you've found out, we're close. We can put a stop to this."

Simon flopped onto the bench, resting his elbows on his knees and his head in his hands. "I've been focused on being someone else since I was sixteen years old, but for once, I want something for myself."

The bench dipped as Ben sat beside him. "Simon, I understand what it's like to want to put everything on the line for a woman, but you need to finish this job first."

Simon lifted his head and met his mentor's eyes. "What if Jo is the one? What if she's my chance at happiness?"

"My daughter died because of these people. Your parents died because of them."

Simon straightened and turned toward Ben. "No, they didn't. My parents died in a car accident."

"With everything you know now, do you still believe that?"

"No." He'd never really believed it was just an accident. He knew what his social worker told him, that his father lost control of his car and it crashed into a guardrail and flipped over the side of a mountain. Even to a ten-year-old, losing control of a vehicle on a clear, dry road in the middle of the day hadn't made sense. His father had been a careful driver. He'd always told Simon that the few seconds he'd save going over the speed limit wasn't worth risking the lives of the people he loved or those of someone in another car.

Ben stood and put his hand on Simon's shoulder. "Simon, we need justice for what these people did to the people we loved. And we need to stop them for everything else they've done and will do. If they find the magic box and open it, literal hell could be let loose."

"I know."

"When Jo finds the book, we'll find a way to keep the book to save Reece and give the council what they need, as well as appease Snake and his group."

"How?"

"I don't know yet, but we will." Ben sat down on the bench and turned to Simon. "Now, fill me in on everything that's happened and don't hedge. Jo told me about the attacks."

Once more Simon followed directions and told Ben everything, including his impressions of Snake, who he now believed was Andrew Smith from the charity event. While he spoke, he mulled over the thought that his parents had been murdered. So many people had died because of these elusive books and magic box. Simon would end it. He'd even walk away from Jo if it meant preventing more people from being killed.

28

*L*ucas huffed out a breath and pushed back his chair as he stood.

"What's wrong?" Jo looked up from the book she was reading.

"Nothing, except that we're getting nowhere. I need to stretch."

She walked over to him and the corner of her lips ticked up in a grin. "I'm sure I can help you figure out a way to stretch." She ran her hands up his chest.

Lucas's chest. He'd shown up as Lucas for the last two days, but she hadn't said anything. Her talk with Ben the other night must have made an impression. It wasn't that he didn't want to be Simon when he was with her, but he wanted her to be safe, and him doing his job was the best way for that to happen.

Grasping her wrists gently, he met her eyes. "Jo, we can't."

"Yes, we can. And it's a great way to release tension."

"You trust me? Even though I lied?"

She dropped her hands. "Why does that matter?"

He immediately missed the warmth of her hands, but this was too important to let it go. "Because regardless of where this goes, I care about you. If you don't trust me and we make love, you'll just be using me. I want more than that from you."

She was already using him to find the book and he was okay with that. It was a mutual win-win. But using him for sex was more personal, even though he hadn't cared if a woman had one it in the past.

"I trust that you won't physically hurt me if you can help it, and you care about me."

"I do care about you." He was falling in love with her.

"You said you wanted to make love to me as Simon—will you?"

That was an easy one. He didn't even have to think about it. Lucas stood and waved his hand toward the door. The telltale sound of the lock clicking in place was loud in the small room. "I put a light spell on the room—it will repel non-magics and warn magics to stay away."

It was just a safety precaution in case someone came looking for them.

"I told you that the first time I made love to you wouldn't be in the library." And it wouldn't be. He had the perfect place in mind and threw the image into Jo's head.

She sucked in her breath and closed her eyes. "I see a field in my mind. Did you do that?"

"Yes. Keep your eyes closed and soak in the image. Flash there."

Jo nodded and then she was gone.

He didn't waste any time and flashed right behind her, his feet touching down on the soft grass.

She opened her eyes and looked around. "This place looks like it could be the same field Jack brought us to when we practiced magic. I learned to flash for the first time in a place like this."

"It's not far outside Blue Mountain, but still secluded." He hadn't imagined the first time they made love would be outside, but he didn't want to take her to Lucas's house.

He conjured a blanket and spread it on the grass, then two pillows appeared. When he held out his hand, a glowing orb appeared in his outstretched palm.

She gasped and then grinned. "A nightlight?"

"Exactly." He returned her grin and placed the glowing ball on the edge of the blanket.

They kicked off their shoes and stood on the blanket facing each other.

"Are you sure?" he asked.

"Yes. I want you, Simon."

Her saying his name when he looked like Lucas didn't feel quite as strange anymore. Like she could see inside him.

He nodded and shed Lucas's appearance, changing light blue eyes to dark green first, then the rest of Lucas's looks disappeared. Simon stood before her as his true self—dark-haired, tattooed, and not as outgoing as the man he portrayed.

He hadn't sent Lucas's bespoke tan suit away and retrieved his own clothes because like so much in his life, this was temporary. He would need to change back into Lucas when they went back to the library.

His eyes stayed focused on her as she reached forward and undid the top two buttons on his shirt. Her breathing sped up, as did his, in anticipation of what was to come. He'd wanted this for so long.

She placed her hand on his memorial tattoo and he knew she could feel its heat seeping into her fingers. "When I see your tattoo, it's like you're both you and Lucas, the best parts of each one," she whispered.

"I once thought I could protect the world by myself. But I was wrong. I think I need you, Jo."

She chuckled softly. "I think you messed up the end of that quote, Superman, but I'll take it."

They were in the middle of nowhere so she didn't need to whisper, yet he understood why she did. It was keeping their world small, like it included just the two of them. She fiddled with the buttons on his shirt, not yet undoing them, and tilted her head up. "Ugh," she huffed out, "you're too tall."

He leaned down and placed a soft kiss on her lips. "You sure it's me who's too tall and not someone who's too short?" he teased against her lips.

"Definitely, Superman." Her voice sounded breathless as he moved his lips to trail kisses down her neck.

Gripping her hips, he dropped to his knees, and she looked down at him. "What are you doing down there? Hmmm?"

"You said I was too tall." He trailed his hands from her hips down her thighs and pressed his face into her stomach.

His hot breath permeated the thin barrier of her shirt. He could smell her arousal and it made him almost painfully hard.

She ran her fingers through his thick, dark hair, and tugged, pulling his head back so he would look up at her. Her forcefulness was another turn on. "Don't tease me, Simon. I've waited too long, and I want you."

"Can I undress you?" he whispered.

She let go of his hair and dropped her arms to her sides. "Please."

He used his magic to remove their shirts, and then the rest of their clothing.

She threaded her hands back in his hair as he leaned forward and kissed her stomach. "Wow, I didn't know that trick," she said with a laugh. The discarded garments laid in a pile on the edge of the blanket.

He laughed softly too, his breath spreading over her skin, and she shivered. "Yes, that one may have been a bit tricky to be taught to you as an adult, especially if you were learning in a group."

His laughter ceased when he looked at her fully naked in the moonlight before him. "You're beautiful. I want to kiss and taste every inch of you." He wrapped one arm around her and supported himself on the other as he lowered them both to the soft blanket.

"I want to taste you too." She wound her hands back into his hair and pulled his mouth down as his body blanketed hers.

"Later." He settled between her open legs and kissed her, nipping and teasing at her mouth, savoring the taste of her. He pulled away and moved lower, spreading kisses on her neck and chest. Sucking one nipple into his mouth, he lightly pinched the other, bringing it to a peak. She groaned and arched into him. He thought he'd never get enough of the noises and responses Jo made. She was passionate and didn't shy away from taking what she wanted.

He lavished her breasts, giving them lots of attention. She squirmed beneath him as he continued his exploration. He showered kisses over her ribs and stomach as his hands trailed behind his mouth, kneading her flesh as he went. She moaned again and her stomach muscles tensed as he moved lower still.

His eyes followed his hands and mouth, and he smiled as he got to her legs and saw the ink on her right thigh. "Wonder Woman. It's exquisite." He breathed the words onto her skin as he continued to kiss down her leg. The tattoo covered her thigh from her hip to just above her knee. An inscription wound around the bottom of the ink. *They'll only haunt you if you forget what they taught you.* He recognized the quote.

Holding her hips, he tilted his head so he could see her face. "That's what Wonder Woman said to Superman after he was lamenting about all those who had died."

"It was fitting. I got it when I was eighteen."

"Amazing," he said as he continued to kiss her and savor the taste of her skin.

She tugged on his hair. "Simon, please, I need you."

Shifting his body lower, his hard cock pressed into the blanket-covered ground. He ignored his own ache and concentrated on Jo. He spread her folds and lowered his mouth, licking and sucking, giving her all his attention.

He lifted one of her legs, positioning it on his shoulder, and snaked his hand underneath, spanning his fingers across her stomach to hold her down.

He inserted one finger into her heat and then another as his tongue continued to lavish her. He increased the rhythm of his tongue and fingers, matching the cadence of her hips bucking up despite his hand holding her down. He loved how she took her own pleasure.

It wasn't long before her breathing increased and the muscles in her legs stiffened as she thrust up against his mouth, her orgasm overtaking her.

Slowly, he withdrew his hand and lowered her leg, then crawled up her body, kissing her soft flesh as he went.

With the moonlight and the soft glow from the orb, he could see the flush of her skin. "You're magnificent." He leaned down and kissed her, taking most of his weight on his forearms on either side of her. If she pressed his lower body into hers, he might explode like a horny teenager. He wanted her so badly that he was barely holding it together.

She wrapped her hands over his shoulders and pulled him

down for a kiss. He feasted on her mouth. He loved the sounds she made as he nipped at her lips.

"Now, Simon. I want you. Now," she said again as she bit into his lower lip while her hands clawed his shoulders.

That was his tipping point—he lost his battle of restraint and lowered his body to hers, his hard length pressed against her. He stuck out his hand and the condom from his wallet landed in his palm. He was addicted to kissing her but forced himself to pull away long enough to sheath himself.

Holding her against him, he flipped them both so that she was now astride him as he lay on his back. He wanted to see his warrior princess above him in the moonlight. She shivered in the spring night's cool breeze. "Are you cold?" he asked.

"I'm fine, you'll keep me warm." She pressed her palms onto his chest as she ground her hips into his groin.

He moaned at the sensation and knew he wasn't going to last. He wanted to be inside her more than he ever remembered wanting anything, but he also cared for her and wanted to make sure she was warm. He let his magic flow into his hands and rested them on her hips. "How's this?" he asked as he let the heat of his magic seep out and up her body to blanket her skin in warmth. He moved his hands up, continuing to spread the warmth, and cupped her breasts, kneading the soft mounds.

"It's better than warm towels from the dryer." He heard her breathing increase as she pushed into his hands and reached between them. Taking his length in her hand, she squeezed him and pumped her hand up and down. "But I want more."

He jerked up and groaned at the amazing feel of her small hand. Gripping her hips, he lifted her up so she could position him and then she lowered herself onto him, inch by inch.

The sensation was glorious and almost too much as he hissed out through his teeth. "I'm not going to last long this first time, my warrior princess."

"Don't hold back."

He didn't. He pumped up into her as she ground herself on him. Their movements were frantic as they both took all that the other gave. When he felt her stiffen around him, he let go of her hips with one hand and wrapped it around the back of her neck, bringing her down for a kiss. He swallowed their moans as they both went over the edge and his world exploded in the best possible way.

When they came down from their high, she was still laying atop him and he didn't want to move.

She lifted her head to look at him, a sly smile on her face. "So… do you have any tension left?"

He kissed her again. "I think I'm good."

"I don't know. I think I might have more tension that needs releasing before we get back."

"Well… we can't have that. I better help you release it." He held her against him as he rolled her onto her back, leaned down and captured her mouth with his again.

LUCAS WALKED over to Jo and crouched in front of her, resting his hand on her leg. "Hey, how are you doing?"

When they'd flashed back to the library, Simon had changed back into Lucas's form and released the spell on the door. He needed to be ready in case something happened. It worked out well when Viktor popped in to say he was leaving for the day.

Jo let her head hang for a moment. "Fuck, I'm tired."

"Want to call it a night? I'm tired too." He looked at his watch and saw it was after ten.

"We can't. This is day three of the warning. Do you think they'll be waiting for us when we leave here?"

He stood, pulling her up into his arms. His kiss was slow this time. "Probably, but we can flash from here."

Jo looked defeated. "I can't. When I used the restroom earlier, I ran into the night guard, so he knows I'm here."

Lucas rested his forehead on Jo's and breathed in her fresh, natural scent. They stood there for several moments before he finally pulled away. "I have an idea we should try. It's a long shot, but I was thinking about how the latest book appeared when we rearranged the spells."

"You want to do that again?"

"In a way." Lucas held out his hand and the book they'd found floated onto one of the standing cradles in the middle of the room. Then he floated another book onto a second cradle.

"Is that second book the one with the spell we tried with Viktor?"

"Yes, the one that seemed to be a dud. I was so sure that the spell seemed right, but then nothing happened. The same with the new book. What if we need to combine them?"

Jo's eyes widened as she looked from him to the books. "Could it be that easy?"

He chuckled. "I don't think any of this has been easy, but it's worth a shot." Lucas gestured to the book with the spell that hadn't worked. "I kept studying the spells, the English translations, and I realized that we didn't say we wouldn't do harm and ask for permission."

"Why do we need to do that?"

"I'm not sure that we do, but the spells are protecting the books, and if we promise to do no harm, it might reveal the spell for us."

"Can we promise that?"

He leaned down and gave her a quick kiss, unable to resist. "No, but we don't have ill intent. I don't want this book to get in the wrong hands either, so it's worth a try. Let's see."

"Wait, don't forget to protect the room. I'll get the lights."

He rolled his eyes and grinned down at her as the lights dimmed. "Right. I'll put us and these two books inside a bubble." He waved his hand, using his magic to create the bubble, and felt the energy shift as it settled into place.

Directing his magic toward each book, he used the same spell as before to see the words. The spell from each book now floated in a bubble in front of them. Choosing the first book, he read both passages aloud:

"For all the magics seeking within be worthy of this book.
To know thine self to know that worth is the right look."

As he read, Lucas looked around the room to see if the spell was working. The words were glowing, but nothing else was affected.

"For the spells of magic herein have been undertaken.
Only by the most rightful and honest will they awaken.
The walls are closed and locked for those who do not deserve.
I pledge my fealty to the gifts within to serve.
Open thine eyes and walls for me to see."

When he spoke the final word, the bubbles disappeared like sand blown in the wind and a glow appeared on the far wall.

Jo pointed to the far wall. "Holy shit, do you see that?"

He looked at the wall and took a couple of tentative steps forward. The air at the wall was swirling in a circle, like a great mass. The circle was getting bigger and bigger, and light poured from the middle, revealing an opening. A book balanced inside the opening as if suspended in the air. It glowed more brightly than any of the spells they'd done so far.

Lucas held one hand in front of his eyes to help shield himself from the blinding light as he stepped closer to the opening and reached out with his other.

Jo grabbed his arm, pulling him back. "Are you sure it's safe?"

"Only one way to find out." He thrust his hand into the gaping hole and grasped hold of the book. It felt cool and weightless against his fingers.

He pulled his hand back and almost dropped the book as its weight increased by several pounds. Cradling the book in both hands, he looked back at the wall. The hole had closed and only the normal wall and bookshelf remained.

"Holy shit, that's it, isn't it?"

Jo removed one of the books from the cradle, placing it on the table behind them, and Lucas set the new book down in its place.

"Yes, I think it is."

He kept back a few feet as Jo walked up to the book. This had been her crusade for months and she had so much at stake. He wanted her to be the first to open it.

"The book looks ancient and yet it's pristine. No dust or marks mar the cover." She gently flipped open the cover and gasped. "The pages are blank!"

Lucas stepped up behind her and looked down as she turned several pages. "I think it's the same as the spell and finding this book. The words need to be revealed."

"Okay." Jo let out a breath and closed the book. "We should get this to Jack."

Simon knew it was the right thing to do and he wasn't

going to stop her. As he watched Jo carefully wrap the book in a protective material, he realized then that he would give up his job for her. By letting Jo take the book, he was sacrificing everything he'd done in the last year with trying to infiltrate Snake's organization and finding out who all was involved.

Jo finished wrapping the book and put it in her bag with her laptop, placing her bag's strap over her shoulder. "You're not going to stop me? You're not going to take it?"

He stepped up to her and wrapped his arms around her, snugging her in close. He placed a soft kiss on her head. "No, I won't stop you. You're more important than any job and you need the book for Reece."

Jo pulled out of his arms and looked up into his face, Lucas's face.

"You mean that?"

"Yes." He gave her another quick kiss and took her hand in his. "Come on, let's get out of here and hope we don't run into a welcoming party."

When they said goodnight to the security guard, Lucas stopped Jo at the library's front doors. "Wait, before you step outside, I need you to promise me something."

She looked up at him and nodded, and in that moment, he knew she was his everything.

"If we run into Eddie or any of his cohorts, I need you to flash home. Don't worry about who may see you. I'll make sure any cameras in the area are wiped clean if you're captured on film."

"I don't know if I can promise that."

"Why not?"

"Mr. Smith threatened my family."

"If you have the book, that won't matter. Get the book to Jack and Meredith and they'll make sure your family is safe."

"And you?" She wrapped her arms around his waist and melted into him.

"I'll be okay," he whispered into her hair. He pulled back and took her hand again. "Okay, let's go."

They pushed open the library doors, Simon a step ahead of Jo. He was looking straight ahead, checking out the grounds, when a blow struck the side of his head.

29

Jo watched in horror as a man clobbered Lucas on the head. She called out as she reached for him but was grabbed from behind and felt the all-too-familiar rope wrap around her hand. "Hey! Don't touch me, asshole!"

"We meet again," Eddie said, coming around to her front. She struggled against the hands banded around her arms to no avail. She focused on Eddie.

"Yeah, lucky me." She realized too late that she'd let the sarcasm rip again, but she really didn't give a shit. She'd had enough of this asshole.

Eddie looked over her head at the goon behind her and cocked his head toward the street. "Let's go. Get her to the car." Then he turned to the guy holding Lucas on the ground. "End him."

"No, wait!" Jo lurched forward but was pulled back against a hard chest. She shuddered at the thought of who she was touching but let it go. "You can't kill Lucas, I need him."

Eddie turned toward her with a smile that was so

smarmy, she shuddered again. "He's not useful anymore. You can find the book without him."

"We found the book." She might have the book, but it was useless to them and that was what she was going to risk hers and Simon's lives on.

Eddie walked into her personal space, his breath hot on her cheeks. "Well, well, why didn't you say so? It seems we don't need you either."

She'd really had enough of this douchebag. "Yes, you do. The pages are blank."

"What?" Eddie ripped the bag from her shoulder. He dropped to his knees and rummaged through the bag, pulling everything out.

"Hey asshole, be careful. You could ruin the book. It's centuries old, dumbass."

Eddie took the book from its protective cover and stood. He glared down at her and then smiled. His hand came up so fast she didn't have a chance to move to the side as his fist slammed into her cheek. If it wasn't for the Neanderthal behind her holding her up, she would have fallen to the ground.

"Not so tough, are you?" Eddie spit the words into her face, and pulled a handful of her hair, forcing her head back.

"I'm a hellava lot tougher than you, asshole! You've trapped my magic and got your goon holding me! Let me go and we'll see who's tougher."

"Jo, stop," Lucas whispered, just loud enough for her to hear.

Eddie released her hair and they both looked down at Lucas. He was on his hands and knees, struggling to his feet, when the other guy kicked him again. Lucas dropped to the ground like a dead weight.

"You should listen to him," Eddie said as he turned to face her.

Her face throbbed like she had a toothache she'd ignored for too long and she once more missed Eddie's fist coming toward her. It wasn't until the guy holding her from behind pulled her to the side to avoid the blow that she realized what was happening.

"Eddie, let's go," the guy behind her said quietly.

She'd heard that voice before. He was the guy who'd blindfolded her and let her go, and he'd just gotten her out of the line of fire. Maybe he'd be an ally again.

Eddie glared over Jo's shoulder, then turned to the guy holding Lucas. "Bring him."

One of Eddie's goons dragged Lucas to his feet and helped him to a waiting SUV. They threw him into the back seat and Jo scrambled in after him. Turning, she tried to get a look at the guy who'd been holding her, but he let her go and shut the vehicle's door.

There'd be time to worry about that guy later. She scooted across the seat and placed her hands on Lucas's face, gently turning his head to look at her. "You okay?" she whispered.

He placed a hand on her wrist and squeezed. "Don't antagonize him," Lucas said, his voice barely a whisper. "And be nice to Rocky, he might help you."

She wouldn't promise that, but she nodded. "Rocky? Is that the guy who was holding me?"

Lucas nodded and rested his head on hers. She snuggled into him, wrapping her arm around his stomach. They stayed like that until the vehicle stopped about ten minutes later and the back doors were ripped open.

"Get out." A hand snaked into the SUV and Jo took it. She was pulled up and out to stand on a sidewalk in front of a tall building. Up on her tiptoes, she peered over the top of the vehicle, looking for Lucas, but didn't see him. "Stay quiet," Rocky whispered close to her ear. "Don't talk to Eddie."

Maybe Rocky was another undercover agent like Simon, but neither he nor Ben had mentioned him. Jo snorted to herself; right—undercover. That was the point. She could only hope. She turned to look at him, but only saw his back as he walked away and someone else grabbed Jo by the arm.

They made their way to the building's top floor and to a condo that looked like it could have been the same one she'd been taken to before. She was getting really sick of being taken against her will. When the door to the condo was opened, someone pulled Jo down a hallway, her feet almost dragging on the ground.

The person behind her shoved her. The action propelled her forward, her knees hitting the hardwood floor. She bounced to her feet and turned around just as the door to the room was shut and a lock clicked in place.

She banged on the door. "Wait, where's Lucas?"

"Don't worry about Lucas, it's too late for him. Keep quiet," Rocky said as if he pushed his quiet voice through the door just for her. Since he was back, maybe he could help her.

"Rocky?" She stood with her ear to the door and waited. Nothing. What was maybe her only hope had left her.

After a few minutes, she looked around at the large windows and saw the same view that she'd seen the last time she was taken. Pulling on her magic, she attempted to flash. Nothing happened. She looked down at her wrist and realized that it was still bound with the magic rope. She pulled on it with her other hand and gasped when the rope tightened, threatening to cut off the blood flow to her hand. "Well, that wasn't a good idea," she whispered to the room.

She walked over to the door and pulled on it—locked. She'd heard the lock click in place, but she never wanted to be like one of those dumb heroines in books who didn't even try to get free.

Looking around, she noticed the place looked like a designer had used oatmeal as their inspiration. The space was furnished in matching beige tones—beige couch and chair, beige throw rug, beige accent pillows, and a beige abstract painting. Not her cup of tea, but she was sure there were worse places to be held captive.

Jo sat on one corner of the couch and tucked her feet underneath her. She yawned and stood back up, pacing the room in an attempt to stay awake. Finally, her exhaustion became too much and she sat back on the sofa.

She must have dozed off at some point because she woke up with a stiff neck. It was dark outside, so it was still nighttime, but Jo didn't know how long she'd been there. Her phone had been in her bag and she never wore a watch so she had no way to tell the time.

The list of magic things she needed to learn was racking up—how to tell time without your phone, what to do when kidnapped and your magic was bound, how to get out of magic ropes, and how to steal back a magic book.

The book—even if she could escape, she couldn't leave the book. Reece needed it. She wouldn't fail her brother, and she wouldn't fail Lucas. It was funny that she now thought of him by which look he sported. It didn't matter anymore that he was two people—she cared for him regardless of who he looked like.

There was a noise in the hallway, like someone had banged against a wall. She stood and moved toward the door, prepared to fight whoever walked through.

Then the door opened, and she stared into the faces of the last people she expected to see.

30

*L*ucas cursed when he was tossed into a room, smashing against a coffee table and falling onto his face. Eddie's people had bound his hands behind his back when they'd pulled him from the vehicle. The rope used was the same as they'd used before, and it bound his magic.

He rolled onto his back and lifted his head just in time to see the door close. Flopping back down, his head thunked on the floor and he grunted again. This night had certainly taken a turn for the worse. It had started out with him making love to Jo—a dream come true. Now, he'd been beaten, tied up, and he didn't even know where Jo was.

Rolling again, he propped himself on his elbow, then hefted up onto his feet. He wobbled, dizziness flooding him. Leaning on a nearby couch, he waited until the feeling passed and tried again. He probably had a concussion but at least they left his liver alone this time. He could feel bruises along his ribs where some asshole had kicked him, but nothing he hadn't had to deal with before.

After a few minutes of steady breathing, he was finally able to haul himself upright. He looked around for anything he could use to cut the rope. It bound his magic, but it was still rope, so maybe it could be cut like regular rope.

The room was beige and sparse, like the last one he'd been held in. All the furniture was soft and cushy, not even one chair or a counter with sharp edges, except for the damn coffee table.

When he finished scouring the room for something to cut the rope with and had come up empty, he sat on the sofa and flopped back into the cushions.

Without his magic, he was useless. Not even his FBI training could get him out of this if he didn't release his magic first. He'd been sitting there for several minutes hoping a great idea would come to him when he heard some commotion in the hallway. It sounded like someone had hit the wall.

He heaved himself forward, pulling himself out of the bottomless pit of cushions he'd sunk into. Listening at the door, he knew he and Jo weren't the only ones in trouble anymore. His situation had just spiraled and because he'd refused to do his job, two more people were now mired in his mess. Ben was right, he hadn't been thinking.

The door swung in and Lucas stepped to the side. He prepared to rush the person, but never got a chance. A fist came at his face and he ducked to the side so fast to avoid the punch that he lost his balance.

"I figured you'd be waiting at the door." Rocky hauled him up by his shirt and pushed him back into the couch cushion death trap.

"Listen to me," Rocky said as he closed the distance between them. "I don't know what's up with you, but you are not who you appear to be."

This day was getting shittier by the minute, but there was still lots of time to go from shitty to totally fucked unless he could turn Rocky into an ally. First he had to figure out what the man knew. He puffed out his chest and put on his best arrogant Lucas face. "I'm a deeply cultured person with many facets."

Rocky put his hands on his hips and stared down at him. "Cut the bullshit. That's not what I meant, and you know it." He glanced toward the door, looking nervous for the first time since Lucas had met him. "I actually don't give a crap about you, but innocent people are going to die if the book is unlocked."

Simon knew that, but he hadn't figured out why Rocky cared since he was on the wrong side of the law. Simon was pretty sure his cover hadn't been revealed, but all the time with Jo had made Lucas a different person, so maybe that's what Rocky meant about him not being who he said he was.

"If I let you go, can you get help?"

"You'd just let me go?"

"Temporarily."

Simon's spirits lifted for the first time in a few hours, and he hoped this wasn't a trick. "Explain."

"I'll let you go, but you've got to be back here in three hours. You can flash out of this room, get whatever help you need, and flash back."

"You'd trust me to come back?

Rocky glanced at the door again. "Not really, but I believe you feel something for Jo. I don't think you'll let her down."

"No, I won't." Rocky was taking a risk with Lucas, and he had to do the same for him. "Why don't you leave? I can help you."

"I can't leave, or I would have years ago and never looked back."

"Because of the healer?"

Rocky ignored his question and grasped the front of his shirt, hauling him up from the cushions, and spun him around. If it weren't for Rocky's tight grasp on his shirt, he would have face-planted on the floor again.

He felt the rope fall away and rolled his shoulders to get the blood moving. He swallowed a groan and turned to face Rocky. "Why are you doing this? Is it just because Jo and the others are innocent?"

"I have my reasons, but if you fuck me over, I will come for you."

"Three hours." Lucas nodded and flashed.

Jo RAN FORWARD when Catherine and Viktor were pushed into the room. Catherine embraced her and then stood to the side to let Viktor envelop her in his arms. "It will be okay, *kicsim*." He kissed her cheek and let her go.

They all walked over to the couches and sat. Jo looked from Viktor to Catherine, visually inspecting them. "Are you hurt?"

Catherine, on the couch beside Jo, reached over and patted her on the leg. "No, we're fine, Josephine. But you're hurt."

Jo touched her cheek and winced. That wasn't the smartest move. "It's just a bruise, I'm fine." She looked between Catherine and Viktor. "How did they get to you?"

"They broke into my house. I was asleep in my room, and they wrapped a rope around my wrist—it blocked my magic before I could flash anywhere." She held up her arm to show Jo a rope similar to the one she had. "I did manage to convince them to let me use the restroom to change."

"Viktor?" Jo asked, looking at him.

"They broke into my house too, but I heard them and

flashed to the front foyer, and then someone got me from behind," he said, frustration evident in his voice.

"Did you see Lucas?"

"No, dear, was he with you?"

"Yes, and I'm worried now that we have the book, they're going to kill him." Catherine gasped and Jo leaned forward and hugged the woman. "Shit, I'm sorry, that was heartless of me."

"No, I understand. I know he's not my son, but I care about him, and I believe you do too."

Jo nodded but couldn't speak around the lump in her throat.

"You found the book? Do you have it?"

Jo shook her head but was thankful to Viktor for taking the conversation off Lucas. "We found it, but they took it from me. Right now, the pages are blank, but I'm worried what they're going to do with it."

Catherine's eyes were wide. "Blank? Oh, the spells are hidden, aren't they?"

"That's what Si—Lucas believes." In her mind, he was both Lucas and Simon and it was getting harder to separate the two.

"Simon and Lucas are the same man." Viktor stated it as a fact, not a question.

She was so afraid to give anything away that she didn't confirm. "What do you mean?"

"I do not know how it is possible, but I believe they are the same person. Some days you are with Simon and some days you are with Lucas and yet they know the same information and continue to find clues. I have never seen magic like this before, but that does not mean that it does not exist."

Jo looked over at Catherine. She'd just admitted that she knew Lucas wasn't who he said he was, and she knew that from Simon too. But neither of them had said how much Catherine knew. "What do you know?"

"It doesn't matter. Let's not worry about Lucas. He's going to be okay, I just know it. Now, what are we going to do about the book?"

Jo shrugged. "I don't know. Do you two have any suggestions?"

Viktor leaned forward, his gaze serious. "Tell us how you found the book and we will go from there."

Jo thought back over the past few weeks and started at the beginning, telling them about the clues they'd found and filling them both in on how their roles helped and what happened when they rearranged the sentences. Then how the vortex had opened and they'd found the book.

She told them about the spells and that Lucas thought the final key was them pledging their fealty and that the book would do no harm while in their hands.

Viktor stood and walked to the window. After a couple of minutes, he turned back, his brows furrowed. "I think that's the key. Promising to do no harm."

Jo frowned up at him. "What do you mean?"

"The book revealed itself when you promised your loyalty and to do no harm. That was the first step, but now I think it needs to hear it again for it to reveal the spells within."

"How do I do that?"

"I think you make another promise, another spell," Catherine said.

"Shit." Jo rubbed her eyes with her hands, exhaustion once more threatening to overtake her. It'd been a long few days and now she'd been up almost all night. "That would be great if I could promise it, but I can't. I don't know what Eddie and his boss are going to do."

"I don't think it matters, dear. You just have to make the promise and if they do something else, that's on them, and I expect the spells will disappear if they break the promise to the book."

"But what if the book disappears because it thinks I lied?" Jo sprang up off the couch, adrenaline coursing through her at the thought of losing the book. "I need that book to save my brother."

Viktor came back over to sit. "Maybe the key is casting a spell that states you won't lie and that the spells will disappear again if someone's intention is to use them to cause harm."

Jo sagged back onto the couch and ran her hands through her hair, tugging the ends. The slight pain helped keep her awake. "I guess all we can do is try. I'll—"

The door opened, cutting Jo off mid-sentence. It was Eddie. "Get up. Time to do your job."

It was two-thirty in the morning when Lucas flashed to the FBI headquarters, not sure where else to go. He hadn't worried about who would see him because several of the rooms used by the magic task force were magically shielded from cameras and non-magics.

He picked up the phone on the desk and dialed the number he'd memorized years ago.

Ben answered after only two rings. "Davis."

"Jo's been taken and I need help. I'm at the office."

"I'll be right there."

Lucas sat down and rubbed his hands over his face, pushing some magic through his system. He was wiped out in a way he'd never been before and could only imagine how Jo was feeling. Probably tired and scared, and by now worried about Viktor and Catherine. He'd heard their voices and knew they were taken because of him.

"Who the fuck are you?"

Lucas looked up to see Jack Knight standing in front of him. Simon had heard through the years that Jack was special because he could do a bit of all types of magic. Now, he was supposed to be even more powerful and could even stop time for a few seconds. At least, that was the rumor. If Simon had ever doubted Jack's power, he didn't now as the energy radiated off the man in waves, and yet Simon hadn't even felt him arrive.

"I'm Lucas Jenkins. Ben called you?"

"Yes," Ben said as his feet touched down softly on the carpet. "I also called in some other agents."

With perfect timing, three more pairs of feet touched down—Lisa Munroe, Javier Cano, and Drew Bartley's—and took a seat around the large conference table. Simon had seen them all from a distance and Ben kept him up to date on what everyone was doing, but this was the first time he'd been in a room with them.

"Lucas?" Ben asked. The one word contained so many questions; Ben was too smart to reveal Simon's real identity when Simon hadn't himself. After all, there was still a mole in the task force.

He looked at Ben where he sat at the head of the table. "I thought it was safest for now." Simon knew Ben would pick up on what he wasn't saying. Likely, they all would, but he didn't care. There were people in the room he didn't know, and Jo's, Catherine's, and Viktor's lives were at stake. Jo's for sure, and since Jack didn't say anyone else was missing, it was a good bet that the other innocents Rocky mentioned were Catherine and Viktor. They both meant something to Lucas and Jo.

"I've got three hours"—he looked up at the clock on the wall—"correction, two hours and forty-six minutes before I have to be back, or something could happen to Jo, Viktor, and Catherine."

Javier sat forward. "I know Jo, but I don't know who you

are or the other two people you're talking about." He looked at Ben. "Sir, you'll fill us in?"

"I'll let Lucas get you up to speed on what he's been working on, and Jack can fill in any other gaps about the book and the council."

Lucas glanced once more at the clock and launched into a skeleton sketch of what he'd been doing over the last year. How he'd worked with Eddie and his crew, who he now believed was working for Andrew Skalbeck, aka Andrew Smith, and looking for an ancient book with a spell to locate a map to a magic box. He never once revealed that he was anyone other than who he appeared to be. He told them about finding the clues to the books and that they'd put them together, but not how. He wasn't willing to reveal any details yet in case the book went missing again.

"Okay, so now what?" Lisa said, looking at Jack and then Ben. "Shouldn't this be a council issue?"

Jack shook his head. "No, the council is still only Meredith and me. She'll probably give me shit later, but I'm not going to bring her in on this unless I have to. She's already been through so much and I'll do anything to protect her, especially if there's the slightest chance that she could watch her cousin Jo die, and Reece as well, if we can't get the spellbook."

"No!" Lucas pushed back his chair and stood. "I won't let it come to that." He glanced at the clock and paced back and forth beside the conference table before stopping and leaning his palms on it. "I need a way to get the book and let them believe they still have it." He turned to Jack. "Is there a way you could clone it?"

"Maybe, but I'd need more time. And I'd likely need the book to do it."

Lucas sat again and looked at the others. They threw

ideas back and forth and Simon's frustration grew. The minutes were ticking down and they weren't getting anywhere.

"My guess is that Eddie and Skalbeck don't trust you anymore?" Javier asked.

"Yes, but they still think they've got me captured, unless it's been discovered that Rocky let me go. I think they want to use me to persuade Jo to reveal the spells."

"Does she know how to do that?" Jack asked. "She's had her magic just under a year and she's still learning."

Lucas smiled for the first time in hours. "Jo is smart and damn tenacious. I expect she, Catherine, and Viktor have already come up with a plan. I just have to figure out how to make Skalbeck think he has the book when he doesn't."

Drew hadn't said anything while they were brainstorming, but now he sat forward, catching Lucas's attention. "I don't know about the book, but Skalbeck is going to kill you now that he doesn't trust you, so you need to be replaced."

Lucas wanted to throttle the man. "Don't you think I fucking know that? But even if we could find someone to replace me, he's not going to trust them, no matter how much of a long game they play. It took me a year to ingratiate myself with them and look how that turned out."

"I could replace you." Drew looked directly at Ben. "Andrew Skalbeck is my dad and he's wanted me to join him for years."

"Fuck!" Jack yelled.

Jack was out of his chair with Drew's shirt fisted in both of his hands, pinning the agent against the wall so fast that Simon hadn't even seen Jack move.

"You're the fucking mole! Because of you Reece is spellbound, Elise is dead, and I have to wake my fiancée up from fucking terrifying nightmares!" Energy swirled around Jack and the papers on a side table danced in the air. "I should fucking kill you right now."

Drew gripped Jack's hands, trying to pry them off. "No, that wasn't me."

"Jack, let him go so he can explain." Ben's command allowed for no argument.

The energy in the room settled and papers floated to the floor. Jack let Drew go, dropping him to the floor, but Jack didn't sit. He moved to the head of the table behind Ben, his arms crossed in a rigid pose.

Ben looked over his shoulder at Jack but didn't say anything before he faced Drew. "Explain."

Drew looked shaky and conjured himself a glass of water, downing the entire thing before he sat down. "Skalbeck is my dad, but I was raised by my mom, Heather Bartley. She died in a car accident when I was ten and she had no family, so I was sent to live with my paternal grandparents. My dad reached out to me when I first joined the FBI, and he contacts me once or twice a year. He wants me to join him, but I always refuse. That's it."

The story was too simple. Simon didn't trust the man as far as he could throw him.

"Any thoughts?" Ben asked, addressing the group.

"I don't fucking trust him," Jack said, echoing Simon's opinion. Jack didn't move from his position behind Ben, like a predator eyeing his prey. Simon was just glad that he wasn't the prey for once.

Lucas looked at Ben. "Sir, I don't think we have a choice and I only have forty-eight minutes before I have to be back."

"Right. We'll use Drew for now. Let's plan."

Forty-six minutes later Lucas had a plan, but it was going to be painful. He wasn't completely confident it would work, and it could get him killed, but if it saved Jo and the others, he'd do anything. Even die.

He flashed back to the condo to see Rocky pacing the room. "You asshole! Cut it close enough?" Rocky flashed to Lucas and had his hands around Lucas's neck before he could react. He threw out a punch, catching Rocky in the gut, doubling him over as he let go.

Lucas sucked in a large breath and rotated his head from side to side. Damn, he was exhausted and not reacting fast enough. "I said I'd be back in three hours and I am. Anything happen?"

"Not yet, but I think Mr. Smith will be here soon. Sit the fuck down." Rocky held out the magic rope for Lucas to see before shoving it in his pocked. "Don't make me regret not tying you back up."

Lucas was more than happy to sit down. He dropped into a sturdy-looking wooden chair that hadn't been there earlier. Not having his magic bound was reassuring, but it wasn't like he could flash away and leave Jo. Nor could he fight back and risk putting her in more danger if they decided to use her against him.

It was only five-thirty in the morning, so he didn't expect Mr. Smith to be around, but he heard some male voices in the hallway. Turning his head toward the door, he didn't see Rocky coming at him with a right jab, spinning his head to the side as pain exploded in his cheek.

He righted his head at the same time the door opened. "What're you doing?" Eddie asked.

Rocky punched Lucas in the stomach, but there was no pain. Rocky had pulled his punch, like they had been acting in a movie. Lucas bent forward and groaned in pain, giving as good a performance as Rocky had.

"The motherfucker was trying to escape, so I was teaching him a lesson."

Eddie walked over and patted Rocky on the back. "Good job, man. It's time to go, bring him along."

Rocky hauled Lucas up by an arm and passed him off to Eddie before disappearing. Rocky may have beat him as a cover, but he'd also helped. Now his only ally was gone and he wondered if he'd even be able to enact his hasty plan or if he was walking to his death.

32

o stared at the blank pages, willing her eyes to focus. She was exhausted and didn't know what to do. Viktor and Catherine had been so sure that she'd be able to figure out a way to unlock the book, but their faith in her appeared to be misguided.

A couple of hours ago, Eddie and his goons had brought her, Catherine, and Viktor into the condo's open-concept area. She was now sitting at one end of a large dining room table. Catherine was on one side of her and Viktor the other. They weren't bound, but they each had a cord of the magic-blocking rope around one wrist.

"Maybe you need some incentive."

Jo blinked and looked up from the blank pages to see Eddie dragging Lucas into the room. He was bruised and slouched over, but he still made Jo's heart speed up. Maybe there was hope after all.

Grabbing Lucas by the arm, Eddie hauled him over to the table by Jo's chair. She bounced to her feet and put her arms around him, resting her head on his chest. "Are you okay?" she whispered.

"I'm fine—"

Lucas was ripped from her arms as Eddie yanked on his shirt. "I thought my boy Lucas could give you some motivation to work faster." Eddie nodded to the goon at his side and the man pulled his arm back and pummeled Lucas in the stomach.

Jo cried out as Lucas dropped to his knees. She heard Catherine scream, but she kept her focus on Lucas. "Stop. Don't hurt him, I'm working. I'll figure it out."

Eddie hauled Lucas to his feet by his hair but had to let go due to Lucas's height. "Not fast enough. Again," he said, nodding at his man.

The goon hit Lucas in the face, sending him rearing backward, but Eddie caught him, holding him upright.

"Stop!" she screamed at Eddie, and the sadistic bastard laughed at her and nodded at his man again. The goon went at Lucas with two more blows while Jo continued to scream.

Catherine cried softly behind her as Lucas fell to the floor. Jo pushed forward to go to Lucas when she was grabbed from behind. She was getting fucking sick of it. She stomped on the guy's foot and spun around. Her sneakers were ineffective against the man's boot but it was enough of a distraction that he wasn't expecting it when she spun and slapped him in the face.

"Stop fucking grabbing me!" she yelled at him. She would have laughed at the stunned look on the man's face if the situation wasn't so dire.

Eddie stepped over Lucas's prone form and got right in her face. She held her breath against his overpowering cologne. "Fucking bitch!" He jerked his head at his goon. "Tie her to her chair."

The man grabbed her by the shoulders and forced her down. Her ass smacked against the chair and then her arms were wrenched behind her back. "Ow! How am I supposed to work without my arms?"

"The old lady can hold the book for you." Except for the magic rope around Catherine's wrist binding her magic, she remained unbound, but they'd tied Viktor to a chair. Not only were these guys assholes, they were fucking chauvinistic assholes.

"It's okay, dear. You can do this." Catherine patted Jo's shoulder and then glanced at Lucas on the floor. "He's strong."

Jo didn't know if she was talking about the real Lucas or the man who looked like her son. She was right. Simon was strong and so was she. They would find a way out of this. Catherine, Viktor, and Reece were all depending on them.

She moved her shoulders to ease the stiffness from her arms being pulled back and stared down at the blank pages again, hoping for some inspiration. She saw movement out of the corner of her eye and turned her head. Eddie had hauled Lucas up and he was swaying on his feet. His nose looked broken and his eye was almost swollen shut.

Eddie smiled down at her, a creepy kind of smile. "You have five minutes before Lucas here gets another beating."

"I think he needs more than a beating."

Jo looked up to see Drew Bartley walk in with Mr. Smith by his side. She'd met Drew many times as he was one of Ben's agents and had even helped them with the unbinding ceremony.

Don't say anything, Jo heard Simon throw the thought into her head. She glanced at him and he gave her a barely perceptible nod. She didn't know what was going on but kept quiet.

"Eddie, I was just telling my dad here that Lucas is not who he appears to be."

Jo held back a gasp as she stared at Drew. She wasn't sure

what surprised her most—that Drew knew Lucas's secret or that Mr. Smith was Drew's dad.

Her head was swimming from exhaustion, the beatings, and now information overload. It was hard to believe that less than twenty-four hours ago she had made love with Simon, and now their lives were on the line and she didn't know of a way out.

"What the fuck you talking about, Drew?" Eddie asked. "He's a fucking cop?"

Drew walked further into the room with his father, coming up to Eddie and Lucas. Drew looked Lucas up and down in disgust. "He's an FBI agent." The corners of Drew's lips turned up in a sneer. "I was just in a meeting with other FBI agents, and our boy Lucas was there. He's been under-cover this entire time."

Jo felt bile rise in her throat but swallowed it back. Drew had been her friend and he'd come to family dinners, but it was obvious he knew everyone in the room. They already trusted him. Drew had been there the day of the unbinding. He must have been the one that tipped off these guys and the reason that her brother was now in a coma.

"The fuck?" Eddie yelled. He pulled back and sucker punched Lucas in the gut, knocking him to the floor.

"No!" Jo and Catherine both yelled at the same time.

"Enough dramatics," Mr. Smith said, somehow projecting his voice around the room without yelling. Everyone went silent. "Josephine, I'm disappointed in you. I thought we had a deal. You needed to find the book for me and in exchange your family would be safe."

Jo wanted to yell that his son was a traitor and he'd already broken his fucking deal, but for once decided to keep her mouth and sarcasm in check. She gestured to the book with her chin. "I found it, it's right here." Her voice sounded shaky even to her own ears.

"That may be, but it's useless as is. You need to make the spells appear."

"I don't know how."

"You'll figure it out, or your friends here are going to suffer," Mr. Smith said.

Drew snorted a laugh. "I think Lucas should suffer anyway. Maybe that will make Jo work faster." He jerked his head at Eddie. "Put Lucas in a chair."

Eddie pulled Lucas, almost carrying him, over to the table and pulled out a chair beside Viktor.

Drew stood watching with his arms crossed, like he was deciding on furniture placement. "No, put him next to Jo, up close, so she can see the torture her inadequacies are causing."

Bile rose in Jo's throat again, but this time she felt like she was going to puke. Her breathing was coming in pants, and she couldn't feel her hands anymore. She knew they were about to have to fight for their lives. Squeezing her eyes shut for a second, she took in a deep breath to steady herself.

"Jo, open your eyes!" Drew demanded.

She did, just in time to see Drew lift Lucas's left hand and slam it down on the table's smooth surface. "Eddie, where's your knife?"

"No! No, no, no!" Jo cried out when what Drew was about to do dawned on her.

Drew ignored her as well as Lucas's struggle to free his hand. "Is it sharp?" he asked.

"Fuck yeah," Eddie said, handing over the knife handle first.

"Stop moving!" Drew yelled and then Lucas's hand was spread like a starfish on the table, completely still—magic holding him in place.

"You look like you don't need your pinky finger," he said as he snorted at his own joke.

"No." Drew stopped, and all eyes turned to Mr. Smith as he spoke to his son. "A pinky is nothing, son. What finger would prevent you from being an agent?"

Drew looked at his father and a shit-eating grin spread across his face. "Losing my trigger finger."

"Exactly."

33

*J*o looked down to where Lucas's right hand, his dominant hand, was now stuck to the table, his fingers splayed.

She lifted her gaze to his. He was breathing fast, sweat beading on his forehead, but his gaze didn't waver from hers.

She realized then that she'd been lying to herself—the worst kind of lie of all. It didn't matter if she saw Lucas's light blue eyes or Simon's deep green ones—she loved this man. All of him. Even when he lied to help others. "I love you," she whispered.

"How touching," Drew said before Lucas could respond. "Maybe you'll work harder now." Drew lifted the knife and Jo screamed. The sounds of her cries blended with Catherine's as she looked into Lucas's eyes, feeling like she was looking into Simon's soul.

It felt like time stopped as screams mixed with shouts, but her gaze stayed on Lucas's until his chin dropped to his chest, a tortured sound coming from his lips.

She felt blood splatter on her face and forced herself to look down. Lucas's index finger lay in a pool of blood as more poured from the stump. The deep red liquid spread quickly across the table.

Drew picked up Lucas's finger and turned it around, examining the clean cut to the end. "A souvenir," he said as he closed his hand around the bloody appendage, and then he opened his hand to show it was empty.

Even knowing it was useless, Jo struggled against her bindings. "You need to stop the bleeding!" She looked up at Drew. "Please, you have to help him." Frantically, she looked at the others in the room. "Someone, please stop the bleeding before he loses too much."

Lucas's chin still rested on his chest, but she could see he was trying to slow down his breathing.

"Please!" she said again.

Mr. Smith walked over to her and put one hand down on the table, right in the blood, and leaned into Jo. "I'll tell you what. I'll stop the bleeding if you make the spells in the book visible."

She nodded several times like a child wanting to get their way, but couldn't make herself speak.

When he straightened, he waved his hand and the blood disappeared from his palm, then he flicked his hand at Lucas's damaged finger. Lucas threw his head back as a cry of agony tore from his throat, like that of a tortured animal.

Jo wrenched her gaze from Lucas's face and looked down at his finger. The smell of burned flesh hung heavy in the air. Once again, she swallowed the bile that rose into her throat. "Holy fuck, you burned him!"

"You asked me to stop the bleeding and I did. I cauterized the wound. Now, reveal the spells. You have ten minutes or our boy Lucas here will lose another finger."

"I need time! I've never done this before!"

"You now have nine minutes and forty-five seconds, so I suggest you get to work."

Jo looked over at Lucas—his chin rested on his chest and his eyes were closed. She took a deep breath and looked back down at the book's blank pages.

Blood splattered some of the edges, the color already turning a rusty brown. She sucked in a deep breath through her mouth, trying not to take in the smell of Lucas's burned flesh.

Jo closed her eyes and focused on everything Simon had taught her about spells over the last several weeks. She remembered what Viktor had said about the spell she needed to create. *The key is casting a spell that states you won't lie and that the spells will disappear again if someone's intention is to use them to cause harm.*

Then she remembered Simon making up a spell to tell the book what it needed. He'd said their magic didn't always need the words; it just needed the intention. She played with words in her head, creating different sentences. Did they need to rhyme? What if she didn't do it right?

"Josephine," Mr. Smith said, startling Jo. She opened her eyes and looked up at him. "You have two minutes left and then Lucas will lose another finger. Or maybe a limb."

Jo felt a tightness in her chest but ignored it. She had to do this. "I'm ready, but I need my magic unbound."

"Fine, we will remove the rope, but we'll give you some extra incentive not to fuck around." Mr. Smith nodded at Drew, who walked up behind Viktor, and then Eddie rounded the table and stood behind Catherine with his hands on her shoulders.

"Don't hurt them!"

"That will be up to you, Josephine. You reveal the spells, and only that, and they will be unharmed."

Jo nodded and felt the rope release from her wrists. She stifled a groan while pulling her hands in front of her, shifting her shoulders to ease the tension.

When she picked up the book, the backs of her fingers slid through Lucas's blood. Another realization came to her. He'd sacrificed everything for her, including his career and his person. Just like her mother and aunts had. When you loved someone enough to sacrifice for them, you loved them enough to lie.

She glanced over at Lucas. *I love you.* She threw the thought into his head, hoping that anyone powerful enough to pick up on a small energy signature was too distracted to notice.

Lucas lifted his head and the corner of his lip twitched up.

It was enough for now. Jo looked down at the book and hoped that the sentences she'd thought of would work.

Holding the book close to her, she whispered the sentences she had decided upon.

> *"The spells herein unlock for me to see.*
> *I offer up this basic plea to give to thee.*
> *Make visible to me who intends no harm and have great need.*
> *Hide from sight of those with intentions of greed."*

When Jo finished her little spell, she looked down at the pages and gasped. It had worked. Spells were visible on the pages.

Lucas heard Jo's gasp and looked over at the book. She had done it. Now, it was his turn.

He squeezed his eyes shut and took a steadying breath as dizziness threatened to topple him.

He'd been punched and kicked more times than he could count. Even almost strangled, but nothing could have prepared him for the constant throbbing that was all-encompassing, like his heart had moved from his chest to his hand.

Intellectually, he'd been prepared to lose a finger, but not his index finger. He shoved the thought aside. There would be plenty of time to mourn that loss later if he survived the next few minutes. That's if Drew had followed through on his part of the plan. A big if, but Simon shoved that thought aside too.

Pulling on his magic, he sent some of it to his hand to relieve the worst of the pain and then sent a message tele-pathically to Jack. *Get ready.* Even though Jack and the others were waiting outside the building, the distance would normally have still been too great for Simon to speak tele-pathically to someone. Lucky for him, Jack's power was no longer normal. When they'd made the plan at the task force office, the new council leader had been confident he'd be able to receive Simon's message, regardless of the distance.

Less than five seconds later, Simon knew his message had hit its mark. *Ack,* Jack said, throwing his acknowledgment into Simon's mind.

He turned to Jo and using his uninjured hand, cupped her cheek and pulled her closer, his forehead resting on hers. Their legs bumped under the table. "Today we don't fight for one life, we fight for them all," he whispered.

She sniffled and choked out a laugh. "You're quoting Thor?"

He pulled back just enough to see her eyes and for the first time saw them swell with tears. He used his thumb to wipe them away. Using his magic to dry them seemed too impersonal. He wanted her to feel him. "Jo," he whispered, but firm enough to have her focus on him.

When she looked directly at him, he transformed his eyes. Gone was Lucas's light blue, and instead, his own bright green shone back at her. He heard her small gasp and kissed her softly on the lips.

"Get the fuck up, Jenkins," Drew said from behind him. His time was almost up.

"I love you," he whispered against her lips and then changed his eye color back to light blue.

"I love you too, and whatever happens, you're stronger than you think."

He recognized the Superman quote and dropped his hand. Drew pulled on his shirt from behind, but he kept his gaze on Jo. Tears streamed down her cheeks and she did nothing to stop them.

A lump formed in his throat as he turned to face Drew, knowing what was coming. He braced himself when Drew raised his hand, a Glock 19M in his hand.

How ironic that he was going to be killed with an FBI-issued weapon.

The bullet hit Lucas on his right side, like a sledgehammer connecting with his chest.

A burning hot pain seared his torso as he fell backward, his head hitting the hard floor. His vision started to blur, the fire in his chest all consuming.

He was going to die looking like someone else when he finally had a reason to just be Simon.

He closed his eyes as the pain took him, but he couldn't pass out yet.

Now. He threw the word out to Jack and the sounds around him disappeared.

THE GUNSHOT REVERBERATED in the room and Jo's ears pulsed with the sound. She stood still for a moment, not believing what she was seeing.

Catherine's scream next to her pulled her out of her shock.

Jo yelled out words that were incoherent when Lucas fell backward. His head hit the floor and he lay still. She scrambled out of her chair and rushed to him.

"Lucas, talk to me. Lucas!" She put her fingers on his carotid artery, feeling for a pulse, but felt nothing. She must have missed it. She put her fingers on his neck again, holding her breath while she waited for Lucas's heart to beat. Still nothing. "Lucas!"

Grabbing him by the front of his shirt, now stained with blood, she yanked him up into her lap and cradled his head. This couldn't be happening.

"No!" She leaned down and kissed his lips, still warm and supple under hers. "Lucas, don't leave me, please! I love you!"

She repeated the words over and over as she rocked his body in her lap. Something was wrong. Her Lucas, her Simon, he was strong like Superman. This couldn't be happening.

She felt a hand on her cheek and gasped, looking up. Catherine kneeled on the other side of Lucas, tears streaming down her face. "He's... he's..." Lucas's mother couldn't get the words out and shook her head.

"No! No, no, no." Catherine was wrong, Lucas couldn't be dead. She continued to talk to Lucas, rocking him back and forth.

The room faded out of focus until it was just her and Lucas.

Shifting so she could support Lucas's weight with her right arm, she ran the fingers of her left hand over his face, stroking his forehead and then down to his eyelids.

His eyes were closed, but she didn't need to see them to know how the light blue lit up when he was his most charming self. Nor did she need to see Simon's eyes to picture the deep green that seemed to be able to look right into her soul.

She remembered the passion in them when they'd made love. And the joy when he laughed. The excitement in them when they'd found the book. The tenderness they'd reflected when he'd healed her.

Her fingers trailed over his cheek. A cheek slightly blue from the beating he'd taken earlier. He'd risked so much to help her and had paid the biggest price—his life. Just like her mother and aunts had done. They'd all lied, but they'd done it out of love, and now they were all gone.

She considered herself pragmatic. Always drawn to history—she had studied it and taught it—she understood that life was finite. People were meant to come in and out of one's life, but some left far too soon, leaving a heart so scarred it sometimes took years to heal.

Jo's life had been filled with death.

The people she had lost would forever be with her. She would grieve and no matter the hurt, she would get on with life.

Her fingers traced over Lucas's lips, and she knew that this time would be different. She would never heal from the loss of this man. Whether he was Lucas or Simon, he was the man she loved—intellectual and nerdy, fun and serious, carefree and caring—and passionate.

Tears hit her fingers and slipped onto Lucas. She pulled him up higher and bent her head so she could kiss her own tears from his lips.

"So long as life remains there is hope…" she whispered, but her voice trailed off as she choked on the last words, not able to finish the quote. She wasn't Wonder Woman and there was no more hope and there wouldn't be victory, as the famous line went.

"Jo." She lifted her head to see Jack kneeling in front of her. Time had stood still for her. She didn't know how long she'd been holding Lucas or when Catherine had left her side.

"Jack… how… why are you here?"

She placed her hand on Lucas's unmoving chest and looked around; the place was teeming with people. She recognized Javier and Lisa, who often came to the family dinners at the restaurant. Ben was there too. Viktor held Catherine in his arms, her head buried in the curve of his neck. Jo looked back at Jack for answers.

"We stormed the building but were too late," he said, looking down at Lucas in her arms, and she tugged his body closer to her. She noticed his body wasn't as warm now.

She pushed magic into her hands and arms to warm Lucas as she rocked him against her chest.

"Viktor told us that as soon as Drew shot Lucas, Andrew —Mr. Smith, well, really Andrew Skalbeck—grabbed the book and everyone flashed. We've searched the premises but there's no sign of anyone. Or the book."

Jo looked down at Lucas and brought her hand from his chest back to his face, her fingers skimming his cheek.

"Oh no!" Fresh tears welled in her eyes. She'd smeared Lucas's blood down his cheek.

Jack waved his hand over Lucas's face and the blood disappeared.

She raised her eyes to Jack, unable to see him clearly through the tears. "He's gone. They're all gone."

Jack nodded and sat with her for several more minutes as the truth of the situation sunk in and her tears continued to fall. She watched as they soaked into Lucas's shirt, mixing with the blood.

She swallowed against the tightness in her throat. "He sacrificed everything for me... He loved me..." She choked on the last word and pulled Lucas higher in her arms and tilted her head down, kissing his lips once more. They were colder than they had been even a few minutes before.

"Jo, they need to take Lucas," Jack said softly. She looked up at two emergency responders standing behind Jack with a stretcher.

"No!" If she let him go, she wouldn't see him again. It would make it real. She couldn't let it be real, she couldn't let him go—she loved him. It didn't matter that he'd lied. She loved both Simon and Lucas—her Superman. If she let him go, he'd be gone forever.

"It's time, Jo." Lucas's body moved off her to lay flat on the ground and she looked up at Jack. He'd used his magic to move Lucas, but she wasn't ready.

Jo reached for Lucas, but Jack didn't give her a chance to protest. He bent down and picked her up, cradling her in his arms. She didn't have the strength to put her arms around his neck, instead laying her head on his chest, her arms limp in her lap.

"It's going to be okay," he whispered in her ear as he carried her out of the room. He was wrong—nothing would ever be okay again.

35

$\mathcal{M}$organa had been waiting for Jo when Jack brought her back to her apartment. Jack had told her that Meredith and Rowena would meet her in Reece's room.

Barely saying a word, Morgana ushered Jo into the bathroom, turned on the shower to an almost incinerating level of hot, and helped Jo remove her bloody clothes. She was too exhausted and in shock to care what happened to her.

"I'll be back in fifteen minutes," Morgana said when she walked out of the bathroom.

Jo walked under the shower spray but didn't reach for soap or shampoo. She felt a lump bubble up in her throat and then a sob erupted from her. Once she'd opened the floodgates, she couldn't stop.

She dropped to her knees, not caring about the pain as she hit the tile floor. She laid both her palms on the bottom of the shower stall, the spray pounding on her back as the sobs were wrenched from her soul. She couldn't close her mouth as the wails continued to pour out from deep within as she sucked in air.

She could see the green of Simon's eyes just before he died, like he was giving her something to remember him by. To remember Simon, and not just Lucas. They were both intertwined for her now and she loved them both—she loved the man within, regardless of what he looked like on the outside.

"Jo." She looked up as Morgana opened the shower door and stepped in fully clothed.

Jo let Morgana pull her up and wash her, not uttering a word. When she was dry, she stood in front of the clothes Morgana had laid out for her on her bed, not wanting to move.

She felt Morgana's hand on her shoulder but continued to stare down at the clothes.

"I'm going to get into dry clothes," Morgana told her softly. "I'll meet you at Jack and Meredith's, okay? Reece is there waiting for you."

Jo waited until Morgana left and sat on the bed, her towel falling to the floor. She closed her eyes and saw the look on Simon's face when they'd found the book. He'd been just as excited as she was. He'd sacrificed everything to save her.

The book was gone, but she wasn't going to let that stop her. Her mother had died to keep her safe, as had Simon, and she wasn't going to let that all be in vain.

She pulled on her clothes and walked out of her apartment. She didn't flash because she needed more time to collect herself before she faced her brother.

A few minutes later, she let herself into Meredith's and Jack's apartment. Rowena and Morgana both rotated on their stools at the kitchen island to face her.

"They're in the spare bedroom, sweetie," Rowena said.

Jo was thankful that they gave her space and didn't try to hug her. She didn't know how much longer she could hold it together.

She pushed open the door to the spare bedroom and her eyes were drawn to Reece lying on the bed, just like he'd been the last time she'd seen him. He looked peaceful, like he was sleeping, but he wasn't the brother she was used to. He was thin, his face pale, and so still.

"Jo, do you know the spell? Lucas said you would know what to do."

She tore her eyes away from her brother and looked up at Jack. Drew had said that Lucas had been in an FBI meeting. That must have been when he'd spoken with Jack, but it didn't matter now. Lucas would never speak again.

She opened her mouth and then closed it, trying to focus on what she had to say. Grief had made her mind a jumbled mess. "I don't know any of the spells because the book was blank. I only managed to make them visible at the end. Simon thought the book needed me to offer my fealty." She swallowed against the constriction in her throat and sucked in a huge breath while she blinked back tears.

She hadn't cried for twenty years and now couldn't seem to stop. For so long she'd been consumed by anger and obsessed with the truth, thinking everything was black and white. She'd been angry at her father for breaking a promise. Angry at her mother for not fighting the mysterious disease before it took her life. Angry at her aunt Elise and then Simon for the lies.

Her childish way of thinking and her anger had stolen so much from her.

Feeling like her eyelids were weighted down, she forced them open and looked up at Jack. "I offered my loyalty to the book, but only mine," she said quietly.

For the first time that day, she almost smiled. Maybe she had beaten Mr. Smith—Skalbeck.

"I don't get it," Meredith said.

Jack huffed a laugh that was more of a snort than humor.

"I think what our Jo is trying to say is that she fucked Andrew Skalbeck by telling the book it could only reveal itself to her."

Jo nodded and held out both her hands, palms up. Feeling her magic within her, she closed her eyes and called on the words she'd created earlier and changed the last two lines.

> *"The spells herein unlock for me to see.*
> *I offer up this basic plea to give to thee.*
> *Take from those with intentions of greed,*
> *And give to me who has great need."*

Jo felt a weight descend upon her hands and looked down to see the book resting there. She placed the old tome on the dresser behind her and held her breath as she opened the cover.

"It worked," she whispered as her eyes welled with tears once more.

"We'll take over from here," a kind voice said from behind her.

Jo turned around to see that Mary, the grand council emissary, had joined them. Passing the book to Jack, Jo stepped back and snugged herself into the room's nearest corner. She would watch, but not participate, hoping the spell could save her brother and honor Simon's sacrifice.

Jo felt a hand on her shoulder and jerked up from where she'd fallen asleep in the chair, her head resting on her arms on the bed. The room was dark now, the light from the hallway casting a soft glow. She must have slept for hours, the exhaustion of the last thirty-six hours finally claiming her.

She looked up at Meredith and then back at her brother sleeping peacefully. The spell had worked, and then they'd removed the magic coma they'd put him in, but Mary said it would take time for Reece to get back to his old self. He'd have to gain back his strength and learn to use his magic now that nothing bound him.

"Come out and talk to us for a bit. Reece will be fine," Meredith whispered.

Jo nodded and followed her cousin into the apartment's open living space.

Jack handed Jo a mug. "Have some coffee. You look like you're going to fall off your feet."

Jo took the proffered drink and hiked her hip onto one of the stools at the kitchen island. She took a sip, breathing in the heavenly smell.

Meredith sat on the stool beside Jo and laid her hand on top of Jo's free one. "I know how you feel about lying, but I need to tell you something."

Jo's eyes felt heavy and gritty as she looked at her cousin. "It's okay. I still don't like lying, but I understand there is a time and a place for it."

"Really?" Meredith asked, her eyebrows almost climbing into her hairline.

Jo nodded and felt that now familiar lump form in her throat and swallowed against it. "Our mothers lied because they felt what they were doing was right and perhaps it saved our lives. We'll never know. And Simon—" Jo swallowed again. "His lie was part of his job, and he did it to help the greater good. It was bigger than just me."

Meredith nodded and turned to her fiancé.

"Jo, we lied to you, but we didn't have a choice," Jack said.

"Okay," she said, drawing out the word. She looked

between Jack and her cousin, waiting for an explanation. "What did you lie about?"

"It's not our place to explain, but someone from the FBI is here to explain it to you."

"But you're with the FBI too. Can't you just tell me?"

One corner of Jack's mouth twitched up like he was going to offer one of his rare smiles, but then his expression sobered. "I need you to flash to your apartment and listen to this agent."

"Now? The agent is in my apartment now?"

"Yes."

Jo didn't want to talk to anyone. All she wanted to do was curl up in a ball and act like everything that happened had just been a bad dream—a nightmare. Then she'd wake up and Simon would still be here.

She decided to say fuck it, she was going to walk and not flash. The person could wait a few more minutes for her. Her apartment was only two floors above Meredith's, but taking the stairs gave her a few more minutes to compose herself.

When she stood in front of her apartment door, she didn't reach for the doorknob. An agent was waiting for her, but she didn't know if she wanted to hear what they had to say and the walk up the stairs hadn't made her any more inclined to talk. She only wanted to crawl into bed and hide.

But what if the agent wanted to give her something of Simon's? Her throat tightened again, and she forced down the sob that threatened to break loose as she took in a big gulp of air and twisted the doorknob.

Determined to be polite to the agent and then hurry them out of her apartment, she braced herself and walked in.

A man standing near the window turned toward her.

"Simon?"

36

Simon heard the door and turned away from the window to see Jo as her eyes widened. He wanted to rush to her and wrap her up in his arms and never let go, but he didn't. He'd lied to her. Again.

His entire career had been spent lying, and he'd been okay with it. Until Jo.

She was everything he wanted—more important than his career or trying to fit in—because with her, he belonged.

"Simon?"

"It's me," he said, unable to keep away a second longer. He closed the distance between them but didn't touch her.

He held his breath as she looked at his eyes as if searching for something. Then she lifted her hand, almost hesitantly, and pulled down the neck of his Henley, laying her hand on his memorial tattoo. She let the shirt go and glanced down at his right hand with its missing finger. Her gaze met his again and her eyes welled with tears. "It is you," she whispered.

Before he could respond, she gripped his shoulders and jumped. He caught her before they both toppled to the floor as she wrapped her legs around his waist and captured his lips with hers.

It was a brutal claiming, and he gave as good as he got, kissing her like his life depended on it.

Spinning them both around, he pushed her back against the wall and moved one hand down to cup her ass while his other wrapped around her neck. They feasted on each other as the rest of the world fell away.

Jo pulled her head to the side, breaking the kiss. "I need you now, Simon."

He'd thought of this reunion from the moment he'd woken up, so grateful to be alive. Take it slow and shower her with kisses and love—worship her—had been the strategy he'd decided upon. Not take her against the wall in her living room.

To hell with strategy; he'd worship her later.

He pulled on his magic and a moment later they were naked, her hot core pressed against his stomach.

A groan erupted from him as she bit down on his neck and then laved at the area. "I still have to learn how to do that. Remove someone's clothes, I mean. I need to add it to my list," she said before her lips came back to his mouth. She bit his lip and soothed the spot with her tongue. "But later. I need you in me now."

He shifted so he was holding her with his left hand and snaked his right hand between them. He stopped when he didn't feel his index finger. The skin was rough where Skalbeck had torched the clean cut of his stump.

Never again would he be able to use his fingers to spread her open and deliciously torture her in the same way he had in the field. He wasn't whole anymore.

"Don't go there," she said, cupping his face, forcing his gaze back to hers. "I love you, scars, tattoos, and all." It was like she could see into his soul and knew what he'd been thinking. She kissed him again and he surrendered.

They were both breathing hard when she broke the kiss and rested her forehead against his. "Shit, I'm an idiot. Did you stop because you were in pain?"

"No, you were right the first time. And there's no pain, Jack made sure I was healed."

She looked him in the eyes, wearing a serious expression on her face. "Then fuck me, Simon. I need you inside me."

Still holding her up with one hand and pressing her against the wall, he gripped his cock with his right hand and positioned himself at her entrance. Lowering her down an inch, the delicious sensation of her heat swamped him.

"Shit, condom." His whole body trembled as he forced himself to stop, holding them both in tortured suspension. "I never conjure them, just in case I don't get it right, and I don't have any to retrieve."

She put her hands on his shoulders and pushed herself down, using his body as leverage. They both groaned at the heavenly feel of him fully seated inside her. "I'm on the pill and I trust that you're disease free. I am too. Now move."

His lips twitched up at her forcefulness. God, he loved this woman and how she took what she wanted. "Yes, ma'am," he said, and started to pump into her with a rhythm as old as time.

Their height difference made it difficult to kiss, but they didn't care, both too consumed with the sensations their bodies made when together. Their heavy breathing matched the sounds of her back hitting the wall as they both fought to bring the other to release.

His orgasm was barrelling down on him, but he refused to experience the blessed peak without her. Moving his free hand between their bodies, he touched her entrance and massaged her clit in time with his thrusts.

"Yes!" she screamed as she once more used his shoulders for leverage and increased the pace.

Her legs stiffened around his waist, and he rammed into her, not holding back. Jo's body tightened around him and took him with her as they both exploded. He shuddered as the incredible sensations echoed throughout his body. *Fuck!* She was everything to him.

After a moment, he dropped his forehead to her shoulder, his breathing still out of control, his eyes closed.

"Holy fuck!" Jo huffed out on a chuckle. "Guh… that was…"

"My thoughts exactly." He untangled their bodies and Jo lowered her feet to the floor.

His magic stirred, like it had the very first time they'd met, reaching for her. She was his.

He held out his hand. "How about we take this to the bedroom?"

She took his hand in hers and led the way down the hall.

Jo pulled back the covers of the bed and turned to face him.

He captured her lips in a kiss, this time soft and slow, before pulling back. "I know we need to talk about what happened today, but not yet."

She nodded and crawled onto the bed, making room for him. He laid down on his back and pulled her so she was sprawled over him and he could look up into her eyes. "I love you, Jo."

"I love you too. I didn't think I'd see you again, I—" She choked on the last word and pressed her lips to his.

Their lovemaking was slower this time as he worshipped her body the way she deserved. He took his time and brought her to climax twice more before he took his own release.

Much later they sat at her kitchen island eating an omelet with the few ingredients Jo had in her fridge. The Magic

Plate had already closed by the time they'd dragged themselves out of bed, and neither had the energy to think about making or conjuring anything fancy.

They were both beyond tired. After Jack had healed him, he'd briefed Ben, Jack, and Frank, the Special Agent in Charge of their division and Ben's brother, for two hours.

They had more questions, but at that point Simon had been barely coherent due to exhaustion and the torment his body had gone through. He'd passed out for four hours in one of the task force offices equipped with a bed for situations just like this until Jack had woken him.

There'd be time later to shed more light on Skalbeck's operations. Seeing Jo had been his priority and Jack was the one who made it happen.

They were sipping their wine when Simon brought the topic back to the events of the morning. Exhaustion was pulling at him, at both of them, but he needed to explain why he'd lied. "I want to explain what happened."

"I saw you die. I saw Lucas die."

"That wasn't me."

"You weren't shot?"

"I was, but then a body was put in my place."

Jo shook her head. "No, I saw you."

He took her wine out of her hand and picked her up. "I've got you," he whispered when she let out a small cry and grabbed his shoulders. He placed her on the couch and sat beside her, pulling her legs into his lap as he'd done before.

She groaned and settled back into the cushions as he rubbed her feet. He needed the ordinary task to ground him as he rehashed what had happened earlier in the day.

"You saw me get shot," he said, picking up the thread of their conversation.

"Yes, and then you died in my arms."

"When you and I separated last night, after we were taken to that building, Rocky let me go get help."

"That's what Drew was talking about when he said he was in an FBI meeting with you… Lucas?"

He rubbed his knuckles on his left hand into the arch of her foot and loved the small groan she made. "Yes, I called Ben and met with him, Jack, and some other agents to figure out what to do."

"Drew knows you're Simon?"

"Fortunately, no. I didn't know who the mole was, so I stayed in Lucas's form. Ben understood why." Simon thought back to the meeting and realized how lucky he'd been that Ben understood what he'd done and brought in the others to help.

"Then Drew isn't bad?"

"Oh no, he's bad." Simon let out a humorless laugh. "He's been working for his father, although we haven't figured out for how long yet. In the meeting he said that he could take Lucas's place because his father had been trying to get him into the business. We went along with it because it would help us solve our immediate problem—getting you, Catherine, and Viktor to safety. Ben and Jack will solve the Drew issue."

"Okay," Jo said slowly, as if trying to process the information. "Was it the plan for Drew to kill you?"

Simon stopped rubbing Jo's feet, and held them in his hands, the stump of his finger a glaring reminder of the plan. "Remember when you asked if anyone else could transform the way I could?"

"You said that you didn't know of anyone, and a spell could help someone transform for a time, but it came with a huge price." Simon watched Jo and saw the exact moment that the realization came. "Holy fuck! The price was a body part?"

"Yes. There is a spell that can transform someone temporarily by using some of their tissue. Drew was supposed to cut off the end of my pinky finger and send it to Jack who would use it to transform a body."

Jo laughed in disbelief, her eyes huge. "You had a spare dead body lying around?"

"Ben has contacts among all types of magics, so they were able to get someone who was recently deceased and would be cremated."

"Handy… Okay, Jack was able to use your finger… well… Lucas's, and transform the body, but how did you do the switch?"

He ran his hands slowly up and down Jo's feet and lower legs, needing the contact and to keep his hands occupied. "Drew was supposed to shoot me, but in the shoulder, so although it hopefully wouldn't have been life threatening, we would play it that way when the bodies were switched."

Jo was too far away; he needed her closer. Reaching over, he hauled her onto his lap and kissed her thoroughly. This was harder to talk about than he thought it would be. "Did you know that Jack had to go through a special ceremony to become a leader of the new council?"

"Yes, and so did Meredith, because they're co-leaders. They both… this has something to do with their increased magic powers, doesn't it?"

"I knew you were smart and quick." He leaned forward to give her a soft kiss and then pushed back into the cushions, settling her in his lap again. "Yes. One of the things that Jack can do now is stop time for a few seconds."

"Holy shit!"

Simon chuckled—he did that a lot around Jo. "That's what I thought, and you're going to have to keep that to yourself." Jo nodded and made the motion of locking her lips and throwing the key over her shoulder. "Since Jack can also receive telepathic messages—"

"I know. Meredith can do it too, and it's damn annoying at times."

"Yes, but in this case it was useful. I was able to let Jack know when to be ready and when to stop time. He flashed in with the body that now looked like Lucas and flashed out with me."

"But the new Lucas was still warm."

"That's easy to do, just like I've warmed you up before."

Jo sighed and rested her head against his shoulder. "It all blows my mind, I can't believe—wait—but you were shot and not in the shoulder. Drew shot you in the chest." She pulled his shirt down and looked at his chest. "Just checking. I didn't remember seeing a new scar earlier."

"There isn't one. Jack and Meredith got to me in time and were able to heal me." He didn't mention how close it was. Jack told him later that he thought they were going to be too late since Drew had shot him in the chest, but slightly off to the right.

"You don't have a scar from the bullet wound."

"Because Jack completely healed me... the wound to my chest, at least." He held up his right hand. He was missing half his index finger and the skin around the end was puckered and rough where Skalbeck had seared his flesh closed.

Simon wrapped his arms firmly around Jo and stood. "I think we've both had enough of that for tonight." He kissed her forehead and walked them into the bedroom.

IT HAD BEEN three days since Lucas had died. Each night Jo had dreamed of Lucas's death and Simon had woken her with kisses and held her until she'd fallen back to sleep. She hadn't been able to let Simon out of her sight for more than a few minutes at a time, needing the reassurance that he was real and wasn't going anywhere.

Having him make love to her almost non-stop was definitely helping.

She rolled off Simon and flopped onto her back beside him. "Holy shit, I think you killed me—I mean…"

"It's okay. I know what you mean." He turned his head and kissed her long and slow. The position was awkward with them laying on their backs, but she'd kiss Simon any way she could get, every day for the rest of her life.

"I can revive you," he said, smiling against her lips before kissing her again.

A while later they laid on their sides facing each other, talking about their day. There was a normalcy and peacefulness to it she never thought she'd have with all the anger that had always been bubbling to the surface within her. She still didn't like lies, but she'd learned there was a place for them. They'd done a lot of talking in the last few days, but she hadn't wanted to talk when he'd gotten home that evening.

She'd attacked him, ripping at his clothes as soon as he walked in the door from his meeting a little while ago. The dinner she'd ordered from the restaurant was still sitting on the kitchen counter, but he'd satisfied a different type of hunger.

She traced her fingers lazily along the tattoo on his chest. The day before he'd taken her to his parents' graves to introduce her and she'd done the same with him. They were both orphans, but they weren't alone. "How did your meeting with Ben and Jack go? Was Frank there too? I know he's a bigwig in the FBI division here, but he's always just been like an uncle to me."

"Yes, Frank was there, and I definitely don't think of him as an uncle," he said as he laughed, "but I get it."

His expression sobered as his eyes tracked to his right hand, tracing patterns on her arm. She took his hand in her own and held it to her heart. She didn't care that he was missing a finger or that he couldn't be an FBI agent anymore, but she knew it wouldn't be as easy for him to come to terms with the losses. "Tell me about the meeting."

"We started putting together the pieces of when Drew had become the mole and how he could have worked with Copeland and his father here. Frank and Ben have agreed to let Drew think we believe he's innocent and is going to report on his father. Ben's team will use him for intel, and feed him what they want."

"Does that mean that you know where Skalbeck and the others disappeared to?"

He flopped onto his back and pulled her over to almost lie on top of him. She loved the position, tucking her head under his chin. "Drew reported that they're in Mexico. It's out of the FBI's jurisdiction, but not the council's, as far as magics are concerned. But for now, Frank and Ben want to see how things play out."

"What about the others? Do you know who they are? Like Rocky and the healer? And what are they going to do now that they don't have the book?"

"No, nothing about who they are yet. As for the book, we didn't give anything up, so they don't know we have it. Drew is being cagey, but we're going with the assumption that they think it disappeared when they tried to use it. Just like the book disappeared when your mom and aunts used it. We still don't know if it's the same book."

"So, for now it's wait and see?"

"Pretty much." He leaned down and kissed her forehead

and she practically swooned. Who knew forehead kisses could make her so melty? "How's Reece?" he asked.

She smiled against Simon's chest as she thought of her brother. "He's still really weak, but Jack thinks that within a few weeks he'll be strong enough to start practicing his magic. Since the spell was cast on him while the previous spell was being broken, he's never been strong enough to use his magic." Jo chuckled. "He was practically chomping at the bit earlier today, and that's putting it mildly."

"I'm glad he's getting better."

Simon reached under her arms and dragged her up further on his chest so she was face to face with him. "Hey, miss me?" She kissed him long and slow before finally lifting her head and looking into his beautiful green eyes.

There had been times over the past few days that she had mourned Lucas—even though she'd never known the real man. Only Simon's version of him—and she now had the best of both worlds. Yet, she'd started falling in love with Simon's Lucas and had watched him die. Her feelings were twisted and it would take a while to come to terms with them all.

Simon tipped her chin up with his left hand. "Hey, where'd you go? I'm right here."

"I know. I was just thinking of Lucas. Even though I never met him."

"I feel the same. He died and no one got to mourn him at the time, but now they will."

She leaned down and kissed Simon again. She'd kissed him as often as she could in the past few days, reassuring herself that he was alive.

After a few minutes, Simon gently moved her off his chest and sat up against the headboard, pulling her up with him. "Let's have dinner in bed."

"What?" She laughed when the tray from the restaurant appeared on their laps, the food already reheated.

They chatted about mundane things as they ate their meals. She loved that they could be normal and there wasn't anything hanging over their heads.

"Jack brought up something I want to pass by you," Simon said after he turned so he was almost facing her.

She bit into the large chocolate brownie fresh from Reece's bakery. "Mmmm. About the council?" she asked after swallowing. She conjured a cup of coffee and took a sip, enjoying the two flavors blending in her mouth.

"That too. He wants us both to be members of the new council and swear us in. I'm not sure what the ceremony entails, but I don't think it's as in-depth as what he and Meredith went through."

"Bummer. It would be good to have as much magic as they do."

He chuckled at her mock pout. "True, but we can ask. Actually, Jack wanted to offer us jobs."

"What? Ouch." She looked down at her naked chest where she'd spilled her hot coffee, but Simon was already drying and soothing her skin. She held her coffee away from her body and leaned over, giving him a quick kiss before she settled back against the headboard. "Okay, let's try that again… what kind of job?"

"He wants us to act as art dealers and appraisers. We'd travel around the world on the pretext of looking for art, but we'd really be helping the other six councils look for more of the magic books."

"Would we get paid?"

"Yes, the councils have money set aside for that. Magics might not be able to conjure money as it would be considered counterfeiting, but conjuring gold is easy. All the councils have a reserve."

It seemed almost too good to be true. She'd still get to do something she loved and be with the man she loved too. She and Simon had both declared their love, but they hadn't talked about anything beyond that. She didn't even know what he truly wanted now that he couldn't be an agent anymore. He could still transform, but whoever he transformed into would have most of his right index finger missing.

"Hey, what's wrong?" Simon disappeared the coffee mugs and tray and pulled her down onto her back so he was hovering over her, looking into her eyes. "We don't have to work for the council if you don't want to."

"It's not that…"

"Then what? I know it will take us a while to feel grounded, but I love you, Jo. We'll get through anything life throws at us as long as we're together."

"It's that, actually. We haven't talked about the future before now. I don't even know what you want now that you're not an agent."

He kissed her forehead, her nose, and then her lips. Another long, slow kiss, making love to her mouth. When he pulled away, he looked at her eyes, and all she saw was love. "That's easy. I want you. You're all I need, Jo. You're my Wonder Woman. I love you and I want to be with you forever."

Her eyes filled with tears, and she didn't blink or try to stop them spilling over her lower lashes. "I want that too, Superman."

As Simon leaned down to kiss her, he magically dried her tears.

EPILOGUE

wo Months Later.

Jo pushed her empty lunch plate to the side of the table and smiled at the server who came to clear the dishes. "Thanks, Jordan." She loved the routine of eating at The Magic Plate and seeing familiar faces.

"Thank you, dear," Catherine said, smiling at Jordan.

Jo waited until Jordan had left and looked across at the woman who had come to mean a lot to her. "Catherine, I'm so glad you were able to come for lunch." She hadn't said anything when Catherine had first arrived, not wanting to make the meeting awkward. "I've been worried about you."

The older woman folded her cloth napkin and placed it on the table before looking Jo in the eyes. "It's been a rough couple of months, but I'm doing well. I've known for a long time that my Lucas was gone, but having a lookalike, and such a lovely one, made it seem like he was still here."

Catherine waved her hand in front of her eyes. To anyone at a distance, it would have looked like she was just talking with her hands. But Jo knew she was magically drying her tears before they could fall.

Regardless of when the real Lucas died, Catherine had still lost her son and watched someone who looked like him get murdered while she was helpless to do anything about it. Jo couldn't imagine what that must have been like.

It gave her a new understanding of what her mother and aunts had gone through. They'd had to stand helplessly by as their husbands and children were consumed by a fire— horrendous and tragic on its own, but to know that it was deliberate and your loved ones were murdered must have made it so much worse.

If that had been her, would she have spellbound her remaining children? Jo had been trying harder to see shades of gray and now she couldn't say with one hundred percent certainty that she wouldn't have done the same as her mother. Especially now that she had seen firsthand what it was like to watch someone you loved die right in front of you, a death that should have been preventable.

She reached over and squeezed Catherine's hand before releasing it. "Thank you for inviting me to the funeral. The service was beautiful, and it was really nice of Lucas's friends to sing."

She had to stop and swallow, blinking back her own tears as she thought of the funeral. Simon had wanted to go with her, but Ben and Jack had asked him not to. They didn't know who would be watching. Simon wasn't the only person who'd ever lost a finger, but being at Lucas's funeral and not having his index finger could have tipped someone off.

So Jo had gone by herself and sat beside Catherine, who was now truly alone, and held her as they'd both cried.

The place had been packed with many there to support Catherine. Maybe there weren't a ton of people who would have come just for Lucas, but that didn't matter. They were there all the same.

The irony was that Jo had never met the real Lucas, and

probably wouldn't have liked him much. But through Simon, Jo liked to think that she'd known some part of Lucas, maybe the best part, even if it was just Simon's version of the man.

She'd been falling in love with that version and had held him as he'd died in her arms.

Jo waved her hand and magically dried her own tears this time. "I think Frank Sinatra's 'My Way' was just perfect. I can imagine that Lucas would have smiled at that. And they did such a good job."

"Yes, it was perfect." Catherine waved her hand in front of her face again and then refolded the napkin on the table before looking dry-eyed at Jo. "Tell me what you've been up to."

"Hello, ladies, may I join you?"

Jo jumped out of her chair and wrapped Viktor in a hug, inhaling his sage and cedar scent. "I didn't know you were coming by today, but I'm glad you're here."

"Catherine told me she'd be here, and I thought I'd give you both enough time to eat before stopping by," he said as he pulled out the chair beside Catherine's.

"I didn't think you'd mind, dear."

"No, of course not. I'm happy to see you both." Jo signaled the server to come over and they refreshed their coffees while chatting and catching up.

"How's Simon?" Viktor asked.

Jo couldn't help the smile that took over her face. "He's good. We're going to be working for the council." She spent the next few minutes filling them in but watched Catherine's expressions carefully, worried how she'd react to her being with Simon.

Lucas's mother had known that her son wasn't who he appeared to be, but she still loved him, and he was gone. It didn't matter when the real Lucas had actually died since, either way, to Catherine he was now permanently gone.

Movement caught the corner of Jo's eye and she watched Simon walk through the front doors of the restaurant and head their way. Perfect timing. They'd talked about Simon meeting Catherine and had both agreed it was time if Catherine was going to stay in her life.

When he reached her side, he leaned down and kissed her softly, just a quick kiss. Then he walked over to Viktor and shook the older man's hand when he stood. "It's good to see you, Viktor."

"Yes, it's good to see you too."

Simon looked at Catherine but didn't say anything. Jo jumped out of her seat and went to him, wrapping her arm around his waist. "Catherine, I'd like you to meet my boyfriend, Simon Hughes."

Jo dropped her arm and took a step back as Catherine stood. Simon extended his right hand. "It's nice to meet you, Catherine."

Catherine clasped Simon's hand with her own. She looked down, still gripping Simon's hand, and turned her own palm up, cradling Simon's.

Jo watched as realization dawned and tears sprang to Catherine's eyes. *It's okay.* Jo threw the thought telepathically into Simon's mind. It was all the encouragement he needed.

Simon reached for Catherine and pulled her into his embrace. "I've wanted to see you for so long," he whispered, but loud enough for Jo to hear. Simon held Catherine for a long time.

Mother and son finally pulled apart and Simon joined them at the table. Catherine was full of questions and she peppered Simon with one after the other, asking about his childhood and about the FBI. She'd known Simon's parents, just as she'd known Jo's. It was a small world, and the magic community seemed to be even smaller than Jo had ever realized.

When Viktor and Catherine finally left, it was with promises to get together again soon.

Jo lifted Simon's hand where it rested in his lap, giving it a light squeeze and bringing it into her own. "How are you? Really?"

"I want to be alone with you. Let's go upstairs and I'll answer there."

The restaurant wasn't busy now that the lunch rush was over, but it wasn't empty, so they didn't flash. "Sure." She took his hand and led him up to their apartment.

When they were inside, she dragged him over to the couch and he laughed as she pushed him back against the cushions. "I like it when you're feisty."

Jo straddled his lap and took her face between her hands. "How *are* you?"

He held her wrists in his hands and kissed her. It was long and slow and she could feel his love.

"I'm good," he said when he finally broke the kiss.

"You sure?"

"Yes, I'm sure. We've got to be back downstairs in a few hours for the weekly family dinner, but I have you all to myself for now." He kissed her again but then stopped abruptly.

"What's wrong?"

"Nothing's wrong… It's just in the last couple of months, you've given me another first, Wonder Woman."

"What's that?"

"A new family."

"You are many to many, Simon." She didn't care that she'd butchered another Wonder Woman quote; she had her Superman.

Using her magic, she placed the spell Simon had taught her on the front door, to make sure no one would pop in unannounced. Then she kissed her man. They were going to be late for dinner and she was just fine with that—he was worth being late for.

MORGANA LET OUT a slow breath to counter the migraine threatening to break her skull from the inside. The headaches had been getting steadily worse over the last few weeks, making it almost impossible to sleep. She didn't know how much more she could handle, but then, she didn't have a choice.

She planned to hide in her apartment all day. Not because she didn't want to see anyone, but because it was becoming harder to hide her increasing pain. The night before at the weekly family dinner, she'd told everyone she had some shopping to do and wouldn't be around today, hoping no one would look for her.

Due to never sleeping much, she was up before the sun and had only managed to shower and eat breakfast before running out of energy. She was cuddled in the corner of the couch with a new romantic suspense novel when someone knocked on the door.

She groaned and then slapped her hand over her mouth. If she was quiet, they might go away.

"Morgana, I know you're in there. Sweetie, I'm coming in."

Rowena appeared in front of Morgana a moment later. Rowena could flash wherever she wanted to go. *Everyone* could flash except her. Well... all magics, except for her.

"Good morning, Rowena."

Rowena conjured herself a cup of coffee and sat on the other end of the sofa. "I knew you weren't going shopping."

She held up her book and stated the obvious. "I got a new book and wanted to read it."

"That's it? You just wanted to read a book? Your headaches aren't worse?"

"It doesn't matter if they're worse or not. No one can do anything about them," she said, hating that she sounded whiny. Jack and Meredith had consulted with other council leaders around the world, and no one knew what to do. She'd had hope that the book Jo and Simon had found would have a spell to help her. It hadn't.

Rowena eyed her over her coffee cup and Morgana had to force herself not to squirm.

"What about good old-fashioned talking? It's extremely common for people with PTSD to have headaches. If you talk about what you've been through and deal with your trauma, it could help relieve the headaches."

"I know." She really did, but she didn't want to talk about what she could remember, and what she couldn't remember was probably what was causing her head to feel like it was going to explode.

"Morgana, you're not my client, you're family. I just want to help."

"I know, I'm just not ready."

"Most people are never ready, but it's been ten months and if you don't deal with it, it will never get better."

If she didn't unearth her past and remember, she wouldn't have to face what a horrible person she was. Her actions had most likely killed the healer. How many others were hurt or dead because of her?

Rowena was right, though—the Williams family did treat her like family. What would they think if they found out their new so-called family member was a despicable, selfish person? Copeland had told her she was weak and useless, and maybe she'd forgotten most of her past because her mind had blocked all the horrific things she'd done. What if he was right? Copeland had been an evil ass, but that didn't mean what he said wasn't true.

"Stop, not right now," Rowena muttered under her breath, pulling Morgana out of her thoughts.

"Stop what?" Morgana asked.

"Sorry sweetie, I was talking to myself." She stood and disappeared the coffee mug. "I hope you think about what I said. Bye," she said abruptly and was gone a moment later.

"Bye," Morgana said to the empty room. She shook her head at Rowena's strange behavior. She'd been talking to herself a lot lately, and whenever Morgana asked about it, Rowena just dismissed it. Maybe Meredith had been right and Morgana was just under a lot of pressure with setting up her new business.

It wasn't like Morgana was one to talk. She couldn't comment on someone else's strange behavior since she didn't even know who she was and some days her headaches were so bad she couldn't get out of bed. Then there was what happened to her if she saw a spider. She shuddered and closed her eyes, taking in a big breath. At least none of the cousins had been around to witness one of those episodes.

Rowena's departures might not seem so strange if she had to take the time to walk out of a room. Maybe her flashing, being there one second, and gone the next, made her behavior seem more abrupt than it was, she rationalized to herself.

If only Morgana could do that. She wondered if she'd ever be able to flash in and out of a room like Rowena and the others.

She felt a familiar tingling in her eyes and reached for the box of tissues on the coffee table. Like non-magics, she had a box of tissues because she couldn't conjure one—but she was magic and that seemed to be the problem.

Shit, she was being a big Eeyore today. Most of the world didn't have magic, and they survived. But then, they weren't constantly surrounded by people using magic. No one purposely rubbed it in her face, but it hurt all the same.

She rubbed her forehead, pushing on the pressure inside her skull. It helped for a second, but she couldn't spend all day rubbing her forehead.

Enough of the morose thoughts—it was time to get lost in a book.

She was on chapter two when someone knocked on the door. This time she made sure to stay quiet, hoping whoever it was would go away.

"Morgana, I'm coming in."

Shit. Damon. A moment later he was standing in front of her. She couldn't even put a spell on her apartment to stop people from flashing inside because she was so useless.

"I knew you weren't going shopping," he said as he towered over her, big enough to block the early morning sun streaming in through the living room window.

"Yes, it's a theme." Obviously, she had to get out and do some real shopping, as she was apparently predictable enough that others could assume what she was and wasn't doing.

His gorgeous face pinched as he frowned. "What?"

"It doesn't matter. What do you want, Damon? And sit down—no, better yet, leave, because it hurts my neck to look up at you."

Damon sat on the couch where Rowena had just been. Maybe she should replace the couch with a single chair to discourage uninvited guests from lingering.

"I wanted to check on you. How're you feeling?"

"I'm the same every time you ask me, Damon. What do you really want?" She enjoyed looking at him—he was big and hot, his shoulders seeming to fill the entire room, and if he wasn't so damn controlling, she might even want to have something with him. Well… she wanted something with him now, but he wasn't right for her.

"Isn't wanting to see how you're doing enough?"

Her bitchiness was in full force today. Two people cared enough to check on her and she just pushed them away. She met his eyes. "I'm fine. Thanks for checking on me." That wasn't so hard.

"I also brought you something." Damon held out his hand and when a book appeared he passed it to her. "I thought you might like this."

She knew she hadn't been fast enough to hide her surprise, so she smiled at him and glanced at the cover. "A paranormal romance? How'd you know?"

He shrugged. "Just a guess," he said and then hesitated as if not sure if he should say more. "It's one of my favorites. I thought you might like it too."

She felt sure her eyebrows rose to her hairline in shock. This big, domineering man in front of her read paranormal romance? Who knew? "You actually read it?"

He shrugged again and a blush appeared under his five o'clock shadow.

"Yeah," he said. "I like the connections between the couples and the paranormal elements make it exciting. I enjoyed that book"—he lifted his chin toward the book he'd given her—"because the vampires are a species and not blood suckers. It was a good twist on the traditional. I also like romantic suspense." He pointed to her new book, still in her lap. "That's another one of my favorite authors. I downloaded that one this morning."

For the first time since she'd met Damon, she was seeing a different side of him. A side of him she wanted to get to know. If his sensitive side would cancel out the controlling part of him, they might be able to be friends.

Maybe even something more. But she couldn't be controlled again.

She glanced back down at the book and ran her finger over the shiny cover. The steamy-looking couple embracing on the cover was nothing but make-believe. As if she needed the reminder that her life wasn't all steam and loving, the pounding in her head picked up its pace. Life wasn't a romance novel with everything working out in the end. She knew that better than most. Any romance in her life needed to stay firmly in the pages of a book.

"Again, thank you. It was nice of you to check on me and bring the book." She lifted herself off the couch and placed both books on the table, hoping he'd get the hint to leave.

"Okay… I'll go," he said as if reluctant, and stood.

She took a step forward to go around him to the door when a sharp pain ripped through her skull, down her neck, and into her back. Her muscles ceased working and she windmilled her arms in an attempt to catch herself as her body pitched forward.

Damon caught her upper arms and eased her onto the sofa. "Morgana, what's wrong?"

"My m—" She couldn't talk as the pain continued to pierce her muscles, like a thousand little needles hitting her over and over again.

"I'll call Jack and see if he can heal you."

"No!" She sucked in a deep breath and closed her eyes, forcing her muscles to relax. "I'm fine."

"Don't be an idiot. Of course you're not fine. Something just happened and you're in pain."

Yes, she was an idiot, but she didn't need to hear it from Damon. She panted small breaths, forcing her muscles to relax one by one. Planting her fists by her sides, she pushed herself up into a sitting position and then stood. "I just get dehydrated and sometimes my muscles seize."

"Dehydration? That's what you're going with?" Damon towered over her again, but she refused to be intimidated by his size.

"Yes. I just need water." She prayed she looked normal as she forced her legs to carry her to the kitchen. She poured herself a glass of water, took a large gulp, and turned back to Damon. "See? I. Am. Fine."

He stalked toward her and she stepped back, her butt hitting the counter.

"You're not fine." He placed both his large hands on the sides of her neck, and if it had been anyone else, she would have screamed the roof off. But this was Damon. He was controlling, but he'd never physically harm her.

His thumbs gently caressed her cheeks and she was mesmerized as she looked into his dark eyes, seeing an inner softness that she hadn't noticed before. If her butt wasn't half perched on the counter, holding her up, she would have melted to the floor in a puddle of lust. Her panties dampened, and in that moment, she wanted Damon to kiss her. It didn't matter that he was too controlling—she wanted his kiss.

He tilted his head toward her and she closed her eyes in anticipation.

"You are special, Morgana."

His lips brushed hers in the briefest of kisses and his hands left her neck and cheeks, cold air rushing in to replace his touch.

Her eyes sprung open. What just happened?

"Here, drink." Damon shoved a full glass of water at her and, too stunned to think, she drank it.

Five more minutes and two more glasses of water later, he left. She didn't mention the barely-there kiss and neither did he.

Maybe he did care for her—like a sister. Why, when he was all wrong for her, did she want him?

She washed the glass and put it away before returning to the sofa and her book.

There was something wrong with her—something that no amount of water was going to fix.

A week ago, as she'd laid on the bathroom floor, her muscles paralyzed, she had come to the realization that her body was shutting down and she was dying.

She'd die without ever knowing what it was like to kiss Damon Stone and without ever knowing who she was.

Thanks so much for reading *Truth in Magic*!
You don't have to say goodbye just yet.
Go to:
https://kjwarawa.com/truth-in-magic-bonus-scene/
to download a free bonus scene with more of
Jo & Simon's HEA.

Then find out what happens when Morgana's memories start to return and whether Damon's determination to protect her will be the downfall of them both in
FOUND IN MAGIC
https://books2read.com/found-in-magic

IN MAGIC SERIES

Lost in Magic

Truth in Magic

Found in Magic

Courage in Magic

Love in Magic

Forged in Magic

Forever in Magic

CURSED TO LOVE SERIES

Cursed to Love

Cursed to Dream

Cursed to Wither

Cursed to Suffer

ABOUT KJ WARAWA

Paranormal romance writer KJ Warawa had worked every job under the sun, including swimwear seller, switchboard operator, legal secretary, sign language interpreter, soldier, massage therapist, and process improvement advisor, before settling into the career she'd always dreamed about: Author.

She still loves processes and spreadsheets, doesn't love massaging feet, and is currently living out her own love story in Alberta, Canada.

STAY IN TOUCH WITH KJ:
Join KJ's Newsletter at
https://kjwarawa.com/free-book/
to receive a FREE book, exclusive deals, special offers, behind-the-scenes info, and learn about new releases, plus more!
www.kjwarawa.com